Wife

by Michelle Monay

Compilation and Introduction copyright © 2011 by Triple Crown Publications
PO Box 247378
Columbus, OH 43224
www.TripleCrownPublications.com

Library of Congress Control Number: 2011920508
ISBN: 978-0-9832095-3-9

Author: Michelle Monay
Graphics Design: Hot Book Covers
Editor-in-Chief: Vickie Stringer
Editor: Marian Nealy

First Trade Paperback Edition Printing 2011

10 9 8 7 6 5 4 3 2 1

Printed in the United States of America

$\mathcal{D}$edications

This book is dedicated to everybody out here that have dreams and everybody in the struggle. Know out of a bad situation something good comes. I must not forget about my baby cousin Deanna Brookshire. You're my favorite cousin. This is also dedicated to you family. Know that we control our own destiny and with strong belief we shall conquer all that we desire and though we come from nothing
we are coming from nothing to make something great.

Acknowledgements

Dear Heavenly Father:
I truly love you from the bottom of my heart to deep inside my soul. You made me Special, Father. You gave me God-given gifts and I thank you for it. You are my provider, my source, my King who goes above and beyond and miraculously make a way for me even out of no way. You're so amazing and you've kept a hold on me even through the troubled times in my 22 years of life. There's no word that could describe the way I feel about you. Since I was a young girl, I always felt your mercy and love. Experiencing the love and protection from you, I know that the love you provide me with is unconditional, undying, and sincere without cost and definitely matchless. All that I have been through you have never failed me. Thank You for all of your many blessings, for all that you have made me, and all that you have made me not. You're so awesome Father God.

To my Lord and Savior Jesus Christ, I remember calling on you on many occasions I when I thought it was over, but you came through every time, on time. I know you are with me forever and will never leave me in spite of my faults. For your blood, I'll always be grateful. To my Mother, you know you must come next, fam-fam. You are my best friend. Let me first say that you are the best Mother that every graced this earth. Tonya Marie Cole. Because through your permanent back injury from your bullet wound, you worked your butt off until you could no longer endure the pain daily and the spasms that took you off your job. I still don't know how we made it, but God always makes a way. I'm proud to say I'm your daughter. You've been so good to me and my sister and I put this on my life, one day I'll return the favor tenfold. You are the greatest!

To my father, Michael "Mike" Walker, you were always there and virtually treated me like I couldn't do any wrong in your eyes. Yeah, I remember! Smiles! Oh, and thanks for spreading the word, I'm happy to have made you proud of me.

To my big sister, Jha'quanna Nevins. Bunk, Bunk you know you my true goon (LOL) and we'd protect each other 'til the death, right or wrong. I guess that's what sisters are for and though we are close sister's we are best friends. You, me and Mama.... All for one, one for all!

To my big sister, Denise, what up fam. To my killa, Sally "Butter" Moore. You my #1 reader, read my story within five hours of you having your copy the day it dropped. And your crazy mother, LMBO. Ms. Mary, I'd never forget my first encounter with an unknown reader. And Brandy though we only spoke over the phone via Ms. Mary, I'd always remember that phone call she made after spotting you reading my book Hood Richest. I wouldn't have ever imagined that somebody I have never met would ask someone they've never met to call me. It was very flattering and believe it or not, it was my first time actually feeling some accomplishments. Thanks to both of you. Gots to shout out my girl, Laneesa Kelly, what up!

To my bad nephews: Brian "Boo Boo" Buchanon and Dana Ellis. My two, know it all goddaughter's Ny Ny and Bre, I love my beauty dolls profoundly.

To my aunties: Aunt Pat, Aunt Shirley and Aunt Linda. I didn't think y'all would even consider reading my creation of young adult fiction and it still cracks me up to know it interest the three of you. I must shout out my Aunt Shawn (thanks for being a best friend to my mother and relaxing our hair back in the day...LMBO), Tamika Mc-Comb (Ms. Debbie) and my little cuz Melanie. I appreciate all of you deeply . To my baby cousin Shy Shy, you even read my story. That's funny, youngin! To my grandfather, Jean Walker. I love you.

To my girls: Alisha Briggs, Laken Gardner, Makenzie G, Tamika

Jackson, Joselyne H., Toni Holmes, Brittany Russell, Kim Alsup and Lanita Henderson. ... I appreciate you ladies for always being good friends and cousins.

To Destinee Odom, we got that dynamic duo bond, family. Know I love you if I never told you before. You're more like my sister than just a friend. I promise if it was a best friend of the year Award you would get it, every year. Many pose as a friend but with you I feel the realness internally and I know envy or phony isn't within you. You're the greatest, Des!

To Jerrica, (one of my bestest friends ever) though you can get on my everlasting nerves virtually more than anybody (that's a good thing, cause I don't take attitudes, ya know... LOL) so what's understood don't need to be explained. I love you fam.

To my friend Montinae, you was there when I was penning Hood Richest at the tender age of 19 and believed in me before I told anyone what I was doing. Always will be grateful for that.

To Ms. Vickie Stringer, I thank you in advance for all the greatness that will be ahead for me. You believe in my work and I appreciate you for that. Thank you Caitlin and the rest of the TCP staff for giving more strength to my stories. Y'all did y'all thang.

To my readers, my supporters and everyone who helped spread the word about Hood Richest. I appreciate the love I've been receiving so, so, so, so, so very much times infinity!

Lastly, I can never forget my fam, Ryan Daniel - we love and miss you, family, R.I.P... gone but never ever forgotten, we all holding it down for you.

If I forgot someone, it truly wasn't that you aren't in my heart and I'll catch you on the next one. I deeply love you all the long way. Blessings upon Blessings!

As my wishes were for the ones that can understand my intricate expression through my pen game to be entertained with my debut novel Hood Richest, I also sincerely hope you all enjoy Wife.

Until my brain meets my pen again! It's all love! One!

Contact me with questions or comments
Michellemonay1988@yahoo.com
Signing off -Ms. Michelle Monay

Chapter One

*I*ndia was infuriated as she slung her cordless phone irritably across the room, trying to get back to sleep. It was 5:30 in the damn morning and the prank calls had been coming nonstop since midnight. She was more exasperated that Sump, her husband of four years, wasn't lying beside her — and the caller was sure to make notice of that verity.

India didn't bother to stress that fact nor pick up the phone and call him either. In India's eyes, it was only a waste of time. She was well aware of her husband's dedication to the street life and knew he wouldn't answer anyhow. Plus, she was absolutely over the long nights of dialing his cell phone number billions of times, only to be met with the voicemail. One thing India knew indubitably was Sump had groupie bitches. Hell, her woman's intuition unremittingly reminded her of that, along with the street chatterboxes. But without exclusive evidence, there wasn't anything she could do. Besides, she rarely cared about the chicks because Sump was taking care of home all too luxuriously. She knew no matter what the streets were conversing about, she wasn't going anywhere — and scarcely tripped on him.

India and Sump had been married since India found out that she was pregnant with she and Sump's second daughter Italy. Everyone in all five boroughs knew India was the wife and had never been a side dish. From the beginning, she was always down, and he was truly her soldier through the storms the duo had weathered.

Early in their relationship, there were lots of obstacles. It seemed that all the chickenheads in Queens only wanted Sump out of all the other niggas in the neighborhood. And like any other young dude, Sump fell for anything easy; his infidelity was well-known. India dealt with the constant losses and unfaithfulness, and tried her best to keep their family afloat.

Following the wedding, their relationship was pretty solid. India hardly nagged him and she never once had to bicker, bump heads or have any form of confrontation with broads over her husband, and Sump dared any chick to confront her or even act funny, lest India feel uncomfortable.

India had learned to accept his infidelity. Who wouldn't? Dude gave her whatever she liked and was at her beck and call for anything her heart desired, allowing her to swagger the city streets in nothing but $300 jeans and $2000 designer handbags or better. It was obvious that she was the flyest chick bred in Southside Jamaica Queens.

All that aside, India was frankly beginning to become fed up with the frequent calls to her house phone, waking her up at night. She had the number changed four times in the past six months and after a while the calls would start right back up. She couldn't fake it. Sump was lavishing her with expensive clothes and posh jewelry, and kept her bags caked up to keep her from complaining. It worked. There wasn't any need to fuss and stress him out because he had enough tribulations to fret about in the streets.

Besides, India wasn't by any means worried about him leaving her for another woman. Her presence alone intimidated most. She possessed a smooth caramel complexion and a delicate angelic face. Her handful of perky breasts commanded attention and her curvaceous body was the calling card of a bad chick. Soft, silky black hair cascaded down to the middle of her back, complementing her chocolate brown doe-shaped eyes and naturally arched eyebrows.

Glancing at the nightstand clock, she noticed that two hours had passed, and she was no longer languid and sleepy. India rolled over and planted her bare feet into the chinchilla carpet, allowing her silk La Perla robe to hit the floor. She plodded to the attached

Triple Crown Publications presents... *Wife*

bathroom to handle her morning business.

Once that was done, she reentered the bedroom and looked around, loving her lifestyle. Dancing her way towards her entertainment system, she turned on the stereo and the flat-screen TV that sat atop her surround sound system. Surfing through the channels, she landed on the music station, tossed the remote control onto the bed and promptly retrieved her blunt filled with purple haze. India lit the blunt and took a long toke, inhaling the herbs heavily. Releasing smoke loops from her lungs, she sat on the edge of the bed, swaying her head from side to side and singing along with Mary J. Blige. India was totally feeling her mellifluous voice echoing throughout their bedroom, voicing every deep and loving emotion she held for Sump.

"It's all because of you ... I'm never sad and blue ..."

The lyrics were fitting her mood perfectly, and they reflected her life so well. Abruptly, she stopped jammin' because she heard her Sidekick ringing. Hopping up from her perch, she reached for the phone and cradled it up her ear.

"What's jumpin'?" she answered.

"Damn hoe, turn that bullshit down. It's 7 in the fuckin' morning," her cousin Kyra screamed.

"Right. What the fuck you doing up so early?" she questioned, turning the music down simultaneously.

"'Bout to go scoop yo' sister up from school. Their last day was yesterday and I think the graduation in about two weeks. Something like that," Kyra replied.

"Oh shit! I forgot all about that, fam. We gotta hit up somebody club tonight to celebrate. I'm so proud of her graduating from medical school, eight years. Gotdamn, she tight."

"That's what I said. Too damn bad school ain't for a bitch like me and luckily I went to undergraduate school for the freaks," she jested.

"Hoe, you crazy." They both burst out into laughter. India knew that Kyra was telling the truth though. Kyra was surely a huge deal with the niggas and known for giving the pussy up without delay. Baby girl had been promiscuous since her early adolescence.

"Anyways bitch, your ass ain't going no fucking where, so stop fooling yourself." She giggled. "Sump ain't having that shit and you know it."

"Guurl beat it. Honey, I'ma grown 26-year-old woman. I do as I please."

"Yeah, what the fuck ever bitch." She sucked her teeth. "Sump gon' let you go out tonight, fo' real?" She really wanted to know.

India chuckled. "Kyra, stop gaming! I'm going, damn hoe. Stop geekin'."

"I'ma paid hoe though! But anyhoo, where is the girls?" She paused briefly. "Never mind, disregard that question; I know their Nana has them."

"You know she love her damn babies," India said, peering into the security camera at the far right of her room, watching Sump emerge from his BMW on his celly. "Bitch, I'ma have to get up with you. My husband coming in the house." India hung up, not waiting on her response.

With butterflies still in her tummy after all these years, India stared happily at the bedroom door entrance. She heard the front door close and the heavy sounds of Sump's footsteps approaching their bedroom. She rose to greet him. "Hey baby, why you look mad?" India asked, concerned. She eyed her sexy man representing New York to the fullest, rocking a pair of Robin's shorts, a white T-shirt and Polo boots.

"Yo baby, I was locked up and shit," he lied, kicking off his boots.

"For what, bay?" she asked nasally, worried.

"Nothing major ma, after leaving from fucking with Gene and 'dem after the club the cops swooped a nigga up. 'Dem motha-fuckas had me in that hot dirty-ass cell since 12:00 last night. I hate the county jail, that filthy-ass place," he said. His phone rang. He retrieved it from his pocket, glancing at the screen.

"Who is that, babe?" she inquired.

"Nobody," he said, flipping his phone back down with a stupid-ass sneaky look on his face. He placed the phone on vibrate and sat it on the dresser.

"Sump, please." India sucked her teeth. This was nothing new for her, but it hadn't happened in awhile.

"Baby that was Meek, if you must know."

India rolled her eyes and knew he was lying through his damn teeth. She could just tell. It vibrated once again, and he ignored. India pretended as if she were walking out of the room and then speedily scooped the phone up.

"India, don't start this childish shit up again. Put my phone down, yo." He scuttled over to her annoyed, towered his tall frame over her petite physique and quickly tussled with her over the phone. He snatched it away. "Don't nobody be going through your damn phone," he yelled, slipping off his shorts. "You be playing entirely too damn much, real talk though!"

"Nigga, you don't start tryna reverse some shit on me, 'cause you know ain't a damn thang in my fuckin' phone."

"Come down off that noise baby girl, be easy."

"Um-hmmm." She shook her head. "I'm not even going there with your sneaky trifling ass today okay, Sump!" She flared her nostrils. "I need some money."

"Oh, what's new India?"

"Aww, I see you on some funny acting shit," she sneered, pulling out a pair of faded Joe's Jeans and a sexy black blouse, preparing to get dressed and leave.

"Where you fenna go?"

"I'ma need for you not to be questioning me." She frowned, still angry and digging for undergarments.

"India, don't fucking play with me! Where the fuck you going?"

"Nigga, that tone of voice don't scare me anymore." India laughed, not at all intimidated. "And why should I tell you? You don't tell me yo' every damn move," she countered.

"Matter fact, you ain't going nowhere." He playfully pulled her onto the bed.

"Sumpter, get off me; I'm 'bout to go," India yelled, trying to get back up.

"Lay yo' punk ass down. It ain't even 9:00 yet." He gently pushed her back onto the bed.

"And nigga, you stay leaving before 9, what that mean?" She gazed into his eyes, sensing the seriousness on his face. "But I'm on my way to your Nana's house to have a girl's day out, if you must know." She squirmed around, trying to rise up.

"That's better shorty. Now give yo' man some of that good-good before you go," he gloated, pulling her thighs apart and trying to kiss her lips.

"Nope." She turned her face, tugging her legs together.

"Stop playing India, c'mon now ma," he implored.

She blushed enticingly and knew she could never deny him anything, no matter the circumstances. At that very instant her pussy was soaking wet. Sump quickly tossed his boxers to the corner and India raised her knees up as he slowly inserted his dick inside her glistening nah-nah. She arched her back while trying her best to hold back her loud moans, gripping tightly on the sheets in pure agony and pleasure. He was grinding her pussy roughly, thrusting his hips, slipping in and out of her with his sinful dick. Abruptly, Sump felt the need to play around and slipped his rock hard penis out of her inner being.

"Uh-uh. Sump, stop playing," India panted, pulling him back inside her, this time clenching her pussy muscles together.

"Damn, baby ... daddy's nah-nah always so damn wet, gotdamn this pussy is the fucking best."

"Ahhh, I know you like it daddy!" she squealed.

"You want me to beat this pussy up?"

"Yeah, beat this pussy up daddy. Oh, just fuck me harder. I love that wild shit! I wanna cum, please make me cum, Sump!" India begged.

As instructed, Sump followed suit and threw her legs over his shoulders. He penetrated her warm, perfectly fit slit as they both shrieked, reaching their orgasmic high place. Flipping her over into a doggy style position, Sump spread her ass cheeks apart and began beating the pussy up aggressively. He pumped her kitty as she bucked in a trance of sheer passion and arched around to watch as his manhood slid in and out of her dripping honey pot. He could barely keep his tool's glide steady, it was so wet. India loved how

Sump handled her body. He took control, hitting the right spots and knowing all her secret places. He admired her pussy 'cause it was fat and stayed creamy, plus she knew how to throw it back. India knew that she had the best pussy, and she knew her head game was proper too.

Tossing the pussy back until they both reached their peak, India swiftly flipped Sump onto the bottom and didn't hesitate to grab his instrument. She placed the swollen tip in her mouth.

"Oh shit ma, do yo' thang," he choked, landing his hands on her head and pulling on her hair. She quickly rose up and grabbed her cup of ice from the nightstand, placing two mini ice cubes into her mouth. India forced Sump's entire dick inside and began to deep throat his thickness, professionally going to work. India knew that Sump loved that freaky shit. Hell, she was doing it to keep his ass around.

"Damn ma, this what's up! Don't stop, I'm lovin' it." He groaned with both hands and moaned in delight. She knew she had him right where she needed him to be. His body began quivering over as he jerked and clutched down on the sheets, and started heaving in ecstasy. "Damn India, I'm fucking 'bout to come ma!" he yelled as India allowed all his kids to fill her mouth and she swallowed.

"Damn shawty, I think you getting better." He patted her on the head.

"Shut up, punk." India blushed, lifting up and staring at him sly. "So, Sump ..." She folded her arms. "This morning your dick tastin' a tad bit like soap nigga, you washed up while you was in the county jail, huh?" She grinned, furrowing her forehead. That would get her some cash because of course he didn't wanna hear all that bullshit.

"Oh, nah, here you go! India how much you need, damn!"

India beamed pleasantly. "I don't know. But I want this new Chanel hobo bag that came out along with this new Versace dress. Plus I gotta grab Italy and Summer some more gear, so I really don't know what that total's gonna be."

"Well, yo' ass need to stop cruisin' and work full time. You always wanting to take your happy ass shopping. What the hell I pay for you to go to RN school for?"

"Oh nigga don't even front," she said, hitting him on the chest. "Your ass the one telling me not to work." She puckered her lips.

"You some shit, man," Sump said as he slightly shook his head and retrieved a wad of money from his safe. "I just gave yo' ass a few stacks two days ago."

"That was two days ago. Don't play with me, Sumpter." Smiling she snatched the wad of money, scampered to the bathroom and hopped into the shower.

After showering for 30 minutes, India returned to her bedroom, gazing at her other half. *I put that baby to sleep*, she thought giggling. Wrapped in her fluffy towel, she plopped down onto the bed to lotion up. She sat massaging La Mer body cream into her smooth skin and pondered on how she was going to pop the question to him. She knew Sump was going to have a damn baby once she asked him to hit the club later on. He hated for her to go anywhere. Not because of insecurities, but because of hating-ass niggas. He was more than certain that niggas went straight for a dopeman's wife first. India knew that Sump's ass was just too damn protective.

Pulling her pants up, she placed her leather gold belt through the loops. She stepped into gold Christian Dior ankle-sandals and approached her husband. Soon as she sat down, his eyes blinked profusely. "What now, India?"

"Sump, I was just wondering was you going out to the club tonight?" She was pouting slightly.

"Nah, why?"

"Because I was seeing if I could go hang out with Kyra and Ton'na ..."

He quickly interrupted. "Nah India, I'm driving to B-more tonight. I gotta handle a lot of business 'round that way, ma."

"But you know Ton'na graduate in a few weeks and tonight we're celebrating. C'mon please baby, just this one time," she pleaded, whining.

"India." He stared into her eyes. "You know I don't like you going out without me. Just let me pay for y'all to take a trip to the Islands, or even a vacation in Europe."

"I'm tired of taking trips, Sump." She smacked her lips. "Damn, can I kick it where I grew up at? Hell, you would think I was European or Bahamian how many times I done visited. Damn Sump, no one's going to try and holla at me." She sighed heavily and rolled her eyes in the back of her head. "I will be sure to let you know if someone does." She conjured the saddest facial expression that she could. She hoped that the technique she used often would work this time.

Her innocent face and beautiful pout was a huge deal and something that Sump couldn't resist. He waited a moment longer and then answered. "Yeah, a'ight India. But don't be on no fuckin' dumb-ass shit. Just hang out for a couple hours. Be home before 1:00 and call me when you get back. Please, ma."

"Thank you, big daddy." She kissed her husband passionately, savoring his lovable taste, and scooped up her car keys. She grabbed her Carlos Falchi bag, whizzed out the door and headed in the direction of her daughters for their mother-daughter pampering at The Village Spa.

Chapter Two

Yo bitch, I can't believe Sump let you drive the fuckin' 57!" Kyra burbled.

"Gurl, boo. He don't know I'm pushing this whip. You know Sumpter would have a fucking fit. Dude be mad buggin', yo," India replied, laughingly. True enough, he rarely drove the car himself. Only time he brought it out was on special occasions because it was too noticeable, and everyone around town knew that Sump had the cocaine white-on-white Maybach with personalized plates that read *My World*. He really didn't like to bring much attention to himself, so he frequently drove his businessman Lexus or BMW.

India scooped Ton'na up close to midnight from their grandparents' house and headed to meet the rest of their girls at the club. In New York, the major folks were just sliding through the doors so their grand entrance would be known. Being so, the girls were running right on schedule. It was Saturday and as always, people were out clowning and the traffic was ridiculous. They had to wrestle their way through just to get to their destination.

Ton'na exclaimed, "Damn, look at all those mothafuckas waiting to get inside the damn club! Is everybody out or what?"

"Most certainly," India said. They reached the nightclub and leisurely pulled up to the front valet parking. They exited the vehicle and surveyed the crowd. Cars were everywhere, bumper-to-bumper around the club. The cars' speakers were playing a little bit of everything, from hip-hop to reggae. India immediately spotted her peoples and they sauntered their way up front. There was no way Sump's wife had to wait in line, and the bouncer quickly unhooked the black velvet rope, admitting them all inside without hesitation.

As the girls sauntered through the jam-packed club like superstars, India bopped, rapping along with Rick Ross blaring out of the huge speakers. *"Limousines, I did that ... two door coupes ... boy, I live that."* All eyes were glued to her as if she were a celebrity, which she was in her own right. What she was rocking didn't much help the attention that she was receiving. Plus everybody knew she was Sump's wife, making her queen of the borough.

India was the shit in black designer jeans, accentuated by a white leather braided belt with a buckle incrusted in black gems. She rocked a fitted white leather vest, an oversized white handle bag, and topped the outfit off with a pair of white peep-toe ankle boots. Her hair was styled in an up-do. Colorless diamond hoops hung from her ears and a costly designer watch adored her wrist.

"This place is jumping, y'all," India's cousin and best friend Nala chimed.

"Yeah, it's definitely a good look," Ton'na voiced, skimming over the club scenery.

"So far so good, ladies." India added her approval of the club's atmosphere. "Packed, but it's good," she said, bumping right into Sump's homeboy. "Meek, hey what up, fam? What you doing out, fool?"

"You know I'm just doing my thang, baby. Handling business with my mans. Nothing too out the ordinary though. But, the question is what are you doing in the club big head?"

"Shut up, punk." She lightly hit him across the chest as Nala intervened. "Meek, have you seen Gene? Is he in here?"

"I don't know. I ain't seen him, Sump or Mac C."

"Sump in B-more so he won't be coming out tonight," India informed him.

"Meaning that I gotta watch you for my nigga then." He winked, slyly grinning as he ushered them to the bar and purchased them all a drink of choice. Once they received their drinks, they dropped Meek and India led the way, trying to get to VIP. She bumped into so many people that she knew or knew of her every step of the way, saying "Sup" every two seconds. It seemed like everybody was showering the crew with mad love. Nah, let's rephrase that. It seemed like all the niggas was showering them with mad love.

All the girls were the shit standing alone, but together they were hot shit and once they got together which was hardly ever they set shit off real well. When they stepped on the scene they put chicks to shame. Most females hated India, Nala, Ton'na, Kyra, and Vanessa 'cause they were guaranteed to take over any broad's show. They could only find one reason why the chicks couldn't stand them. It had to be because they all stayed fly and were always on the arm of a boss, which made their high-class status possible.

The girls had kicked it since they were kids and were all connected some way as family. They all got branded as bourgeois hoes, but it was pure jealousy 'cause it didn't take nothing for a nigga to wife them up. Even the freaks of the clique, Vanessa and Kyra, still got wifed up when they were in a one-man mood.

As soon as they found a table, India and Nala, who were infatuated with hip-hop music, stood in the center of the floor and began moving their bodies rhythmically, chanting along with Trina. *"Money over everything ... I'm all about my change ... ."*

"Oh, hey now. Y'all, this is my shit," Kyra screamed, snapping her fingers in the air and joining in on their anthem. *"See, I'm still running over bitches ... still fucking over niggas ... ."* Kyra yelled over the blaring music, "I'll be back, y'all!" She disappeared to the dance floor.

The DJ was obviously doing his thang because the girls danced to six straight hip-hop tracks. After beginning to get hot, India placed herself inside the booth, not trying to sweat out her hair.

She sat sipping on Patron as she scanned over folks in the club. Somehow, she didn't scan for long and her eyes landed on one of New York's biggest ballers, a guy named Scrappy. She tried her hardest to keep her composure but she couldn't. Scrappy was appealing.

At that instant, she felt the same feeling she had when she used to creep with him back in the day. He wasn't the finest thang but

Triple Crown Publications presents... *Wife*

over the years he had grown ... and there was something about his demeanor that demanded her attention. *Damn, it's crazy what money can do for these niggas*, she thought, closely eyeing his figure. He stood 6-foot-3, with a soft toffee complexion and some funny colored eyes. He sported long braids and possessed a good grade of hair. He was rocking a red Artful Dodger T-shirt and baggy denim shorts with a fresh pair of crisp white-on-white Uptowns.

India didn't know how he had spotted her, but he did and without hesitating he quickly approached her. "Yo, what up India baby?" Scrappy said, leaning in to hug her neck.

"Hey Scrap, what's been good with you?" India greeted amiably, knowing he was Sump's rival and that they both despised each other to the zenith of hatred.

"Nothing baby, just kicking it and getting this money. What about you?"

"I'm good."

"I'm surprised yo' mans let you out the cage." He chuckled.

"Boy, bye. I'ma grown-ass woman."

"Yeah, that's what ya mouth say. How's your marriage doing anyway?"

"Oh, it's good, we good."

"Damn, I thought I was gon' be able to rumble with you tonight. Shid, I haven't seen you in forever, can I?" He was blatant.

"Scrap," she scrunched her face up. "Nigga, I'm married and Sump will kill me and you, plus you know we're in love, check the band." She flashed her eight-carat platinum diamond solitaire cut wedding ring; different hued stones filled the pendant.

"Yo, shawty. The ring is fat, and Sump's one lucky nigga. But just in case the nigga fuck up though, like before ..." He winked. "Baby, holla at cha boy." He licked his lips, passing her his business card. She accepted and placed the card in her bag knowing she would never call his butt. Her cell phone rang almost concurrently. "Hello, baby," she answered with an erratic heartbeat, already knowing who it was.

"India you still in the muthafuckin' club? It's damn near 2:00!" Sump roared through the phone. She felt the anger in his voice.

"Babe, calm down. I'm sorry ... we just got here about 30 minutes ago, I'm cool though. Meek 'n 'dem in here," she told him.

"I don't give a fuck if God himself was in there, Indy." She knew he was hot because that was the only time he called her that *Indy* shit. "Man, when I call you in another hour, you better be at home climbing your monkey ass in the fucking bed," he screamed. "Hard headed-ass bitch," he whispered underneath his breath.

"But Sump ..." It was too late, he had already hung up. Now India was pissed. *Niggas always tryna fuck up somebody damn night, fuck him! Bet I won't answer when he call,* she thought. A bad feeling ran through her stomach. Something was going to happen, but she didn't know what. *Fuck that, this nigga got me fucked up. I'm staying till it fucking closes,* she decided after debating with herself.

A moment later, all her girls came and sat inside the rounded booth. "Yo, why you look like you just lost your best friend?" Ton'na asked.

"Sump bitch-ass just called, talking 'bout I gotta go home!" she yelled angrily as tears welled in her eyes.

"What? You better not start crying!" Vanessa flared her nose. "Fuck Sump's ole insecure ass. He needs to stop trippin'! You haven't been out kickin' it with us in months of Sundays, and now you get out the house for one night and his black ass gotta problem with it. Fuck that bullshit. His lame ass can beat it," Vanessa yelled, being the most outspoken one of the crew.

"Nessa, leave that shit alone. That's between her and bra. Stop down speaking that damn boy all the damn time," Ton'na chimed.

"Fuck that nothin' ass nigga. He stay jumping without India day in and day out. So she can at least enjoy partying sometimes without his ass tagging along."

"That's all I'm saying. But I just don't feel like beefing with that nigga when he gets back tomorrow," India whined as Gene and Meek approached the table.

"What's up ladies?"

"Hey," they all replied.

"What up baby, I missed you." Nala stood and greeted her husband.

Triple Crown Publications presents... *Wife*

"Roll up, nigga," Vanessa suggested, knowing Gene always kept that fruity fruit.

"Ay, I got this round, Sump left me with some of this purp he got from Uptown," India said.

"That's what's up," Vanessa replied.

India fumbled through her bag for her ounce of kush and a cigarillo. She filled the blunt with the best purp in New York and blazed up. India took two long drags, then passed it to Vanessa who sat to the left of her.

"Damn bitch, this is some good shit," Vanessa said in between coughs.

"I know," India replied as she saw Kyra approaching them with a huge cake.

"Happy, happy ... what you call it!" Kyra screamed, feeling every bit of the blunts she smoked and the bottle of Patrón she drank. "Hell, let's just give it up for Ton'na. The big doctor in the house! She done did her eight years and congratulations to my big cousin. Ton'na, big babyyyy!" Everyone applauded and congratulated her success.

"The only hood chick I know that's done made major power moves like this." Nala giggled.

"A real sassy-jazzy, classy bona fide hood bitch 'bout to be a damn doctor. Get it bitch," Vanessa complimented excitedly.

"Right, sis wasn't gonna play wit 'em," India said. Ton'na couldn't stop smiling; she was ecstatic.
"She done missed out on eight years, studying hard while we was out partying. But now we can all say that it has finally paid off." India beamed.

"Sure have, monkeys. I'm ready to party like it's my fucking birthday. Shoot, every day is my damn birthday," Ton'na gushed, happier that she had ever been.

The fellas stayed a second longer and bolted over to the dice game in the back room.

Everyone was partying hard, having a good ole time. Unfortunately for India, the night was coming to a close. She knew her and Sump would go toe-to-toe for this shit for weeks, and there wasn't any telling when the next time he would allow her to go out would be. Walking out, people were shoving and squeezing through to reach the exit.

Finally making it outside of the club, India, Kyra, and Ton'na hugged their peoples and told them they would holla at them tomorrow. They walked across the street to their car.

"Ay, fam, hold on," Kyra yelled to her cousins. She spotted a prospective sponsor for her expert services. She acted like a straight up dude. If Kyra saw something she wanted, she hollered, not at all timid. She walked in the opposite direction of the car to go see what was up with homeboy pushing the triple black Land Rover.

The girls sat patiently waiting on Kyra in the Maybach '57, receiving mad attention as they pulled up alongside of the club's front entrance. People were standing around as if the party wasn't over. Ranges, Benzes, BMWs, and all sorts of trucks were riding up and down the boulevard as if there wasn't any other street to cruise through.

After a minute of showstopping, Meek approached the car.

"Hey, what's good Meek?" India said, rolling down her window.

"What up, what y'all waiting for big head?"

"For Kyra's jigging ass to come the fuck on. Sump already gon' kill me."

"That nigga ain't gon' kill his India. But he will kill over yo ass 'dough, most def." He nodded, agreeing with himself. He still held lust in his eyes. "But, what up Miss College Grad?" Meek leaned his head slightly inside the window, observing Ton'na.

"Nothing much." She cut her eyes, really wishing that Meek wouldn't try to get her to leave with him because it surely wasn't happening with all the eyes glued to the car.

"Yo, ma ... I'm getting ready to bounce up outta here. You wanna roll with me?" he inquired, praying that she would. He definitely wanted some of her pussy since he couldn't get what he really wanted. Ton'na wanted to accept his offer, but she would loath for people to see them leaving together — and she definitely didn't want their little one-night-stand secret to surface. Besides, she hated to be the replacement and knew she had to decline his offer.

"Meek, you know sis ain't even gonna fuck with you on that level, my dude."

"Shit, I don't see why not," he said cockily.

"Because you know she's not, nigga," India giggled.

"Yeah she be on that bullshit. But it's cool ma, I'll get up with y'all later. Oh, and I'ma tell Sump you was up in all these niggas' faces. I know he don't know you whipping this '57."

"What nigga? Meek, stop playing," she belted out.

"Yeah, well you better put me on Ton'na," he jokingly said.

"Shut your silly ass up. Bye, boy."

"Bye, Meek," Ton'na cooed.

"A'ight then ladies." He tapped the car and moseyed on off. Not even a second later, Kyra appeared, excited. "Ay y'all, I got some slam on deck, so I'll holla at you hoes tomorrow, or maybe the day after tomorrow, 'cause I think I can drain this nigga."

"You know what, Kyra?" India was heated. "That's why I don't be fucking with you. I could have been gone. Bye." She skidded off into traffic.

"Did you have fun, girlie?" Ton'na asked.

"I did. I'm just salty 'cause it seem like time flew by so fast."

"Right, it was so many niggas in there tonight."

"I know, right. Too bad I'm happily married, because it would be on and poppin'." They both laughed.

India continued navigating through the city streets. Drake crooned from the speakers as India thought about how Sump was going to act a straight fool once he got home. She wondered for a minute if she should have left when he instructed her to. Then she obliterated the thought from her mind because she hardly ever tripped on him. He shouldn't be mad at her hanging out for one night. Whatever happened, India knew he couldn't be upset forever.

They must have been a few blocks away from their grandparents' place when a dark SUV abruptly pulled in front of the car, cutting them off. Their hearts instantly dropped as two masked gunmen jumped out the SUV, automatic weapons in hand. All the sisters could do was scream and kick while being pulled out of the car. The masked men threw the girls in the backseat of the SUV and one guy hopped in the '57. As quickly as it happened was as quickly as they disappeared through the clear night air.

Chapter Three

India Jones had always been the big thang poppin' around Queens, New York, where she lived all her life. Yes ... she was a hood chick, but her father practically owned the city streets. So she was cool with that fact because that very borough was certainly their territory. India didn't want for anything, and acquiring the last name Jones explained it all. The one and only person she had to keep up with was her damn self. She was always considered a daddy's girl, and when it came to India, her father gave her anything she yearned for.

India's body had sprouted out soon as she hit the early age of eleven, and it made her Dad a bit nervous. He didn't play any games though, and would've killed anybody who looked at her wrong. No nigga would dare stare at India too long.

She had a slew of family members from all over New York, making her connected to families that she didn't even know. Every year, her father held his famous Memorial Day cookout for all the niggas he lost in the game. It seemed as if Denel Jones had all sorts of shit going on in the community. Everyone in the hood enjoyed fireworks on the Fourth of July and on Halloween, everybody had costumes. Dude showed everyone mad love. He would have given anything anybody asked for no matter how big the request was, even if it was the last thing in his pocket. He was a good nigga. Once every season he would give away a car and sometimes even passed out raffle tickets and the winner would receive five

thousand dollars in cash. On Christmas, he was like the ghetto Santa Claus 'cause everybody in the projects woke up to presents. Not little trinkets or bullshit-ass gifts. People were receiving Nintendos, Polo gear, Jordans for their footwork, and every trend that was hot at the time.

It wasn't shit to get a million back in the day. Hell, Denel knew he couldn't take no damn armored truck to the funeral home, so he didn't mind sharing the wealth. He was a nigga that never had shit and once he got it, he flaunted and distributed the paper with all who came into his presence. India understood how her mother had fallen in love with such a charismatic hood nigga. Her mother Marla and Denel were young lovers and their relationship resembled India and Sump's a lot, welcoming Ton'na into the world when Marla was only 15, then two years later welcoming their other princess, India, to earth.

Growing up, India yearned to have a dude to take care of her as her mother did. She loved the way her father dropped cash on her mother, giving her rolls of hundreds just to shop, having her riding too damn lovely. Everyone in the neighborhood knew that Marla was the head bitch in charge and surprisingly Denel never once cheated on her. Marla was all he ever needed and being that he didn't too much trust people, he didn't get involved with other women at all. He had heard way too many stories of bitches setting niggas up. He prevented all the extra drama and just kept his main lady underneath his wing.

Although they lived in the projects, they lived like it was the suburbs. Denel had two apartments as one in their apartment building. He had gotten the walls knocked down and laid the place out. It was decked out with only the top-of-the-line shit. His philosophy was, *Ain't no money like dope money*. Denel and his crew lived by that maxim and hustled hard for theirs, reigning over the Queens drug trade. He was big time; a millionaire nigga who was rolling with cats getting galore money too. Cocaine was the main moneymaker during the '80s. Money was coming from everywhere, but heroin was what satisfied his hunger for that fast money, transforming him and his comrades into multi-millionaires.

That's how India was introduced to Nala and Sump. Both of their fathers were rolling with Denel heavy. Sump and Nala's fathers were brothers and were the craziest niggas Denel knew. Rumor was, they killed their own father at the ages of 9 and 10 for beating up on their moms.

Sump's father Mark took his stepfather's last name, Jones. That was Denel's great-uncle. That fact made India happy once they wed because she never wanted to get rid of her father's surname. They all wanted their pops's legacy to live on. The only thing it could be was legendary.

Denel and his partner's time ran completely out when the Feds came in and took over everything. It was a hassle because Sump's father wasn't surrendering when the peoples came to round him up. He had the police on standoff for two days and finally came out busing his AK, taking a couple officers out with him. Sump had to admit he liked how his pops went out, on some straight up G shit. Luckily, Nala's father and Denel got off, being that they snitched out the entire police force and government officials who were working for them. For that, the men were placed into protective custody somewhere on the other side of the globe.

Sump knew from that point he was going to be the king following in their footsteps. With a plan intact at 12 he took on the game, bringing along his childhood friends Meek and Gene and cousin Mac C. The years he spent around his father allowed him to know the ins and outs of Queens's goldmine, setting the perfect tone for his turn in the streets. In due time he had Queens and its surrounding areas in his palms; on lock as the street kings once had.

India wasn't trying to chase after the gotdamn American Dream with the white picket fence and the prince waking up every morning going to work at his Fortune 500 company. Fuck that prince charming fairytale bullshit. She was from the ghetto and that lifestyle wasn't real in the hood. That fake dream was all movie script. Her expectations of life were far away from that and it suited her well.

India wanted herself a boss. She already knew that starting off as a young hustler like her father did would produce major wealth in the future. Being that Sumpter Jones was already her childhood boyfriend, the one she used to always get caught humping on, was a boon for her. It seemed as if they had been together forever because neither of the two remembered when it was that they officially hooked up. All they knew was, he popped her cherry when she was 13 and impregnated her with their first-born, Summer, when they were just 14 years old.

Both of them were ecstatic about India being pregnant, but Ronnie, his mother, was pissed beyond belief when she learned there would be a new member being added to their family. She hated the fact that her only child was having a baby and he was just a baby himself. Ronnie was the mother that chicks hated and to date, she and India bumped heads every time they crossed paths. Sometimes India wondered if Ronnie wanted to fuck her own damn son. But that was a worry she didn't take seriously. Ronnie wasn't even attracted to men. She had only been with Sump's father once and she despised it. Ronnie and Mark met when she was 16. He didn't wanna do anything else but get between her thick chocolate thighs.

Ronnie knew she was fooling herself hella hard because all her life she eyed chicks. But just to make sure that's what she solely wanted, she gave it up to Mark, the infamous heartbreaker. And a heartbreaker he was. Mark was beyond irate when he was informed that Ronnie was pregnant with his son. He tried offering her money to get rid of the baby, to paying street chicks to fight her. That was a waste of his money. Ronnie came from a family of six brothers and whooped every bitch who tried to step in her area, yapping about *nothing*.

Once Sump was born and Mark saw himself living within the boy things changed drastically. Mark loved his son dearly, sometimes even fighting with Ronnie over who would raise him. As his toddler years came, they both knew they had to put their differences aside for the sake of their baby boy. Even though Mark and Ronnie didn't get involved sexually, he still stepped up to the plate and took good care of her and his son. He paid all the bills and kept cash in her pockets.

Triple Crown Publications presents... *Wife*

India always knew Sump's sexy ass would be something major. He was always a determined type of dude and never gave up on what he called his American dream. He promised himself that he would be the man, but knew that anybody could get up and begin selling dope. But, Sump was far from a gym shoe hustler and craved for the hot whips and major cribs. He always could see himself in the limelight of the game and dreamed about it damn near every night. He deeply devised his plan and by the time he turned 13 he was moving ounces of drugs biweekly and the old heads had much love for him because of the name his father had in the streets.

Besides, it seemed that hustling came natural to him. At the age of 16, Sump had his hands in many markets. He peddled pounds of pills and bricks of crack cocaine and heroin. Being a young dude, he was bringing in plentiful cash and purchased himself a 96 Range Rover, also copping India a 1990 Lexus. Ronnie didn't trip about him hustling because she knew it was bound to happen. Sump was amid drug dealers far too long for him not to have the ambitions of a hustla and he earned his own street credibility swiftly.

By 18, all of Queens was his and he quickly bought a house out in Jamaica Estates. He was the youngest dude getting that rich white man paper and on his 21st birthday he purchased a bigger house. He was living too good, moving out to the beautiful mansions in Long Island, New York. The house was breathtaking.

The moment India saw the place she damn near fell out. By the huge manicured front lawn, she knew she was finally settling into the life that she deserved. The expensive castle-styled double wooden French doors didn't much help and the farther she traveled the better their domain got. The place held six bedrooms, five full bathrooms, a home theater system, a playroom for the girls and a massive pool with Jacuzzi in the back yard. Every room throughout the house had off-white marble flooring with authentic crystals encrusted within, except for their bedroom and the main living room, which had off-white chinchilla carpeting. White Italian leather furniture decorated the main living room; even the beautiful fireplace bricks were white. A total of six crystal chandeliers surrounded the entire house. They added flat screen TVs to each and every room including the dining room. The dining room was off-white and silver with an off-white and clear dining room set imported from Russia.

Their crib was definitely decked out and major, but Sump's ass constantly left India in that huge house and she was bored out of her damn mind. She had to admit that she was well pleased and very grateful, but sometimes she also felt forlorn. He would stay out to the wee hours of the morning and every now and then he wouldn't come home for a few days. She couldn't stand it, but that cycle was old and she was done nagging his ass after they exchanged vows. India knew no matter what he did out in the streets no bitch could top or replace her. So although he wasn't there often he wasn't going anywhere either, she knew that for a fact. She indeed loved his protection and the way he took precautions. India just thought that he went overboard with the rules a little. Nobody was allowed to visit their home unless it was close family, meaning immediate family only. Hanging out on the town was very limited without him being present and certainly she couldn't ride around certain parts in New York City's perimeter without him.

But, it was the price she had to pay to live the lifestyle that was so appealing to her. Even with what had happened with her father, India was enamored with the life. Many girls from the hood dreamed of being crowned the kingpin's wife. The pleasant trips to France and Italy, the extravagant shopping sprees on Rodeo Drive, and splurging at the Mall of America were well worth it all. India had gone from princess of the hood to queen of the streets.

That was one thing that Sump hadn't inherited from their fathers. He didn't shit where he ate. Living in the inner city at such a high status was prohibited. It wasn't because he was afraid; he wasn't easily intimidated. As a matter of fact, just the mention of his name scared folks. He was known in the streets by not to be fucked with as he carried on his pops' legacy. The seriousness that he wore on his smooth chocolate face was what got him noticed. He had the same killer instinct look that his father had possessed, and certainly would kill at the drop of the dime if need be. Although he was presented to the streets as mean and arrogant, he was much different to India. Her man was sexy and sweet; though they battled to no ends at times he was her best friend, her confidant and other half.

India just loved the muscular build that reached six-foot stature. Sump's cheekbones were chiseled and she lit up every time she saw his sleepy light brown eyes. He owned the sexiest lips known to a woman. He rocked his hair cut into a fine Caesar with deep waves without a lick of facial hair. Sump was that nigga with the perfect swag to match.

From the beginning of time, it was a love connection that they felt would never wane. Sump knew India was his soul mate and his Nana reminded him of that. If he didn't listen to anyone else in the world, he made sure that he took heed in any and everything that his Nana said   and learned a lot by doing so. Nana loved her some India too and it showed in the way she cared for her girls.

Sump was everything that India ever wanted, and she had gotten dazzled by the glitz of the life, forgetting that nothing lasts forever   especially if it's not right. She utterly lost sight of all the bad situations drug dealers are faced with by the reintroduction to the glamour. She completely forgot that jail shouldn't be an afterthought, and death should be the biggest thought   if nothing else a fear. She never thought she would need a plan because Sump was smarter than her father had been. He was careful. He kept family and the streets separate.

India was in love with the man of her dreams and truly enjoyed spending the dope money. Loving it, and sometimes wondering if she loved it more than she loved herself. But she rarely questioned if the street lifestyle that they were living would actually turn bad – as it often does ... and it was a price that many have to pay, just by being a part of the game.

Chapter Four

Wake "Wake up! I got yo' bitch nigga," the kidnapper mimicked laughingly, as he found it comical to imitate Dame from State Property. Here it was 5 in the fucking morning and Sump was awakened by the piercing sounds of his BlackBerry Storm going off. The first few times he ignored, surmising that the restricted call that displayed on his caller ID screen was India trying to explain herself. There wasn't anything that she could have said or done for him not to be extremely upset with her, and he held onto his word up until this very instant.

"What the fuck!" He moved Lilly from underneath him and jumped up out of bed, hoping that he was only dreaming. "Hello, what the fuck you just say, nigga?"

"Nigga, I'm sure you don't wanna start playing games with me. We don't have time to talk. Yo' bitch kinda cute and I don't know ... if you keep stalling I might have to fuck her." The kidnapper spoke through the phone again chortling at his replications. "Now, $150 bans, son. You have an hour and a half to get them ends together nigga. There's this black van in the alley off of Queens Boulevard and Willard Drive. Leave the cash in the backseat. Come alone, no police, and try any bullshit   these bitches are dead." *Click.*

Sump stared at his screen for five minutes after the caller had already hung up. Lilly sensed there was a problem, observing him frantically pace back and forth. The instant stress and heartache was written all over his face. But she elected not to speak because the menacing glare steaming from his eyes informed her not to fuck with him.

Who in the fuck would do some shit like this? A jumble of thoughts danced around Sump's mind as he allowed another five minutes to bypass, desperately trying to figure out what envious-ass nigga would have enough balls to pull this stunt. He was clueless to the fact because he had entirely too many known enemies and didn't even wanna surmise the covertly serious ones. He glanced at the nightstand clock. It read 05:09 a.m. He had no idea how he was going to be able to collect the entire $150 G's from his crib in Long Island in an hour and half. He was laid up on the upper side of Manhattan with his mistress, knowing that it was impossible even if he tried.

Damn, why I have to lie, I just should've gone out with her. Then this shit wouldn't have happened. Fuck, why she didn't just leave like I told her ass to? Sump thought as regret plagued him. Disgusted and full of fury, his chest caved in at the thought of one of the guys fucking his wife. Anger and jolts of energy filled his body. His head was pounding a mile a second and he knew he had to do something and something fast.

"Ay, Lilly how much money you got here?"

"$15 thousand in the safe, why?"

"Let me hold that," he whispered. She shot up without delay and headed for her safe. Sump frenetically scrolled through his contact numbers and dialed his best friend. "Yo Gene," he spoke into the phone. "How much money you got on you right now, nigga?"

"Why, what up?"

"Somebody done snatched India up, and all my real fuckin' bread at my safe in the Islands. I need some paper a-fuckin'-sap, son." His voice cracked. "Talkin' bout I got an hour and a half and it's impossible for me to grab the cake from out there and be back in an hour and half. I got $15 G's right now, $30 G's in Jamaica and $25 stacks at Nana's crib. I need $80 more."

Gene was in a state of shock because he couldn't imagine how Sump was feeling, knowing if it was Nala he probably would've blown some shit up in New York.

"Bra, did you hear me? They got India, son!"

"All I got is $30 G's here and some dope."

"Get that and meet me at the spot immediately. And call Mac C. Fill the nigga in and tell him be there too and grab some dough."

He quickly hung up and phoned Meek. Meek was surprised. He had seen India less than thirty minutes prior and now she was in the hands of a kidnapper. That shit fucked him up too. "Son, that's fucked up. I just seen her and Ton'na right before they pulled off from the club. Man, we gotta get shorty back."

"I know." He sat down and leaned over with his hand on his face. One solitary tear raced down his cheek as a qualm overwhelmed his stomach, almost expelling the contents from it. "Man, I just gotta get this bread quick, fam. I gotta get them back, yo."

"I got $50 bans for you. I'ma meet you at your spot in twenty."

*****

India's body shuddered violently. Her hands were bound tightly behind her back by rope and her legs were duct taped in an unloosening restraint. Fear blazed from her eyes and snot dripped down her nose as she anticipated death. She didn't know what would become of them. Uncertainty of what the captors were going to do with her and her sister lingered in the air like a dark plague.

"Y'all niggas must really got a death wish!" Ton'na snarled. "Y'all know Sump gon' kill you niggas after this shit over with, right?"

"Yeah, yeah ... all that rah-rah shit and the nigga still ain't came through."

"Ton'na, just be quiet," India demanded through sniffles, already knowing the drill.

"Yeah, listen to your people if you know what's good for your asses."

Ton'na always had a smart mouth and never feared anything in her entire life. As death stared her in the face, she spewed rudely and unflinchingly. "Fuck you, pussy nigga!"

"Ton'na just shut up," India shrieked as tears poured from her eyes. *What the fuck is takin' this nigga so fuckin' long?* Trembling with fear, she looked around the dreary basement with the moisture and grime overlaying the concrete flooring. Her nose burned from the foul stench. India wished there was some way she could summon Sump to rescue the two of them because she was almost sure that Ton'na wouldn't shut up.

India knew the high risk the kidnappers were taking by holding her for ransom money. Sump with all certainty would kill everyone involved in the worst way if he ever learned their identities. But, it was obvious that the mothafuckas didn't give a shit. That's why she just hoped that Ton'na would be quiet because it was evident that the niggas didn't care about Sump or what he stood for.

"Oh this li'l' bitch got balls. You think you tough?" The captor walked up to her and forebodingly glided the barrel of the gun down her face. "I'ma show you how to respect grown-ass men."

Not even a second later, Ton'na felt a blow to the left side of her face. Then the gunman repeatedly struck her in the same spot with the pistol. Instantly blood oozed from her mouth onto her pure white Coogi dress. The agonizing pains coming from Ton'na's face only caused her to curse him out further. She tried to squirm around, but she couldn't go too far because her hands were tied behind her back and her feet were intertwined closely to each other. The gunman continuously kicked her with his steel-toed boot, forcing her head to hit the back of the wall.

India knew she couldn't do anything because she was tied up. It hurt her to just sit and watch. She tried wrinkling out of the rope with piercing screams, but froze when the other gunman forced the barrel of the gat to her head. "Bitch, stop moving." India did as she was instructed and rocked herself back and forth against the wall with tears streaming down her face. The gunman towered over Ton'na and roared, "Bitch, I bet you won't disrespect nobody else."

Despite Ton'na's injures to her swollen face she glared up at him, clothes gory and blood gushing from her mouth. She spit disrespectfully into his face. "Betcha I will, bitch made-ass nigga."

A knee-jerk reaction pulled him instantly to the trigger and without hesitating he fired three shots into Ton'na's body, causing blood and body fragments to splatter everywhere.

"Oh my God! Oh my God!" India screamed as the sounds echoed throughout the basement. Blood was oozing from the corner of

Ton'na's mouth and streaming out of her nose and eyes. India couldn't stop herself from screaming as she saw her sister's body trembling uncontrollably. The world had appeared as if it had stopped and even the shooter's acquaintance looked astounded.

India listened, traumatized. The sound of footsteps grew closer.

The orchestrator appeared behind a mask and noticed India still breathing, but Ton'na's body slouching over in quivers.

"Yo, man what the fuck just happened?" he screamed at his henchmen.

"Fuckin' bitch spit on me! Man, shit was my reflexes. I didn't mean to kill the bitch," he said as Ton'na took her final breath.

The voice stifled by the black ski mask sounded very familiar, but India was in such emotional shock she couldn't put her finger on it.

"Son, that shit wasn't the fuckin' plans, this shit is about Sump you always beefing with bitches, man." He shook his head, disappointed. "I can't believe this shit. Always fuckin' some shit up, nigga." He paused briefly and continued. "The nigga just made the drop. Let's get India and get the fuck ghost, fam."

Triple Crown Publications presents... *Wife*

Chapter Five

*I*ndia was a complete wreck and her presence was that of a zombie. The condolences of the funeral attendees overwhelmed India as they came one after the other. She sat on the front pew silently. She was unable to respond and hid her devastation behind a pair of oversized Tom Ford sunglasses.

Ton'na Jones was being laid to rest on the south side of Queens, exactly one week from her graduation day. Her funeral was huge. Outside resembled more of a car show than a funeral service. Inside, the vast church was even more packed. There weren't any seats left and hardly any standing room. May's weather produced a nice breezy spring day, as mourners poured in by the droves to say their final farewells.

It was one thing that Ton'na was well known around their way, but people were coming from all five boroughs as well. When news of her hateful murder hit the streets, the black community came in for support. India was grateful that everyone came out to say their goodbyes to Ton'na. She saw a lot of her sister's homegirls from school, and even a few of her professors. The Dean even came to give a speech on Ton'na's behalf. All of her peoples were showing love in paying their last respects. Mostly everyone in attendance rocked pictures of Ton'na on their attire.

Sump made sure that Ton'na was going to be buried like a queen and ordered her a custom made diamond-trimmed and platinum-plated coffin. White roses and lilies surrounded the

church, along with pictures of her. He paid for everything, showing how much love he really had for someone that he considered blood. Sump wanted to make sure she was sent off like a queen. Nobody knew it, but Denel had made it to the viewing. He somehow managed to see how beautiful India had gotten as he admired her exiting the limousine.

Marla had flown in from California where she was residing. She was taking it terribly because she knew that she would be in Queens, but thought it was to see her daughter stride across the stage, not to be buried and gone forever. She lost control and broke down at her beloved daughter's casket. She couldn't take the horrible sight of her baby lying dead in a casket any longer. As she was being escorted out of the services, she spotted Sump through the sea of faces and didn't hesitate to rear her hand back and slap the shit out of him.

"It's all your fault my daughter is dead!" Tears rained from her eyes as she turned to India. "India it's not worth it, get away now — having a drug dealer isn't the way out sweetie. You can never win with them no matter what route you take; they're bad news all around sweetie. Find you a good man, baby." Marla spoke from her heart, hoping her daughter would take note before it was too late.

India dropped her head, too hurt to even act upon the situation. She said a silent prayer for her sister. *Dear God, Please welcome my sister into your house with open arms. Care for her, love her and protect her, God. Give her peace. I know you want her with you, but tell her I will see her soon. And please help her to forgive me. I'ma love her forever and one day we will reunite. In Jesus' name, I pray. Amen.*

The preacher spoke his last words as everyone made their last views, and then they closed the casket. The pallbearers carried the coffin out to the hearse and the family let off five hundred white doves before they departed the church.

There were four miles of cars following the four stretch limos. A platinum Hummer hearse carried her body with a huge screen atop. A slide show of her life was being showcased; she always took beautiful pictures.

Once they lowered Ton'na's body into the ground, a piece of

India went with her sister. Before India and Sump crawled despondently into the limousine, her grandfather approached them.

"Sump and India, sweetheart?"

They both turned around simultaneously. "Yes Papa?" she answered.

"Please, you and Sumpter don't go blaming yourselves for what happened to Ton'na, okay," he spoke, being a true believer. "You all know the Lord calls on his children according to his purpose. Only God knows the purpose and he was ready for her. So don't go blaming yourselves or the animals that done this. God will handle all fools, believe me kids. And I say again, we do not blame neither of you. It was just Marla wanted to see her daughter accomplish something, but we never know what God has planned for us. So I beg that you kids not hold yourselves at fault — just take care of them beautiful children and live life, 'cause it's certainly a short one this day and age. Move on, because if I don't know anything else I know God has her. I know she's better there and in a greater place where she don't have to worry." He took their hands in his and said a prayer over them both. Tears fell from India's eyes as her Papa embraced her, saying goodbye.

Sump rented out a banquet hall for the repast and they had a DJ, food and drinks. Sump sat by India's side, not once departing. They both felt so responsible; *ifs* and *should-haves* roamed throughout their minds relentlessly. India's mind was spinning out of control. She only stayed for an hour or so. She had to go because the agony was too much to bear. Before she left she walked over to embrace her mother and grandmother again. Marla wound up apologizing to Sump, and explained she really hoped they got out of the game. Marla was a product of misfortune in the game and knew the outcome was never good. In her eyes, it could only end in three ways: death, jail or getting out before it was too late. She just hoped that they would opt for the right direction. They all prayed together and after their goodbyes to everyone, the pair left.

India and Sump headed straight home. She really didn't know how she would be able to move on without her sister. They had had so many plans for the future, and now it was all over with.

India took a fifth of Patron to the head and she sniffled all night as Sump rubbed her back soothingly for hours. With the morning light peeking inside their room, she finally fell asleep in Sump's arms.

Triple Crown Publications presents... *Wife*

Chapter Six

The summer months were ending quickly in New York, welcoming fall in with a cold chill. India still was messed up behind her sister's death, completely blaming herself for the awful tragedy. Ever since the kidnapping Sump made sure that he was by her side. To India's surprise, he was home more than he was out in the streets. When he did go out to handle business, it would be for a couple of hours and he would return before she took notice.

Sometimes he went out just to try and search the streets for the people involved with the murder and kidnapping. Sump was fueled by anger. He was determined to avenge Ton'na's death and in foresight he saw blood for the abductors. But he knew that it was all a part of the game and for now, Sump decided to chop it up as a terrible loss, but would never allow it to leave his mind. It was unforgettable.

Sump tried doing everything to make India happy and to leave the past in the past. Starting off, he replaced her Beamer for a brand new bulletproof cranberry-coated 2010 XJ Jaguar with cocaine white interior, complemented by 22-inch rims. India didn't want for anything.

One morning in particular, Sump had had enough. India never saw mornings and would be in bed by 9. He was sympathetic of her deep depression but fed up with the moping. Sump wasn't having it any longer and was determined to get her out of the house. They were going to enjoy the entire day.

It was 11:21 p.m. after Sump got dressed. He watched as India slumbered, seemingly still in emotional agony. She was still adorable, pouting miserably in her sleep. He felt the need to start her off in the way she would usually start off his mornings to allow her to have a delightful day. Deftly, he made his way underneath the silk Versace sheets. Being that she never slept with undergarments on, he dove straight in and proceeded to give her one of his phenomenal state-of- the-art performances. He felt India's body tense up, wetter than ever. He inched his tongue in deeper and deeper as she grinded her hips in a steady circular motion until she squealed in pleasure and over-climaxed. He slurped up all her sweet juices.

"Damn you started the day off good, baby!" India cracked a half smile.

"That's because I love my wife." He smiled affectionately. "Now get up," he spoke in a demanding tone. "Get dressed cause you gotta get up out of the fucking house ma. Gene out front waiting for me now, we fenna handle something with the connect. Go and swoop up Nala, y'all go shop somewhere or somethin'." India had to agree herself. She was tired and needed to get out before she went mentally insane. "Make sure you grab the burner just in case a pussy-ass nigga try to run up! Once you finish come down to The Chop Shop. I should be there 'bout time you finish. I left you some money – it's in your top drawer." He kissed her forehead and jetted out.

After showering, India gazed at her sister's picture and kissed it. Then she voiced out loud, "I love you sis, always, forever and ever." There wasn't any need for her to weep over the death of Ton'na anymore. She had come to her in her dream the previous night, and told her to move on, she was okay. That's all India needed and she knew she had to let it go. Sitting home everyday had definitely become a serious bore. She was tired of lounging around in her pajamas; that wasn't her at all. She usually made sure she was dressed to impress and wouldn't get caught dead looking a mess.

Although no gift or trip could replace the love she held for her sister, India also knew Ton'na wanted her to move on with her life. She knew that God sometimes made his calls in wild and devastating ways.

She retrieved her outfit from the closet. It consisted of a cropped white-and-chocolate brown leather jacket and white button down mini-dress that tied in the front and could be worn as a shirt. A pair of wide-legged faded designer jeans and white wedge heels completed the look. She smoothed her hair up into a neat high ponytail and right before she left she grabbed the chrome .380. She placed it inside her Loewe brand handbag that Sump purchased for her, called Nala and was out the door to scoop her up. She only lived ten minutes away.

Two and a half hours later, after hitting up Jamaica Avenue for some light shopping, they were shopping on Fifth Avenue in Manhattan like maniacs. This was something that India hadn't done in forever, but was used to and never got bored doing so. The first stop was Gucci, where she went shopping crazy. "Yo, this New York bag is so fucking major." India held it up for Nala, whose eyes widened.

"Oh yeah, babes. That bag mad presidential, I gotta cop that," Nala said with much excitement.

"Right, me too!" India hissed. "Oooh look Nala. They even got the matching damn peep toes. Oh yes." India beamed.

India was at ease, and it felt really good to be able to enjoy life as she once knew. She was so blissful that her life was back on the right path, she wound up hitting a few more flagship stores. She picked up Nana a few items, Sump's two younger cousins and her two daughters four designer outfits a piece with shoes and bags to match perfectly. Sump never forgot about her when he shopped and it was vice versa. She picked him up two dozen luxurious boxers and a bottle of costly cologne along with picking herself up another bottle of Clive Christian fragrance, which cost her well over a G.

After departing the mall she called to see where Sump was. He informed her that he would be at "Super Cuts" in another hour. India decided to swing by Nana's place to drop off their gifts. India was always happy to see Nana; she was the sweetest person India had ever known. Of course, Nana was always excited when India stopped past. She knew that her grandson loved India deeply, and Nana loved him dearly so she carried the same love as if they were one.

"How's everything going with my baby? You all right, sweetheart? Sumpter stopped here earlier and gave the girls some money. Come on in here get comfortable. How are you feeling bab-yyy?" India loved visiting Nana and ever since she could remember Nana always been as sweet as she could be, giving off a friendly impression with her honest personality and warm smile. "Yes honey, Sumpter dropped of some money earlier, 'bout noontime. The girls said they wanted to go shopping and then to the movies. I told him he didn't have to, that I would pay, but he insisted and showed up anyway." Nana was one of those talkative older ladies and India could barely comprehend her, but her swift words managed to register.

"Oh, you don't have to take them shopping. I grabbed my girls some stuff, and T'ionna and Brianna also," India told her.

"You know they still gon' wanna go somewhere, child," Nana said. "And how is everything going Nala? Where is Gene, he hadn't visited me in a few weeks now. Tell him Nana gon' get him." She balled up her little fist, playfully jabbing the air with a smile.

"I'ma make sure to tell him, Nana. And how is your dialysis coming along?"

"Oh, honey I go twice a week. It's fine child."

"Nana where is the girls, outside? 'Cause I got their stuff inside the car," India asked.

"Brianna, T'ionna, Italy and Summer," Nana hollered. "India down here; she got y'all something." It was like it was an earthquake in New York City; the entire house shook. Entering the living room, the foursome looked precious.

"Hey, Mommy." Italy jumped right into her mother's arms. "Hey Momma." Summer hugged her neck. "What up India," T'ionna and Brianna said at the same time.

"Hey girls, go grab the bags outta the car."

The girls ran outside and quickly rushed back in, going straight through the shopping bags. "I'onna, give that Chanel bag to Nana," India told her.

"Well thank you, India. You're such a sweetheart but you really didn't have to." Nana sat the bag next to her because she was not really into material things. Instead she watched her grandbabies gleefully go through the bags, seeing who had what. Nothing else made Nana happier than to see other people ecstatic. She just wished they didn't drown the girl's minds by lavishing them with such expensive gifts.

"Ay Mommy, I think you forgot to get me some Prada sneakers," Italy hissed.

Everybody laughed because Italy was only four, and you would've never thought she was because of how clearly and knowingly she spoke.

"You don't like your D & G kicks I got for you Italy?"

"Yeah, but you know Pradas are my favorite. Did you get me some Juicy Couture tracksuits and some Joe's Jeans Mommy?" Italy asked sternly, pulling items out of the bag one by one. She beamed widely. "Oh, okay here they are. Thank you Mommy." She paused momentarily, pulling out a white box as a huge smile spread across the young child's face. "And thanks for the VVS stones Mommy!"

Nala couldn't stop laughing. "Yo kids getting so big and grown girl! That Italy is something else. And look at Summer over their looking just like you and even standing like you. If that ain't your twin, B." She swayed her hand from side to side.

"Girl tell me about it, they all looking grown. Brianna and T'ionna in eighth and tenth grade, looking like college students. Nana is feeding these kids that soul food fo'real. And let's not get on Summer looking 15 and only going on 13." India smirked.

They laughed, really finding the children this day and age funny. The designer jogging sets they all rocked with their hair down made them look older than they actually were. Nala and India had to admit that they all were gorgeous.

"Y'all coming home this weekend?" India questioned.

"Nah Mommy, we'll pass. We gotta keep Nana company," Italy explained. She was the youngest, but still the spokesperson of their little close-knit crew.

"Okay forget all of you. Y'all never likes kicking it with your mother. But it's cool. I'ma stop buying all four of y'all heffas stuff," she joked.

"Uh-huh, Mommy." Italy twisted up her lips and followed her

sister and cousins up the flight of steps.

"Dang, can I get a thank you!" India shrieked.

"Thaaanks!" they all said simultaneously bolting up the staircase.

India and Nala said goodbye to Nana and before they climbed into the car Sump's mother Ronnie and Aunt Ronetta cruised up. Now Ronetta — Brianna and T'ionna's mother — was India's girl. She loved her to death. She was cool, a very down to earth lady who wasn't nearly a full-blown hater like her sister Ronnie. India loathed even looking at Ronnie's boyish ass.

"Hey India baby, you look gorgeous and you stays sharp girlie. I see life treating you good as usual."

"Yup, thanks to my damn son, you fuckin' moocher or leech — whichever you prefer!" Ronnie giggled.

"Ronnie don't start with me today, I certainly ain't on yo' shit." She cut her eyes at her.

"India, don't roll yo' eyes at me cause I'll knock 'em to the back of yo' fucking head."

India and Nala both doubled over into laughter. It certainly wasn't going down like that. They were always taught that if one fight they both fought, so that's how they rolled.

"Ronnie, you'll get your fat ass jumped out here today," Nala agreed, nodding her head.

"Let me go in the house 'fore you go crying to my son and I have to cuss his ass out too. Netta don't be out here kissing ass too damn heavy now." Ronnie flicked them off, rolling her neck.

"Your sister so damn childish." India shook her head, sliding inside her car.

"I know. You have to excuse her sometimes; she just jealous of you and Sump's relationship."

"Well, her time to stop it should be well over due, me and that nigga been together for so many years. We done had two damn kids and been married. What the fuck! She needs to seriously beat the block. On the real though."

"Right, girl. But I'ma let you go. I know you probably in a rush. Call me later on." She closed her door and India pulled off and headed towards The Chop Shop barbershop. It was a hang out spot for niggas more than a barbershop. Super, the owner, mostly had it for a front and handled a lot of drug activities during the day.

Soon as they pulled up they both saw their men deeply engaged in a dice game directly in front of the shop. India and Nala parked and decided to roll up before they climbed out. They noticed a young girl who looked horrible, seemingly from the drugs she was begging all the dope boys for. India and Nala were half-high when the girl finally approached one of the guys. He looked around to see if anyone was watching and scurried off with her like roaches did when the lights flicked on. They cracked up, laughing knowing that the nigga was about to get his dick blown by a dope fiend.

After their men lost a few racks to some street corner hustlers, they gave up and went inside to get their hair lined up. Once the girls finished up their blunt, they strolled inside too.

"Damn, you ladies looking very sexy," Super greeted, joking all the time.

"Hey, hey, now Super — don't even greet my wife," Gene said. Nala walked over to her husband. He was just getting out of the chair smiling one of his Colgate smiles, pulling her right into his embrace.

India kissed Sump as he walked over to Super's booth and got his trim started. She peeped at Meek sitting in the waiting area yapping on the phone, waiting to get his hair cut.

"Who you on the phone making love to, nigga?' India approached him, retrieving Vibe's latest issue and taking a seat beside him.

"Let me call you back." Meek immediately hung up on the caller. "Aww, that wasn't nobody important," Meek said. "I see you big head, you looking nice. I'm glad to see you pulling through this shit."

"Yeah, I don't have a choice, Meek. You know I can't keep sobbing and being depressed."

"I know that's right ma." He smiled and slowly licked his lips.

India just loved the way Meek licked his lips. Da'Meek Hamilton was truly hella sexy to India and many others. Not only sexy, but he exuded a mean swagger with the most attractive personality she ever saw. He was just so meek and hood wrapped all in one. His whole demeanor reminded her of T.I. the rapper. For years she secretly had a crush on him, but never would act upon it. She respected the G-code and her man for the most part. Although Meek sometimes threw flirtatious hints at her, she'd never engage in any sexual performances even though she wanted to like hell. Besides, Meek was a dear friend of hers, and they often discussed problems when things were growing sour in one another's lives.

India couldn't bear to be in his presence for too long alone because he was so damn fine. She stood, told Meek she'd see him around and went where her man was. Super was dusting hair to the floor when India reentered the room.

"You ready baby?" Sump stood, arrogantly checking himself in the mirror.

"Yeah, I'm ready. Nigga get your conceited ass outta the damn mirror." She laughed.

"Quit hatin' boo," he gloated, patting his face smugly. "Now, c'mon India. We 'bout to spend the day together." She beamed excitedly as he grabbed her by the hand and escorted her outside. They climbed inside her vehicle and headed out to eat.

*****

An hour later the pair arrived at Mr. Chows and were both greeted warmly by the supervisor, Lee. "Hello! Our most loyal customers haven't swung through in some time now. I was wondering what happened. Usually you guys dine here at least once a week. What happened?"

They smiled and India held her hand out to be kissed.

"We stopped through a few weeks ago and they said you was on vacation," Sump said.

"Oh yes, I had to get a break from this place."

"I can definitely dig that, homie." They chatted as Lee led them to their booth.

After they were seated they ordered chicken satay, Beijing chicken, lobster tails drowned in garlic butter, fiery shrimp with garlic, brown rice, steamed broccoli and pan fried bread. It was their favorite spot to eat and India loved being in attendance every chance she got. The food was excellent and the atmosphere would always relax her mood. She could chill there anytime and enjoy a delightful meal with her husband. India was always happy to be in his company and he would have loved to accompany her each and every day, but that wasn't possible because of the business he was involved in.

India knew that she could never love anybody like she loved Sump. He knew her like no one else. He knew her weaknesses, her strengths and also knew how far to take things before she would renounce the premise and utterly flip out. Every time she was in his presence she remembered why she loved him solely. There wasn't any difference with her because he most definitely felt the same way. India was his all and everything. Making her smile and allowing her to be happy with the lifestyle she adored was all he cared about. There wasn't a soul in existence other than his Nana that he trusted fully except for India. Words or gifts couldn't even explain how much he loved her. She knew it too and that's why she allowed the haters to hate. Without a doubt she was the twinkle of his eye, the sky to his earth; just seeing her would make his day greater. India was more than his lover; she was his best friend and his core reason for grinding heavily and going hard in the streets. He would easily die for her and would certainly kill any nigga that disrespected her; the bond the duo shared was so strong and unbreakable.

The intense love they held for each other was true. Although India loved spending the drug money, she knew if shit was to ever hit the fan and he went broke, she would stay. She felt as long as he was her man and stayed loyal to her, she would still be in love.

"Yo, bay. You 'member when we first came here you was 'bout to damn near faint?"

"Yeah, nigga. Back then I had never seen a place this formal and sure enough not an expensive place like this just to eat at."

"Right, that was wild though, we thought we were doing it big, at what 18?"

"Yep, baby, and right after that you bought me my first Prada bag. Ton'na snuck and wore it out to her school homecoming and it got stolen two days after you got it for me."

"Hell yeah, ma." He chuckled. "I had to buy your ass another one then Ton'na made me cop her one too."

"Then Ronnie found out and was pissed. Then you had to get her one, knowing she don't even wear bags." They both doubled over into laughter.

"Yo' remember when Ronnie cussed us out talking about y'all mothafuckas ain't having no damn baby over my damn dead body, y'all ain't."

"Yeah I do. She was salty that her momma's baby was having a baby," India teased. "Why your moms still be wildin' out though? I seen her hatin' ass at Nana's and she was talking heavy crazy," India said, laughingly. "Me and Nala was gon' jump her big ass."

"Y'all stupid. I don't know why that woman still acts like that. Something wrong with Ronnie seriously, but I love the hell outta her ass, fo' real."

"You know what I never asked you? Guess it never dawned on me till now."

"What, bay?"

"Babe, why do you always call her Ronnie? Have you ever called her momma, mother or something?"

"C'mon India, you know I love Ronnie to death. But she never once acted like she was a mother so I never called her momma," he asserted truthfully. "She more like a sister and Nana my mother. You know I been calling her my mother since I was a little nigga."

A disappointed facial expression appeared on India's face. "Why you looking like that ma?" he asked, concerned.

"I think I should force the girls to start coming home. I just don't want them to be havin' to look at Nana as a mother. Not saying that Nana isn't good, but I don't want them to think I just put them on her like your mother did."

"India." Sump gently grabbed onto her hand and gazed into her eyes. "The difference with that is I wanted to roll with my momma 'cause she used to be in the streets and Nana's house was boring to me. Italy and Summer love being over Nana's house 'cause they can hang out with their older cousins. So if that's where they wanna be, don't make them come home if they don't want to. That's mainly why I don't look at Ronnie like a mother. She placed me in an environment that I didn't want to be in. I know for a fact that the girls hate being far away because they really can't go out and play with the people that they know. Hell, they barely like attending school out there, let alone be out there all damn day. So never look at it like that, baby. You take good care of our daughters, and Ronetta's girls also. They just like hanging 'round the way and plus Nana loves for them to keep her busy. She don't have nothing else to do."

"Yeah, I guess you're right." India smiled pleasantly, feasting her eyes on the waiter who held the tray with their food atop. The waiter carefully placed each dish on the table. They both attacked, devouring the meal as if they hadn't eaten in weeks.

"Baby, you know I've been thinking lately, and I think we should try to have a boy," India commented, wiping the side of her mouth.

"What made you want a boy now? I can recap a few heated arguments when you said you wasn't having anymore children." He furrowed one eyebrow up in concern. "Don't front India, you must not 'member talking about, 'Sump who the fuck you think I am? We ain't 'bout to be running around like the Jackson Five, the Huxtables, and surely not the damn Brady Bunch.'"

"Shut up, punk." She laughed, playfully hitting him on his arm. "I've just been thinking 'bout it cause I got my playmates although they don't fuck with me like that." She giggled. "But I just think you should have a li'l nigga to kick it with and I shouldn't be so selfish. I am your wife so if that's what you want then we can try again, bay." India beamed excitedly.

Sump sat thoughtfully. He felt it was her decision because she was going to be the one carrying the baby for nine months, not him. A moment later, he voiced graciously, "If you want to have another baby, it's up to you mama."

India perched up optimistically and hugged his neck. "I love you so much Sump. It's almost crazy! And a son you will finally have. He will make our family complete."

"I love you more, baby." He kissed her lips. "Now go grab that bag that's in the backseat of the car for me."

India rushed out speedily, assuming that the bag carried something special inside for her. She returned five minutes later. "Here, bay." She handed him the bag and took her seat again.

"Nah, ma. Look inside." Sump shoved the bag back towards her.

Doing as she was instructed, India slowly looked inside. Retrieving the black box, she inquired, "Oh my God, Sump! What is this?"

"Open it and see."

India did as she was told and opened the box, wondering what it could be that he was presenting to her. The box possessed a wedding band identical to the one she already flossed on her left ring finger, only carrying an extra carat.

"Wow, Sump! What is this for baby?"

"You know we gotta renew our vows on our fifth anniversary, baby girl."

India couldn't believe he remembered their promise to each other, which was to renew their vows every five years.

"Sumpter, I didn't think you 'membered bay," India exclaimed.

"Yep, it's in 'bout five months, but I decided to get a jumpstart on it now," he said. "I'm so happy that it's soon to be our five years of marriage. People these days don't last that long, baby. And even though we done been though some serious shit, it can only get better ma." He grabbed the ring and slipped it on her, right hand's third finger. "I love you so much I wanna marry your other hand." He smiled sincerely. "Plus, you my right hand ma so it is only right if I put a ring on your right hand too."

"Dang. It feels like the first time you proposed to me." Tears formed in her eyes.

"Don't cry shorty. I just love you, that's all." Sump leaned in and kissed her eyes. "We gotta celebrate tonight. But in the meantime I gotta head out with Gene to handle something then we all going out to Club Hypnotic."

"I just love you so much," India gushed, feeling at total peace again.

Triple Crown Publications presents... *Wife*

Chapter Seven

After India dropped Sump off to Gene, Nala popped in with her and they jumped back on the expressway. They headed to Brooklyn where Vanessa lived. India's stylist Leslie was out of town so she had to get her hair done in Vanessa's basement, which wasn't bad because Vanessa was cold with hairstyles. Every time she picked up a hair utensil, she created magic. The girls didn't understand why Vanessa never moved out of the Brownville section, knowing that she could afford an upgrade. She never seemed to become frustrated with the sporadic incessant gunfire, the hustlers on the block, fiends or roaches living in her abode.

When they finally arrived to Vanessa's house it was a quarter till 7. They walked in and headed straight down to the basement, which was set up like a beauty shop. Two hair booths sat in the far right corner, and five hairdryers sat to the left of the room. Everything was in view of the flat screen television mounted on the wall. A sectional sat nearby with a table full of magazines and a bathroom was right behind the two booths. Vanessa's crib was the hangout spot for damn near everyone. She welcomed anybody in; Vanessa was the realest chick India knew and by far the most ghetto. She also said whatever was on her mind and never bit her tongue, no matter who she was going to hurt in the process. She just told shit as she saw it.

It was Saturday so India knew that Vanessa was bound to have a few gossiping chickenheads' hair to do, ghetto fabulous. "I figured your punk butt was going to be doing *somebody* hair." India rolled her eyes, flopping down onto the empty chair beside Vanessa.

"Don't come in bitching today. I'm done with her, girl." She placed the last buckle wave into her client's hair. "Now c'mon, you damn complainer." Vanessa quickly shampooed her hair, rolled her whole head up, and placed her underneath the dryer in record breaking time.

India sat under the dryer with her eyes glued to the television screen, watching "American Gangster." Vanessa's voice interjected her thoughtless brain. "Oh gurl, you ain't gon' believe this shit here. I knew I been meaning to tell yo ass something."

"What, Nessa?" India responded, distinguishing in her tone that it was some bullshit that she probably could've cared less to hear.

"Bitch, why me and She-She was in Manhattan Mall and she ran into a Mexican looking bitch that she used to attend school with years ago, and they got to chopping shit up. She-She just so happened to have asked her did she have any kids and the bitch told her yeah. You know She-She nosy so she asked her who her baby daddy was." Vanessa swayed her head from side to side. "Man, India I don't even wanna tell you this 'cause this shit gon' hurt."

At that moment India's soul fell out of her body; she knew exactly who Vanessa was going to say. India yelled snottily, "What, bitch? Don't game around; you done basically said it now!" She flared her nose up, and just couldn't understand why bitches always got so geeked up to spill the beans on her husband then choked up like they didn't wanna hurt her feelings, knowing they would be glad to see her stressed out and all messed up in the head.

"Well yup, you know I'ma keep it one hunnet. She said Sump."

"How you figure it's *that* Sump, Nessa?" Nala queried.

"Bitch." Vanessa flashed them both a dumb look. "You know once the hoe said Sump I investigated thoroughly. Turns out it's Sump that drives the '57, Lexus, BMW truck ... the list goes on. And the nigga roll heavy with Gene, Mac C and Meek." Vanessa twisted her mouth, nodding her head slowly. "Sounds like the only Sump in the NY to me." Vanessa placed her index figure on her chin. "Hmm ... sure do."

"Nessa, I don't even know why you telling India this. You know how many bitches done said that Sumpter fathered their child?" Nala hated when situations like this arose because she often went through the same dilemma. What everyone had failed to realize was that it was the chick's word over their husband's. "Seems to me that the nigga only claiming two kids on this end. So if the broad does got his child she dumb as fuck." Nala shrugged dismissively. "Hell, if she wants her baby to be a secret then that's on her silly ass."

Vanessa snapped. "Well if y'all bitches gon' put up with it then so fucking be it. Better y'all than me 'cause I'm good." She began going off. "The same shit y'all getting, I'm sure bitches get tricked on just as good and get just as much time as the wife if not fucking more," she said sternly. "Hell, I fuck plenty of niggas that got wives and girlfriends and I'm almost certain that I get more play than the main steady ones. Being the wife ain't always good when y'all niggas going to the next bitch discussing y'all problems."

"Hold on V, this conversation going into another direction that's not even called for. If Sump is out fucking bitches I know for a fact that that's all it is ... because he's not gonna discuss me to no broad about shit. Fucking is one thing, but time is another." India cocked her head back, cutting her eyes. "I know bitches could never get time with my husband like I do, so what are you saying, my nigga?" India was beyond heated at this moment because she hated that Vanessa was so outspoken. To be honest, she could have kept it all to herself.

"Okay — what the fuck are you getting all hostile for girl? I'm just telling you what the girl was saying muthafucka! The li'l foreign looking bitch said that her baby daddy is Sump and the chick got the same exact Japanese symbol standing for Sumpter that you got on the back of your ear on her neck. She said that she know he got a wife, but she don't care because he taking care of her home also." Vanessa paused and continued. "And she an older chick. She thirty."

India rolled her eyes so hard it wouldn't have been a surprise if they got stuck. She knew deep down that the girl's description was

Sump and everything matched up to a tee. But India wasn't going to let Vanessa know that she was sweating it to the point that she wanted to kill Sump. She also knew that several hoes in the past had cried wolf, saying that they were pregnant by the notorious Sump, lying just to get some attention and recognition.

"Damn, that's messed up if it's true," one of Vanessa's clients stated. "That's why I fucks other bitches' niggas, 'cause I would hurt a bitch that fucks my nigga."

"Yo playgirl ... I'ma need for you not to even comment on this shit here. Is it really your concern?" Nala spoke angrily, because they didn't know this chick from Adam. Vanessa's client was astonished by Nala's bluntness and didn't mumble a word. "Exactly. So if you nasty whores wanna keep fucking everybody's nigga, do that. But I'ma tell you like this: Stay the fuck away from Gene or that's where the problems come, sweethearts."

India burst out laughing. "Nala, you are retarded. We ain't even talking about Gene."

"I'm just warning her. Shit, she the one said she fuck other bitches' niggas. I'm warning her because I'm sure she knows Gene and he is surely off limits. Flat out, my dude."

"Nala, stop starting shit," Vanessa yelled.

"V, I ain't startin' anything. She the one talkin' 'bout she'll hurt a chick for messing with her man but she messes with other females' niggas." Nala paused, squinting her eyes. "What, she think the next bitch don't feel how she feel? She think the next chick sleeping on their nigga?" Nala really wanted to know. Nala wouldn't stop; she was a beast at debating and loved it. She had a Communications degree and she was president of the debate team all four years of high school.

"Don't mind her, she loves arguing. I don't know why she won't get into politics. Hell, least you'd get paid for the yapping." They all cracked up laughing.

A second didn't pass when India's Sidekick began to ring. Of course it was her husband.

"Hello, baby."

"Where you at, still over Vanessa's house?" Sump asked.

"Yeah, she almost finished though."

"Well, I'll be at the house so I guess we can leave once you get here and get dressed. I'm 'bout to take a quick nap before we head out."

India started to ask his ass what the fuck he needed to sleep for, but she noticed that all eyes were glued to her so she simply replied. "A'ight baby. I'll be there in 'bout an hour and a half."

"A'ight. I love you ma."

"Love you too, babe." She hung up.

India still held the thoughts in her head, but she was too polished to allow anybody to see her sweat, so she immediately changed the subject.

"So, what up fo' the night V?"

"You know Miss V hitting up the club. I need to see what I'ma come up on. What, you going out tonight or somethin'?"

"Yeah, Sump wants me to go. Talking 'bout we celebrating our five year anniversary early. He got me this ring." India extended her hand and flashed it proudly. "This one just carrying an extra carat than my wedding band. We gon' renew our vows on the day of our anniversary."

Nala laughed. "Tell that shit to Jackie Chan sister, now."

India shook her head giggling as Vanessa unrolled her hair and allowed huge loose curls to frame her face. India hugged and paid her cousin and was happy to finally be out of her house.

*****

After India left she dropped Nala off and headed home. She was still steaming from the information Vanessa had presented her with. Once she got home she didn't even speak to Sump, which was a key sign of her being vexed. She hopped straight in the shower and they both dressed without one word being exchanged from India. She started to spaz out on him, but she refused to allow her little girl ways to resurface and she didn't wanna jump to conclusions. She had been down that road plenty of times. Besides, she wanted to enjoy her night out, but she was sure to get to the bottom of it once they returned home that night.

Sump really didn't know what was bothering her. He just

surmised she was thinking about her sister, so he allowed her to play the silent treatment with him. He tried sneaking in a few words as they put the last touches to their appearance, but opted to just leave it alone.   After Sump parked his black-on-black Aston Martin DB9 coupe at his reserved spot alongside the club's front entrance, he and India entered via the VIP double-glass doors. He slid the bouncer two hundred to let them inside with their pistols. The pair sauntered through as the city's finest and the couple received mad love. India swagged stylishly in a silk crème button-up blouse. The front cut close to the crest of her perky beasts, showcasing her tattoo of Sump's real name. To complete her outfit, she rocked a pair of skinny jeans, and crème thigh-high stiletto boots that matched perfectly. Four-carat diamond hoops draped from her ears, complimenting the platinum Audemars Piguet wristwatch.

Sump wasn't too far behind her. He was high maintenance in a white striped Armani button-up, distressed jeans, and exclusive sneakers. A white NY fitted cap tilted from his head and he rocked so much ice he could've created an ice rink. Gleaming from his ears was a set of squared diamond earrings, chain filled with ten-carat diamond cuts and a matching $100,000 Audemars Piguet watch.

India couldn't fake it; she was happy to be ambling through the club with her man by her side. Females were everywhere and they all seemed to envy the married couple. India never tripped because she knew she was all her husband ever needed, well at least that's how he made her feel. Meanwhile, she was going to enjoy her night. Sump spotted his peoples chilling and popping bottles in the VIP section upstairs. Everyone in the hood knew what had happened with them and most showed a lot of love as the pair made their way up to VIP.

"'Sup, monkey!" Nala screamed, hugging her girl.

"Damn, y'all mothafuckas poppin' bottles without me and my man!" India teased.

"Right baby, it's cool. Excuse me miss." Sump flagged down the VIP barmaid. "Can you get me two bottles of Louie XIII and a bottle of Cristal?"

"Baby." India nudged him. "I don't want any nasty-ass Cristal and I really don't drink Louie XIII, either. Just get a bottle of Patrón too."

"And a bottle of Patrón, thanks." He turned to his partna. "Damn, what up Gene. I see you copped that $200,000 chain."

"Yeah, you know how we do nigga." They slapped hands.

"Look at India." Gene smiled, picking her up and twirling her around in the air. "You funky fresh, baby girl." He placed her back onto her feet.

"Thank you, Gene." She laughed.

"Ay now nigga, don't be staring at my girl too long," Sump joked.

"Forget him Gene. He hatin'," she cooed.

"Damn big head, you ain't gon' speak?" Meek asked, eyeing her voluptuous thighs.

She puckered her lips. "C'mon now. I was working my way down the line, nigga."

"You better not be on that fake shit, shorty." He smiled sexily.

India stretched her arms out wide, continuing. "I'm not, and you really look nice."

Nice was an understatement. The boy looked absolutely gorgeous. He sported a white T with *Hope for Haiti* written across in blue-and-red letters. Covering his eyes were a white pair of tinted D & G frames. On his legs was a denim pair of distressed jeans and high top kicks. He didn't wear any jewelry and didn't have to; his power emanated from his confident yet humble stature.

"C'mon India, let's go meet Kyra and Vanessa at the door," Nala told her.

"Sump, I'll be right back baby." She kissed him.

"Don't be gone too long."

"I'm not, baby." India kissed him again and walked off.

"Girl, it feels so good to have you back hanging out with us."

"I know, I haven't been out in forever. It feels good to be here," India admitted as they continued boppin' towards the front entrance.

"I know and I missed you dearly, family."

"Damn, I just wish Ton'na was here."

"India, believe me she's smiling down on us, protecting us from evil. I know that wound may never heal all the way, but it'll all be a'ight," Nala said assuredly.

"I just miss her, Nala." She shook her head and tears welled in her eyes.

"Bitch, you know Ton'na don't wanna see you sad. So suck it up and party as if Ton'na was here. Now let's forget about the sadness and be happy."

"Yeah, you're right. Let's enjoy ourselves!"

Once the girls reached the door their cousins were coming through dressed like the hoochies they were. "Hey, chickens," India yelled over the music, getting the girls' attention.

"Oh, there they go over there," Kyra said to Vanessa, walking in their direction.

"Damn, I think y'all left y'all clothes at home," Nala teased.

"No, I think you put on too much clothing," Vanessa joked back.

"Forget you, bitch." Nala laughed, putting up her middle finger.

India led the way back upstairs. She spotted her boo and sat on his lap. Rolling up a purp blunt for Sump, she filled it with some of the finest herbs.

An hour, three triple shots of Patrón, and two purple blunts later India was fucked up. But, she was always able to handle her liquor and her highness well. Wanting to be seen in their outfits, India and her crew made their way downstairs to mingle with people they knew.

"Girl, is that T'ionna over there?" Nala pointed to the young copper-toned girl.

"Oh, hell nah. Sump gon' wring her damn neck. C'mon over here with me y'all." They slithered through the crowd and made their way right over to T'ionna, who was standing by a group of seemingly upcoming ballers.

"What are you doing in here TT?"

"Oh, hey India what's up?" She hugged her. "I came with my boyfriend."

"How in the world did you get in here?" India asked, surprised.

"Girl, the same way we used to get in back in our youngin'

days," Vanessa answered for her.

"India, I'm not drinking. I'm cool. He just wanted me to hang out with him tonight."

"So where does Nana think you are?"

"I told her I was going to Brittany's party. Which I did, but we all came here afterwards."

"Well, I hope you know Sumpter in here and if he sees you ..." India gave her the look.

"Oh my God, Sincere." She turned around and yelled over the loud music. "We gotta go bay. My big cousin Sump in here and he will definitely embarrass me if he knows I'm in here."

"A'ight ma. Hold up." He tugged on her belt loop. "How y'all ladies doing?"

"Fine," they all replied.

"That's what's up." He smiled, turned back around and focused in back on his niggas.

"We gon' leave in a minute. Please don't let him know I'm in here; he will flip out."

"Gurl, you ain't gotta tell me shit, you just better get outta here a-sap and make sure you call me when you get in the house."

"Okay." They hugged again and the girls found themselves a seat at the bar.

"Damn, that li'l dude T'ionna was with was fine as fuck. And the nigga look and smell like new money. Ain't nothing like brand new money, feel me!"

"That li'l' boy! Kyra, shut up," Nala said, prodding her leg.

"Did you see how sexy he was? Hell, I know he at least 18 so his ass legal."

"Right, I'll fuck the shit outta him or one of the cats from his crew, ya dig." Vanessa chuckled.

"Give me some, girl." Kyra and Vanessa burst out laughing, exchanging high-fives.

"Y'all are seriously retarded." India shook her head laughing.

"This song is that major shit, yo," Nala yelled over the loud music. The girls jumped up, bopping to Young Jeezy's raspy voice. *"I know you thinking in your mind, you got every right, I know you*

thinking in your mind I'm out every night ... " The foursome danced methodically to the hot track, and they were surely working it out. They all knew they could dance their asses off.

After seriously perspiring India and her girls began making their way back to where their peoples were. "Who the fuck is the bitch all up in Sump's face?" Kyra yelled over the music. All the girls shifted their heads, trying to figure out what was up.

"Ooooh, India that's the bitch we saw in the mall. Word to my mutha. That's her, son," Vanessa said, gaping.

"Damn," said Nala. "I know that Asian bitch ain't who you were talking 'bout?"

"Yup, but I thought she was Mexican." Vanessa chuckled. "I don't know the damn difference."

"I can't believe this shit, B," India said to no one in particular. "This shit never fuckin' fails. I promised myself I wouldn't let shit get to me anymore. It was just too good to be fuckin' true not battling with hoes over his ass for a few years. I guess the nigga feel I done rested long enough." Fire blazed from India's eyes.

"I been tellin' ya ass for the longest that the nigga sorry as fuck. He'll never change and believe me ... just 'cause y'all married, shit ain't changed ... you just don't get it though. Acting like the shit new or some shit," Vanessa stated.

India sighed. "As many bitches I done beat the fuck up for messing with him, they should all know by now. Damn! What the fuck!"

Vanessa didn't make the situation any better by egging her on. "He's so fuckin' disrespectful! The kid is most definitely clowning with this shit. That's her too," she confirmed.

India laughed, mad-like. "I just know that ugly-ass bitch ain't the one. I swear on my daughters this better be a misunderstanding." India fumed, knowing that the girl was far from ugly. As a matter of fact, they stood on the scale evenly. The girl just lost a few points from her spacey teeth, and being that she wore a Hollister jogging suit with Adidas didn't help in India's eyes. But she gained mad points because her black and Asian heritages allowed her to have a beautiful radiant light cinnamon skin tone and long wavy jet-black hair.

India knew Sump couldn't have seen her coming because she saw him corner posted all up in the chick's face, somewhat arguing. It was true. Sump was becoming very frustrated with Lilly because he didn't know when India would return, and he didn't need for there to be any bullshit.

"Go'n, bra. I told you I'll get with you tomorrow, Lilly. Go'n 'fore I beat yo' ass, my wife in here, yo," he roared, clenching his jaws together.

"Sump, I'm your kids' mother too, and you haven't spent time with us every since that bullshit happened to your wife. You haven't given us any money, we need some money," Lilly whined, knowing she didn't need any of his money. She just wanted him to come around. "Now me and my kids gotta suffer cause of this," she pouted as tears slowly welled in her eyes. "When is the last time you seen your sons?" Lily asked, with her arms crossed tightly.

By the time Sump was about to spaz out on Lilly, India was dead smack in his grill. "Nigga, I just know you ain't fuckin' disrespecting me by talkin' to this funny looking-ass bitch in front of me!" She placed her hands on her hips, weight shifted to one side. "Sumpter, you really don't wanna see me clown in this muthafucka. You already know how I do, my nigga."

"Calm down baby, this ain't nothing," he said, attempting to wrap his arms around her neck.

"Get the fuck off me! Do not muthafuckin touch me!" India snatched away. "Who the fuck is this bitch, Sumpter?" she asked, scanning in between the two.

"I can be that bitch. But I'm the mother of his children just how he's yours, India," Lilly spoke coolly.

"Man India, this bitch lying." Sump wanted to kill Lilly, making a mental note to beat the hell out of her later.

"Oh, so she lying and she know my name. Fo'real?"

"Yep, I know all about you honey ... more than you would ever know."

India was extremely pissed by this point, and mortified. She knew Vanessa was standing right behind her gathering notes. India didn't even think twice. She stole on Sump, and then punched the girl right in the face. Briskly, Gene escorted Lilly out of VIP, not even giving her a chance to react.

"Sump, I swear to God if that hoe telling the truth, I'm done! You just better hope she lying like Kim and all the rest of them hoes. All I ever told your crab ass was to use condoms if you ever got the urge to fuck a bitch. And this Asian bitch screaming she's got yo' kid, nigga!" She flared her nostrils. "Bitch, you got some major mothafuckin' explaining to do." She stormed off.

Needing to clear her mind, India walked outside to get a breeze of the fresh midnight air. She couldn't believe the situation. It was one thing to fuck a bitch, but a whole 'nother story to knock the bitch up. She knew no matter what, if the girl was telling the truth she was done with his no good ass. Too many years had passed by and she could certainly say she was fucking beyond fed up. She tried to lie to herself and act as if she didn't care what he did. She constantly reminded herself that she was really wifed up and nobody could replace her. But nothing could compare to the inflicted pain that tugged at her heart when hearing that foreign chick say she was the mother of his kids. Knocked out of her deep thoughts, Meek approached her.

"India, you a'ight?"

She rolled her eyes. "Meek, does it look like I'm a'ight?" She stared at him stupidly, folding her arms underneath her breasts.

"Ma, calm down on that hype shit. Sump told me to come out here and make sure you a'ight."

"Fuck Sump and just tell me something Meek," India said, water obscuring her vision. "Is it true that he messes with her and that girl has his kids?"

"India, real talk, I don't know that man business. I be doin' my own thang." He paused, knowing he knew that Sump courted Lilly, but really wasn't certain about them sharing children. "I'm sure if y'all talk it out he'll let you in on the situation."

India swayed her head from side to side. All the battles and fights she been through with this dude, she knew he better convince her that it was all a lie or there were going to be some serious problems. "Meek, can you just take me home?"

"Yeah, let me go holla at Sump 'dem and tell 'em I'm 'bout to drive you home." Meek handed her the keys to his wine-berry hued SL600 that was parked behind Sump's whip. She sadly ambled over to the car and climbed inside, immediately fumbling through his CDs. India knew they had a long ride and she wanted to be relaxed. Hell, if she would have known that her night was going to be a disaster she would've stayed her ass home. She found Plies's CD and hurriedly placed it into the disc changer.

Climbing inside his vehicle, Meek couldn't help but to admire India with a hard on bulging through his pants. Her full lips were so juicy, he just wanted to jump over and kiss her passionately. The way she swayed her head to number 13 turned Meek completely on, because he wanted her to "Please Excuse His Hands" all right. India was collecting the same naughty thoughts as him, only she was embarrassed because he was one of her husband's best friends. Her panties were drenched as she thought about Meek handling her body. India closed her eyes as her mind wandered; she couldn't believe that she was actually lusting over Meek. Suddenly, she felt a gentle hand rubbing her thigh; she blinked profusely and looked over at Meek.

"You a'ight ma?"

India couldn't find the words to escape her mouth. Just the sensation of his hand caressing her thigh could've had her explode alone. "I'm ... I ... I'm good," India stuttered, not moving his hand. That was confirmation that she enjoyed it. They didn't exchange words the entire ride home and before they took notice they were pulling into her driveway.

India took a deep breath before opening the car door. Climbing out, Meek tugged her back down. "Ma you ain't gon' say thank you?" He smiled charismatically.

"Fo'sho, Meek. Thanks for the ride." India could barely breathe as she could hear her pussy's heartbeat throb in her head.

"Anytime, India." Meek caressed the side of her cheek flirtatiously. Without warning, he leaned in, kissing her passionately on the lips. It didn't take India long to get used to the excitement of his thick tongue and she relished his hands massaging her already hardened nipples.

"I swear all I need is one night, India," Meek mumbled frankly.

India could feel her pussy juice overflowing her panties with wetness and cream. His warm tongue felt so good flicking along with hers, causing her to quake and lightly moan. She felt totally out of control. India was tripping and she knew it. She was married and Meek was her husband's best friend, but the moment was very enjoyable and desirable. She envisioned all the possible positions Meek would place her in as her pussy screamed out to bust a nut and her clitoris distended.

India soon found herself unbuttoning her pants, yearning for him to touch her fat juicy tunnel of passion. Caught up in the moment, she grabbed Meek's free hand all the while gently kissing him. She slid his hands down into her panties when the bright light approaching brought her back to earth. Realizing it could be Sump, she jumped out of the car without saying goodbye. She whizzed inside the house, unbelievably shocked at the action she was engaged in. Regretful she wasn't; she was more astounded than guilty. It actually allowed her to come down from off of her high of pure anger than anything.

India smiled at the vision of Meek's sexy ass and stripped out of her clothing. Entering the sparkling white and silver bathroom, India switched on her custom-made Kenwood surround sound system. The sounds of Keith Sweat's mesmerizing voice soothed her mind as she stepped into her stand-in shower. The soft drops of stream massaged her silky skin as the elating aroma of Miller Harris shower wash filled her nose. She lathered her body, covering her smooth skin with foamy soap bubbles.

Once showering and washing her hair, India stepped out, feeling refreshed. After she patted her frame dry she applied La Mer body lotion to her skin. As she slipped into her silk robe her phone vibrated on the dresser and she elected not to answer. After the second time it rang, she figured it was Sump with some lame excuse, but to her surprise it was Meek. "Hello," she answered.

"Yo', I was on my way in the house and couldn't get my mind

off the shit that happened."

"Me either Meek, and I feel really odd."

"Look, me too. That's my nigga and if y'all wasn't together I would definitely try to make you mines. But y'all are. So we're just gonna forget about what happened even though I wish like hell you could be my shorty. On the real though."

India blushed. "Me too. But I'm glad we cleared that up though. Our little secret?"

"Fo'sho big head ... one."

*****

Sump didn't arrive home until around 4:00. He had already pre-pared himself for the heated debate he knew would certainly take place. Yup, India couldn't wait until he stepped foot in the damn house; she was sure to be down his throat. Sometimes she won-dered what it was that kept her around because all Sump seemed to bring other than gifts was anguish and a damn headache. But she also knew that she couldn't live without him. Without him was like her heart pumping without the body, and just the thought caused serious heartache. He was her air to breathe.

All India wanted to hear was that everything the chick was saying was a lie. As soon as he stepped through their bedroom door, she jumped up in his face, throwing the calmness she previously practiced out the window. She needed answers. She didn't give a fuck about the fight about to go down, and could have cared less about him hitting her.

"Bitch, why you just standing here like you don't owe me a damn explanation?" India poked him in the head.

"Indy, I swear to God don't fuckin' touch me, you already was on some reckless shit letting everybody in on our fuckin' business. You lucky I didn't beat your mu'fuckin ass at that fuckin' club."

"Pussy ass nigga I can touch you if I wanna." Tears rushed down her face. "What the fuck you gon' do?" she screamed, poking him again.

"Indy, gone." He pushed her, walking towards the dresser.

"I swear to God I hate you so much!" She plopped down on the bed.

Instead of fighting India, he ignored her. He removed his jewelry, peeled off his clothes, then left the room to take a hot shower. India desperately wanted to go after him, but elected against it. Even if she tried, she couldn't muster up the strength to do so. India was so upset she wasn't seeing clearly. Her feelings were so hurt she couldn't even think straight. All she wanted was for Sump to tell her it was all a lie and he was so selfish he couldn't even tell her that. What had she done that was so fucked up, mean and cruel that had him acting so dumb? India really thought they had an understanding, and were certainly past all the bullshit. Yet Sump's actions proved that he was basically still running the streets like a bachelor.

India blamed herself because she tolerated his infidelity as long as he kept it a secret. She hated him for allowing himself to go as far as possibly having a baby on her. Now she knew she would be the topic of every bitch's conversation.

30 minutes had passed before Sump reentered the room, trying his best to avoid her. He was pissed at how India performed at the club like she didn't know any better. She acted as she was the chick on the side. She knew she was supposed to act like a woman in public, not the ghetto chick she really was. Sump had to admit that he was at fault, but he also felt they could have settled their differences once they reached their home.

He knew India deserved an explanation. More than anything, he wished he could turn back the hands of time. He wouldn't have slept with Lilly on a regular basis nor carried on this long affair. *Fuck it though; it's too late for that,* he thought. The worst part was done now. Only thing left for him to do was tell India what was up now, or lie to extreme measures and hold this vast secret back. Never in all his time did he intend to intentionally hurt the rock that carried his family. Sump loved India more than she knew it, but by the way he acted, India felt he didn't give a fuck about her feelings. He hurt her constantly.

India watched him with a tear stained face as he dried off and slipped into a pair of Burberry boxers and a silk robe. Sump turned on the stereo system. "When It Hurts" by Avant crooned from the speakers, filling the room. As much as India wanted to curse him the fuck out and fight with him, she couldn't. The tranquil expression on his face left her feeling like there no point in her sitting there with agony digging tormenting twinges through her heart. If he didn't give two fucks, why should she? That wasn't the case though. Sump actually cared, and it pained his heart to know that she was hurting. The problem was he didn't know what to say, what to do, or how to approach her without looking like a complete fool. To see her emotionally drained literally tore his insides up.

Sump loved it when India just understood shit. He liked her when she never mentioned or queried him on his street life. Outside of his father and husband role, he figured she shouldn't have one thing to agonize about. It didn't matter if he fathered ten kids — that could never stop or replace the unconditional love he held for India. All he wanted was for her to understand that he was a street nigga and sometimes shit happens. Selling bricks, getting money, purchasing expensive material shit, and fucking bitches all came with being a dope dealer. He never showed her less attention or affection. He still showered her with the finest trends. So what the fuck was the problem?

Too much stuff was going on for him to be battling with his wife. He still had to look out for the haters and definitely had to make sure he protected his family. Sump knew India too well, and if he said the bitch was lying then the bitch was lying till further information. She would roll with it until she could prove otherwise. He knew one day his skeletons would come to haunt him. He just hoped and prayed that day wouldn't come at the wrong time, and sure didn't want it to come on her fresh wound. Plus, he just wasn't ready for war.

"India," he said, finally breaking the silence. "Baby, you know that girl lying just like the other hoes so what are you tripping for?"

"Oh, so it took you this long to talk!?" She swayed her head from side to side, disgusted.

"Man India, don't start the bullshit. I told you the bitch lying!"

"So, if she lying why didn't you just explain to me like you usually do and just let me in on the bullshit?" She jumped up, getting in his face.

"'Cause India, I know you be on that dumb shit. Besides that, I was pissed how you showed your ass tonight like you some lame jump-off. I told you about that ghetto-ass shit."

She flashed him a dumb look. "Okay, I wouldn't have to show my ass if you wouldn't have been disrespecting me chatting with the hoe like I wasn't even at the damn club." India rolled her neck, choking back on her tears. "So Sump, you sound real fucking stupid!" She mugged, folding her arms underneath her breasts.

"Hmmm, a'ight you got me on that one. I'ma admit I was wrong for the shit India, but I love you and you know that I love you." He pulled her into his chest, knowing exactly how to manipulate her mind. "I know you gon' be mad but I did fuck the girl a couple of times, but that was it, all that other shit is fictitious. You know I will never do anything to purposely hurt your feelings. You know I love you more than anything ma so the trippin' needs to cut back. I'm grinding hard out here every day for us to eat."

"But ..."

"Shush." Sump placed his finger on her lips. "Everything else is irrelevant, baby. I know I fuck up from time to time and that's why I don't fight with you anymore. Every time I see your face I know I fucked up, fucking bitches every now and then and shit. But India when I'm in the streets anything is liable to happen," he said. "But when I come home and see how innocent my baby is I realize that shit. Then a nigga start hurting 'cause I know once you find out you gon' be heartbroken."

"You really don't understand though, Sumpter. I knew about the damn girl before I even saw her. Vanessa told me that she was running off to her step-sister She-She that she got your kids or kid ... and she get things just like me. That shit just crushed my heart, knowing that everything Nessa was saying was true. You just don't realize how dumb that makes me look. You really don't."

"Yes I do, but the thing is it's all a lie India. I hate when mothafuckas tell you shit. Fuck them bitches; they're just miserable. You know can't nobody that walk this earth get what I get for you, India. Bitches that I done fucked gets nothing and I swear on my father," he partially lied. "What's a sack of purp or a twenty, to that Jag, to all 'dem expensive-ass bags? What I look like paying a hoe to fuck?"

"But why do you have to play me period, Sump? We're married. How would you like if I was messing around every now and then?" Tears filled her eyes because she really wanted to know.

He slightly dropped his head and smacked his lips. "India, you putting words in my mouth. I'm just saying I never paid bitches and what me and you have is for life. We have been together forever, and for you to constantly worry about what people talking about is crazy. I told you to ignore that hatin' shit, gurl. You understand me?" He gently cupped her chin. "Oh, and if you ever play me I'ma kill you and that nigga." He laughed, kissing her forehead, eyes, nose and lips.

India burst out laughing because her baby was funny, and at that instant all her pain went out the door. She kinda felt bad for kissing Meek, but being that she got fucked up at the club; she blamed it on the alcohol. Not thinking about it a second further, she sexily led Sump towards the bed and assisted him out of his boxers. India knew that some good head would settle their dispute.

Sump's penis was damn near screaming as India erotically licked all over his erection. She placed the head of his shaft into her mouth, stroking the remainder of his long pole with her hand at the same time. He positioned his hands on her head, and she followed suit wrapping her entire mouth around all inches of his manhood and going to work. With his hands having her head motioning at his pace, India still managed to slip his balls inside her warm mouth. She knew he enjoyed her freaky side.

India continued slurping on his dick as his eyes rolled in the back of his head. India felt his body spasm up. Knowing he was reaching his peak, she bobbed her head faster. Sump couldn't take it any longer, grunting loudly as he released a warm load of semen all down her throat.

Naked with his penis still in her hand, she straddled his lap.

Slowly easing down on it, she began riding him like a professional cowgirl. Winding her hips at a fast but gentle pace, she whined in total ecstasy. She gained speed now throwing fast and hard strokes. Helping the speed, Sump clutched onto her waist and slapped her ass as she glided, sliding up and down his pole. Her dark nipples and caramel titties bounced everywhere, and juices flowed down her thighs as she exploded.

Swiftly turning around with his dick still inside her vagina, India rode him backwards. He loved how India stretched her legs out into the splits and the way her big beautiful ass plucked down onto his lower abs. The colorful butterfly tattoo that covered her entire back was enticing to Sump, and the three mini butterflies that sat on her left ass cheek weren't bad either. Finger fucking India in her ass, she leaned her body farther up and cried out gleefully The combination of the two had her begging to cum all over his dick. A moment later, she came. Sump had allowed her to run the performance. Now it was his turn to beat it up, showing he was really in control.

Flipping her onto her back, he positioned her legs on his broad shoulders, roughly grinding his penis in and out of her creamy pussy. Her nah-nah was so wet it was hard to keep a steady motion. He bit down on his bottom lip, banging her pussy in and trying his hardest not to holler out like a bitch. Their bodies intertwined as he placed her onto her side, pumping her back out. She held one leg in the air as he massaged her throbbing clitoris while caressing her breast with the other hand. She felt him breaking walls that she never knew existed. Sweat dripped from their pores and they both heaved, catching their breath as they both reached their climax.

Still not quite finished, Sump hastily placed her on all fours, spreading her ass cheeks apart this time. He wanted to come with more intensity, plunging his dick inside her sweet pot of honey.

"You like it when I hit it from the back baby?" He stroked her hard and slow.

"Ooooh, hell yeah! Beat your pussy up and make me come, big daddy! I fucking love you!" She wailed, throwing her pussy back while toying with her nipples. He banged her up vigorously while slapping her ass with one hand and then the other. He watched as his dick slipped in and out, loving the view of her fat pretty vagina lips.

"Tell me who pussy this is!" he demanded, pounding her love box without remorse.

"It's yours, yours baby!" India squealed as he sent her to orgasmic bliss.

"Is this really my pussy?"

"Yeesssss!" she screamed out as her legs began quivering. "Ahhh, Sump baby I'm 'bout to come," she screeched, clawing the silk sheets.

"Where you goin' baby? Come fo' daddy!" He groaned heavily, pulling her back and forcefully thrusting his hips from side to side, surely hitting all the walls before he burst his nut. "Now you gotta stop tripping on a nigga a'ight ma," he demanded.

"I'maaa stop daddy I promise I'ma stop," she whined.

"You better." He fondled her body. "Now come on daddy dick," he ordered as his body jerked. He felt a load of semen form up at the head of his penis.

"Fuckiiiinng shiiittt!" India shrieked, convulsing as juices flowed out of her womanly opening.

"Damn, ma. What you doing to a nigga?" He collapsed alongside her.

"Pleasing you how a wife supposed to!" India smiled at a job well done.

"You love me baby?" He panted heavily.

"You know I love you no matter what you do!" With that said, she yielded. Sump kissed her passionately and devoured her juicy lips as she did the same. He pulled his wife close to his chest and she nestled her soft naked body against his. Wrapped inside his embrace, they drifted off to slumber, delighted and greatly pleased.

Chapter Eight

*I*ndia woke up feeling nauseous that November morning,
well familiar with the queasy feeling and the extra sleepi-
ness. It was evident that she was pregnant. She had an appointment
with her gynecologist the following day.

India was surprisingly ecstatic. Things were more than great
between the two and had been for awhile. For some reason, India
felt as if she was having a boy. With her two girls she didn't gain any
weight until her third trimester, but Sump had stressed a couple of
times that her butt was growing way bigger and her small breasts
were now huge. She hoped that she didn't have an ill pregnancy like
she had with Italy. India couldn't do anything, and stayed sick the
entire nine months.

India signed in and twenty minutes later she was called to the
back. She stripped right out of her clothes and placed on the gown
as they both patiently waited on Dr. Osmanski to arrive. India and
Sump loved her; she had been India's gynecologist since their daughter Summer. She was an older, friendly Korean woman.

Just as Sump's phone rang the nurse walked in. He ignored the
call. "Hello, Mrs. Jones. What brings you here?" Nurse Willard asked
flipping through India's file. "Oh, your annual pap smear?"

"Well, that's what I was coming for, but I'm almost certain that
I'm pregnant." The nurse asked the standard questions and excused
herself. Shortly after, Dr. Osmanski entered with a huge smile on her
face. "How are my two favorite patients?" Her accent was thick.

"I'm good, Doc," replied Sump.

"I'm fine." India beamed.

"Well, good. Lie on your back so I can see what you got in that tummy." India followed suit and lay back on the examination table. Sump loved watching as the doctor squeezed the cold blue gel onto his boo's stomach. India was even happier as she placed the monitor on her stomach, and they both saw the 3D image of their seed pop up on the screen. The doctor was closer so she detected something they hadn't.

"Hmmm," Dr. Osmanski mumbled as she circled the monitor around her stomach, then down to her lower abdomen.

"What's wrong?" India asked, nervously.

"Congratulations. It looks like you have two babies in here."

"Real talk?" Sump hopped up, eyeing the screen.

"Oh. Two at once?" India sounded unenthusiastic.

"Yes, ma'am. It looks like you are around twelve weeks."

"Woow!" She was completely stunned.

"India I can tell you this ... it's usually too hard to tell the sex of the baby at this stage, but this one here ... has the legs wide open. A girl doesn't have those parts," she laughed.

"So, that one is a boy?" Sump questioned.

"Yes and most likely the other one is also, but of course we will not be certain until the delivery," Dr. Osmanski said, wiping the gel from India's stomach.

"That's what's up ... so most likely since she's carrying two she will have to be restricted from several things like our last daughter Italy?"

"With the risk of the previous pregnancy the process is the same. This one may be more severe in a way because one baby may be receiving more food than the other. Or one baby could possibly not be receiving any food ... so the complications are now higher. I will have to see you every three weeks to monitor this pregnancy, and I'm going to prescribe you with regular prenatal vitamins and iron pills because of your anemia. Stay away from fast food and stick to baked everything, minus the heavy seasoning, and consume lots of fruits and vegetables daily."

"Well at least I don't have to sit in the house all day."

"Once you reach your third trimester you will have to go on bed rest."

India smacked her lips. "Really? I hate bed rest."

"You here it coming from the doctor's mouth, so you gon' have to stay inside India," Sump teased.

"Ha ha funny, and you're going to have to stay inside with me," she countered.

"Now, I have to head out to my other facility, so I'll see you all in three weeks. Here's your scripts with two refills each."

*****

India was somewhat disappointed that she was having two kids at once, because she didn't know how she was going to manage. She knew she had cursed herself by wanting a boy and got exactly what she wanted, plus an extra one. The thought of not being able to blow her head back with some purp pissed her off even more. Not to mention she knew Sump's over exaggerating ass would make sure she ate and did everything she was supposed to do beyond correctly.

After she called everybody and shared the news with them, they were happier than she and Sump were. Nana assured her that she would help her out. India knew Nana helping was more than helping out. But, this time India wasn't going to allow her sons to be attached to Nana like her girls were. She would allow her to see the boys, and even watch them sometimes, but she would make sure it was limited. In all honesty she wanted to see how it felt to raise children. She had two kids and never experienced motherhood except for buying them material things.

As the days passed, India got used to the fact that she would be giving birth to two li'l ones — and the excitement of them having the same mocha skin color as her daughters with good hair and sleepy eyes like their father made her day. She knew it would be fun to get her li'l mans fresh to def, rocking everything like their father. India figured there would be some kinda animosity once she informed Sump of the names she chose. The boys would be Denel Tony Jones and Mark Ton'nel Jones, naming them after their grandfathers and Ton'na. India assumed that he would flip out because from the beginning he always wanted his son to be a junior. Instead, he was delighted when he found out she was naming them after family members. India was ecstatic to be giving Sump his first sons. Life was really moving on, and well, for the married couple.

One lazy day, "Keeping Up With the Kardashians" was the highlight. It was one of those days when Sump was out handling business. She had just finished cooking baked chicken breast, rice and cheese, steamed broccoli and a side spring salad. She fixed her plate, poured a glass of punch, grabbed a bottle of water and entered her living room via her kitchen. She placed her drinks and plate atop the oval-shaped table and plopped down comfortably onto her sofa, covering her body in a purple cashmere blanket.

After wolfing her food down and cracking up at the craziness, her phone rang. She glanced at the screen, and not recognizing the number she answered, concerned.

"Who dis?"

"Hey, Pretty Lady, who you want it to be?"

"Man, who is this?"

"Damn India, don't kill me. It's Scrappy."

"Boy, how in the hell you get my number?"

"You know I bought it for a couple hunnets from your people."

India shook her head, knowing that Vanessa or Kyra had sold her damn number for some money. She laughed. "Boy, you a fool. What's up though?"

"Yo nigga around?"

"Nah, but what up?"

"Shiiiit you ... I wanna see you tonight."

"Scrap, you know I can't see you, dude."

"Why not?" he asked, as if he really didn't know why.

"First off, I'm married and me and my husband are doing fine. Then me and you haven't kicked it in what five, six years. What makes you wanna kick it with me now out of the blue and shit! Kid, you trippin'?"

"Every since I saw you that night at the club, you 'member? I gave your ass my number... the one you never used," Scrappy said humorlessly.

She chuckled. "You are silly, but you know my husband will kill me if he knew I was on the phone with a nigga. Let alone your ass."

"Fuck that nigga. What he don't know won't hurt 'em," he expressed.

"But, I'm not even gonna give it a chance so I'll see you in the streets." India rushed him off the phone. She never knew what Sump was up to and never wanted to chance it. Although she knew they were cool, these days you couldn't be too sure on what a nigga would do to catch his bitch up.

He laughed lightly. "Aww, you just gon' H me, huh?"

"Boy, bye, I'ma holla at you in traffic, H." She hung up, cracking up laughing. Scrappy was comical. She seriously couldn't believe that he still wanted some from her after nearly six years. She was so bored that she did want to kick it with him over the phone light way, but something just didn't seem right. Five minutes later, her Sidekick vibrated; a text message came through that read:

From (212-555-8746)   *Message:*
DAMN BABY U JUS GON HNG UP ON A NIGA LIK DAT, WE CNT EVN CHT
10 MINS N U H A NIGA, WAT DID I SAY SMTHN WRNG, GT WIT ME WEN
U OFF DAT BUL!! STIL LUV U, SEXY!
Received on: Nov 11 11:09pm
REPLY   *OPTIONS*

India laughed, closed her phone and took her dishes in the kitchen. She reentered her living room, laid down on the sofa, covered up and drifted off into a stuffed and light slumber.

*****

As nighttime approached, Sump made his way over to Lilly's crib to wish her a happy birthday and to see his sons, 20-month-old Sumpter Jr. and 9-month-old Marquis. They were kept a secret from his family except for Ronnie. Lilly had been his sideline chick for the past two and a half years. He met her one night when he was in the club. At first Lilly tried to front as if she wasn't paying him any mind, but frankly she and her crew were checking for he and his niggas, noticing them when they first sauntered through. He sensed it and hollered at her. She low key dissed him, but by the end of the night, Sump had her and the rest was history.

In the beginning, they started off as friends — she knew he was married with children. But it didn't take long for Lilly to fall completely in love with Sump. After two months, their friendship turned physical and eight months later they welcomed Sump's first son into the world. He banged up galore chicks in his day, but Lilly was the only chick who actually got more than a fuck out of him. She gave him what India had yet to give him at that time; a son.

To Sump she was exotically fine and independent with a personality to match. She was a bit older in age and mature. At the time, Lilly was 28 years old, thick with a nice shape. Her 34 DD breasts always called out to him, along with her little onion. Independence was what gained his respect the most. In his entire life he never saw a chick that held herself down like Lilly had. She worked two jobs, was attending school, lived in a nice part of town and was pushing a Dodge Magnum that she purchased herself. He admired her for that. Although India was his number one, Lilly filled in the second slot warmly and not at all forcefully.

After awhile she considered herself damn near in the same category as India. She received gifts, took trips, and got time right along with India. Lilly even had a profitable designer handbag boutique that she received as her graduation present. There was never any need for her to step out of her place because she knew his marital status from the door. And just how he stayed with India some nights, Sump stayed with her on others. Maybe not as many, but long as he kept his other life straight everything was good. She played the position of being the mistress the first two years perfectly. But once she felt Sump's distance she would sneak and go through his phone while he was slumbering to search for his house phone number, along with India's cell phone number. She would actually play on the phones. Hell, the nights he wasn't lying beside her she couldn't get to sleep. So she made sure if she was stressing and feeling miserable she would call their phones and allow them to feel frustrated like she was ... until they turned their phones completely off.

Sump was still pissed at Lilly from the stunt she pulled at the nightclub but he never mentioned it to her. It took everything in him not to beat her muthafuckin ass, opting not to because he knew it wouldn't accomplish anything. He just killed her in the worst way and didn't speak a word to her when he stopped by to visit his sons. He would chill with them for an hour or so and bounce out. Lilly needed to be taught a lesson and leaving her alone was the best he'd come up with.

Lilly would curl up on the couch and cry her heart out, wishing that she never showed her ass like she wasn't aware of the game. Agony sat on her heart being that he wasn't dealing with her at all. She'd rather still receive phone calls throughout the day instead of no calls at all. She fucked up and she knew she had to make it up to him. She would have done anything for his forgiveness.

When he pulled up he noticed a couple of cars in the driveway, which only made matters worse. Sump hated when Lilly had chickenheads chilling in her crib. All he knew was his kids better not be inside the house while they were drinking. He took a deep breath before sliding out of his Lexus, ambling onto the porch. He placed the house key into the knob and turned. The coast was clear downstairs, but the sounds of laughter blared from upstairs as he ascended the staircase. Opening the door, he peek his head through scrutinizing Lilly seated at her vanity mirror with her back towards him, applying soft gold eye shadow to her eyelids.

Lilly and her friends didn't even notice him standing there. They were too busy gossiping about nothing. Sump was still angry at her, but the way she laughed, happily swaying her head, and how her tan colored skin glowed underneath the bright yellow lighting, made his dick rise through his jogging pants. No doubt India was lethal naturally, but Lilly was lethal in an exotic way. Hands down, India was the hottest because she was a natural beauty in his eyes, but there was still something about Lilly that was very striking and different.

"Yeah, the 40/40 Club gon' be poppin' tonight," Deanna said, dancing around on the bed. As she rose up, she walked straight into Sump. "Oh, my God Sump, you scared me!" She giggled, holding onto her chest.

"My bad," he said dryly. "Lilly, where are my kids?"

"Up, let me go. We'll be downstairs, Lilly." Her other two girl-friends quickly walked out of the room.

"So you finally decided to swing through, huh?" She continued applying eye shadow.

"Man, Lilly I just came to holler at my kids and just on GP wish you happy birthday."

"Well, thank you and the kids are at my mother's," Lilly said, puckering her lips and coating on brown liner. "So you ain't going out tonight?"

"Nah, I'ma head to the crib and chill out with my wife."

"Hmm," she said, slightly heartbroken.

"Look, though, I grabbed you a li'l somethin' when I was out earlier." He retrieved the small blue box from his pocket. "Here, man."

"Oh thanks, you didn't have to," she replied, opening up the box and finding a pair of three-carat diamond earrings and bracelet to match.

"I know I didn't, but I really do appreciate you taking good care of our sons. Although you get on my nerves I still had to do it outta respect." He chuckled lightheartedly. "Even though you ain't got respect for a nigga no more."

"Sump, pleasssse." She paused briefly and continued. "Look, you know I'm sorry for stressing you that night. I know everything good between the two of you now. So can you just forgive me already?" She perched up, walking over to him.

"Lilly I'ma keep it real. That shit was too close of a call and I just wanna keep a tight friendship for now ... till a nigga clear his mind."

"So what are you saying?" she inquired, tears welling in her eyes.

"Shiiittt, we can be cool as fuck and I'ma still help you no doubt. But far as fucking and the feelings, Lilly, it's a wrap," he said, not totally sure.

"Oh, so that's your word?" She stared him blankly in the eyes.

"Yeah man, that's my word. So you can go do whatever you try'na do wearing that li'l skimpy-ass dress you got on."

"I'ma need for you not to be worried about nothing I'm wearing Sump," she said. "But I am glad you let me know what's up. The thing about it is I'm not even mad," she spoke frankly.

Lilly was honestly running him the truth, she wasn't mad. Just a little disappointed with herself for allowing him to constantly play her. Truth be told, Lilly wanted a change. Being that other chick was starting to get old and she was seriously fed up. Hell. Lilly was tired because although India was his wife, in her eyes she still never amounted up to the woman she was. Lilly often asked Sump why he never purchased India her own business and he would simply reply, "She don't want her own business." The way Lilly saw things was India was idle and spoiled rotten. She couldn't understand what Sump saw in her lazy ass. India never lifted a finger unless she was shopping, traveling, receiving spa treatments or getting a pedicure and manicure.

Plus, she was the one who took long drives to DC, Miami, and New Jersey to get his work, not India. She was the one stashing his different products and hustling the streets with him, not India. He proclaimed that India's ghetto behind was his down-ass bitch but she never delivered anything when it needed to be. Sump never taught her how to cook up the dope and package it. Her ass never did shit but spend the dope money and that was something Lilly couldn't fathom.

It wasn't supposed to be like this and Lilly knew it, but she also knew that she couldn't keep allowing him to play with her heart. She could recall all the nights clearly when she couldn't sleep and would cry in pure anguish. The girl was deeply in love with him. She stressed so badly to the point of her hair shredding like she was a cancer patient and losing weight as if she was a dope head.

She had asked God day in and day out for Sump's forgiveness for several weeks, and that he granted her, minus the relationship they carried on for the past two and a half years. But she was finally cool with that fact and knew she had to learn to cope with it. The girl was ready to wash her hands. She was rather glad that he made the decision on their relationship because she was tired of his bitching when she went to the club and the constant questions. *"Who tried to holler at you? What you wear out? Did you give your number to one of them niggas? I'ma fuck you up if I heard you was out acting a fool all up*

in a nigga face!"

Lilly was now a single woman and could do as she pleased. She knew it wasn't hard for her to pull a dude, especially rocking what she was wearing that night. She was never into the fashion trends, but when she felt the need to be fly, Lilly got sexy. She was wearing a Herve Leger yellow and gold mini-dress that draped open in the front, revealing her gold star belly ring. The back was completely out, showcasing the two tattoos of her sons' faces. Her hair was pulled back in a sleek ponytail with one big curl, complementing her huge star earrings. She wore a long gold necklace with a star pendent around her neck. Her size seven-and-a-half feet sat high in a pair of suede yellow and metallic gold ankle boots. To finish her outfit, she carried her gold clutch purse.

"Oh, so now since we ain't together you wanna dress like a li'l hoe?"

"Sump, please. I can dress how I wanna dress. Don't worry about me."

"Lilly you better change outta that shit now! I don't give a fuck if we're together or not. You got my kids and my bitch ain't gon' be going out dressed like she walking the strip in fucking Vegas. It's cold as fuck outside, dumb-ass hoe."

She chuckled madly. "You be confusing your damn self. One minute you say we cutting feelings and the relationship over, now you say I'm your bitch." She tried to walk away but he pulled her by the back of her ponytail. "Get the fuck off my hair nigga!" she yelled, stumbling back. "See that's where you got me fucked up at, I don't be on that fighting with you Sump. I'll leave that up to you and that ghetto-ass hood rat that you call your wife," she snarled.

"Bitch, I know you better take this bullshit off fo' I beat your mu'fucka ass ... and Lilly I'm not fucking playing!" he exclaimed, yanking her hair harder and finally slinging her onto her bed.

"Now, you tryna fuck up my day because you going through something." She choked back her tears. "I can give a fuck what you going through nigga. I'm going out exactly like this and what the fuck you going to do 'bout it?" she challenged, smugly.

"Oh, I see bitches wanna try a nigga out. Lilly I grant you, you won't be wearing this outfit." He laughed, angrily. "Not tonight!" He snatched the dress of her, leaving it hanging from her body, ripped. Her hair and clothes were disheveled.

She shook her head. "So you a hater, bitch-ass nigga!" She laughed lightly. "Don't be mad 'cause the niggas going to wanna take me home tonight, oh, or better yet make love to me in the club!"

"So you wanna go out there and be on some hoe shit, bitch." He mugged her in the face. Every time she tried to get up, Lilly would easily get mugged back down. "You better shut the fuck up fo' your ass won't be going no damn where. Now try me if you want to!" he dared.

"What the fuck you mean?" she snapped. "It's my day! I bet you I go or I'ma be calling India ass and tell her how you salty cause another bitch going to the club, how about that?" she threatened and went for her phone.

"Oh, so you wanna threaten a nigga? I wish the fuck you would." He mugged her face again. "You know what ... fuck you bitch, go on out and dress however the fuck you want to. That's on your low budget ass, fuck bitch. I'm cool on you, you fucking whore."

"I'm cool on you too. Actually been cool," she yelled, getting up. "I swear to God I wish you would die!"

Everything in Sump wanted to beat Lilly to the ground, but her homegirls were there and he didn't need the police on him ... so instead he reared his hand all the way back and backed handed her in the mouth, causing her to fly up on the bed. "You ignorant-ass bitch, I hope you die! I'm up." Sump stormed out.

Livid beyond intense belief, Lilly lay there perplexed. One thing she knew was Sump played too many mind games, but this one she didn't comprehend. Once she'd accepted the fact that he was done with her, he acted as though he wasn't finished. What kind of shit was he really pulling? Lilly didn't know but just wished that Sump would make up his damn mind because she loved him. One minute he wanted to be with her and make her his wife, being that she held hers down as a wife should. Lilly was always submissive and satisfied his every want and need. The sad thing was she knew India and Sump had history and he wouldn't leave India for nothing in the world. Yet knowing that information, every dream he sold Lilly bought from him ... mostly to make herself feel better. She was finally through, finished, and now he wanna bring along some damn confusion!

Something had to give. Here it was, going on three years, and he was still starring in two separate lives. Lilly was tired of her mind being in a jumble of confused thoughts over Sump. It was her day so she got up and found something to put on. She wasn't sure if Sump was going out and she didn't wanna get embarrassed in the club so she elected to wear a fitted cowl-neck sweater and a pair of Seven jeans. She and her girls were out the door.

*****

After chilling with one of his project chicks at a sidebar, Sump arrived at home around 2:00 in the morning. He was hoping that his love was up so he could present her with some gifts. There wasn't any way Sump had purchased a chick something without grabbing his wife something too. He knew India would flip the fuck out if she knew he was carrying on a relationship with Lilly, let alone buying her expensive items. It was just hard to escape a relationship that he'd carried on for so long.

He never meant for Lilly to become permanent in his life and damn sure didn't expect to grow to love her because the only chick he ever loved long was India. He always fucked bitches 'cause sticking with the same ole pussy made things sort of boring for him. Of course, India's sex game was the greatest. Hell, he was introduced to that first but to Sump there was never no pussy like some strange pussy. He always knew home was home and the streets were the streets and he loved India with all his heart. He just messed up with Lilly and if it could be a secret to the grave then that's what it would be.

Sump made his way upstairs after bashing his dinner and found his beautiful wife cold knocked out in bed. There wasn't anything left on except for the huge built-in fireplace. Wanting to cuddle up with his baby, Sump placed her gift on the mantelpiece, stripped out of his gear and climbed into bed with her.

Sump couldn't help but to look at India sleep; she was just the cutest little thing. The way she slept peacefully with a slight smiling expression plastered on her face each night made his days better. He knew he was on some lame shit when he would just observe her for long periods at a time, but India was his wife. He loved and cherished his prize till the death. Sump couldn't imagine life without her. Wanting to feel her, he gently lifted up her shirt, caressing her small round belly and softly planting kisses on her face. "Get, up ma." He pecked her on the lips, instantly waking her up.

"Hey, baby," she whispered, turning onto her side as he caressed her face.

"I got you something when I was out. A nigga was missing his boo."

"Thanks, and I been missing you too, bay. What you get me?"

"Some jewelry ... but you can check that in the morning, baby. I just wanna hold you."

"Well, I wanna do it, let me get on top." India got straight to the point.

"C'mon," was all Sump said. He was drunk and just as horny as India had been all day. As soon as India got a whiff of his Cartier cologne, her kitty cat was throbbing. Sure enough, he was the lifesaver and couldn't wait to dive inside. Straddling him, India speedily came out of her negligee and helped him out of his boxers. He was rock-hard and didn't waste any time placing her onto his manhood. As she slowly eased down onto it, the feeling of pain and pleasure traveled throughout her body. Sump wanted to make love to his baby so he made sure the process was slow and gentle. Plus he wanted to enjoy that pregnant pussy. She was wetter than usual and with each stroke more creamy juices dripped onto his thighs.

Lost in a world of bliss, Sump was abruptly knocked out of his trance by the shrill sounds of the phone ringing.

"Damn, ma! Who calling your phone this time of night?"

"Don't know," she purred, really not caring who it was.

He ignored it, figuring it was Nala or one of her peoples calling to gossip. He softly flipped her onto her back and gently stroked her nah-nah, which was now hot and gushy.

"Ooh, daddy, you gon' make me come!" she squealed.

"Yeah. Tell daddy how it feels, ma?"

"Too damn good!" she moaned. "Aaahh, ooh, yeah, too good baby!"

"You gon' come for daddy?"

"Yeah, daddy. I'ma come all over my dick."

"Tell me you love me and how much you love this dick," he groaned, thrusting his penis in and out, side to side and all around. Juices were pouring out of India as if her womanly opening was a water faucet.

"Ooh, baby, I love you and I love this dick, I'm fenna coooome!" she screamed.

"Come with me baby." Sump bit down on his bottom lip, jerking and pounding in and out of her climaxing. He fell to the side and collapsed. Coming down from their orgasmic high, they lay side by side happily until India's phone rang once again.

"Who the fuck is blowing up your phone at 3:00 in the fucking wee hours of the morning?" he questioned, now pissed. He was ready to curse out Nala, or whoever it was.

"Calm down off all that racket noise, boy. Answer it if you're so concerned."

Wasting no time, Sump quickly grasped her Sidekick from the nightstand. "Who the fuck is this?"

Click, the caller hung up.

"India you gon' make me fuck you up! Who the fuck calling and hanging up?"

"Don't play. It's prolly one of your hoes playing on the phone, mu'fucka."

"Try and flip shit if you want to and I'ma fuck you up, India," he said, gawking at her suspiciously.

"Boy, I'm not the mothafucka that commits adultery. So please don't go there with me. I really don't feel like arguing with you about a petty-ass hang up."

"Okay, let's see what you got going on in this phone, since you ain't got nothing to hide," he said sarcastically, surfing through her call log. India couldn't believe that out of all days, this nigga wanted to investigate shit when she forgot to erase her call log. She could've slapped herself and passed out. Quite a few dudes had her number and from time to time she'd kick it over the phone with them, nothing major – just casual conversation when she was bored.

"India, who the fuck is this restricted caller you was talking to for 48 minutes and six damn seconds?" he asked. "And I swear to God you better not say Nala or none of them 'cause y'all ain't talking after no damn midnight. And their numbers show the fuck up. Now who the fuck was it, India?" he screamed. Sump was heated now. It was as if a bomb had exploded inside his body. Homeboy was fired up.

At that very moment, he didn't care about his infidelity because he took good care of her ass. Sump wanted India to himself and as long as he provided her every need and want, she shouldn't even speak to a nigga. Besides, he frequently warned her about dudes in the streets. He taught her from the beginning to not communicate with niggas. Part of him was being selfish, but another part of him was protecting her from the cruel streets. Sump knew the game too well and knew exactly how niggas operated. He was damned to allow a bitch, his wife or anybody to become his downfall. And India chatting with different dudes, ones that he didn't know at that, was too risky. He trusted India without a doubt. She was the only person he trusted after his Nana ... but what he didn't trust was niggas.

From jump niggas in the neighborhood was checking for her. They wanted to snatch her up to claim her as their own trophy. It was just something about India's demeanor and swagger that they digged. She had a hoodish swagger but a suburban attitude and Sump smugly took pride in being the only one who had her in every way. He loved claiming her as his leading lady. Just the thought of her talking to another man drove him insane.

India was annoyed because she felt Sump was taking it too far. She sat up, scrunched her face up and cocked her head back. "Are you serious, dude?" She really wanted to know.

"Nah, this for play. Yo, I'm dead fucking serious so who the fuck was you talking to? And please don't make me ask you again, India muthafuckin' Jones!"

"Boy, I don't have to explain shit to you. Do you tell me who the fuck you be talking to?" she snapped, getting out of bed.

"Who the fuck you talking to like you done lost your rabbit-ass mind? I don't gotta tell you who I'm talking to or fuckin'," he bellowed, jumping up in her face. India started getting a little scared because he looked damn near demonic.

"Oh, so you can just fuck whoever and it's cool? It is 3-somethin' in the morning. Go'n with the bullshit." She walked away.

"Aw, now you wanna be on some bullshit and don't wanna let a nigga know what's up. You must got some shit to hide. You got something to tell me, India?"

"Naw, fo' real, though, Sumpter ... go'n."

"Sumpter, go'n?" He paused for a second. "So you want me gone India? That's what you want?" He jumped in her face again, this time pushing her.

She stumbled, almost falling. "Oh hell nah you done lost your mind pushing on me and I'm pregnant."

"So you fucking some other nigga now? What nigga you protecting, huh?" He pushed her again.

"Bitch, you better quit fucking pushing me!"

"I'ma keep pushing you till you tell me what nigga you fucking?"

"Boy ... I don't know what the fuck you are talking about and can care less. I really don't understand what the problem is!"

"You my problem India, that's my damn problem! Keep on lying and I'ma show you the problem when we're in court," he threatened.

"Court?" India was stunned. "Pussy, we can go to fucking court. What the fuck, you want a divorce? So what ... I'm 'posed to cry 'cause you want a divorce? Shid that's cool if that's what you want. What we going to tell 'em? We getting one because you're constant cheating on me along with your insecure ass?"

He shook his head in disappointment. "That's how I know you fuckin' somebody 'cause you ain't trippin' and crying about the shit. Who are you fucking? Just let a nigga know so I can bounce right now. Slut!"

"Nigga you must be feeling real guilty about some shit or one of your bitches got you pissed 'cause I haven't did a damn thing to your ass. I was talking to muthafuckin' Kyra and you trippin' about nothing. Calling me a slut?" She chuckled. "Psshh, niggas wish I was a slut."

"Yeah, speak that Kyra shit if you want to. Just make sure you speaking that shit when we get that DNA test!"

Crushed beyond belief, India just stared at him.

"Yeah, don't just stare muthafucka."

"Boy, you done really lost it. But it's cool 'cause you know it's nothing. I can go chop this baby up very quickly, nigga. So fuckin' fast it'll make your head spin. I was trying to make you happy as my husband having a son for your lame ass! But you flipping on me for no apparent reason. I haven't did nothing to you, but be the best wife I know how to be and you push me while I'm carrying your kids! I'ma tell you like this, my dude. Don't touch me no muthafuckin' more or it surely can be War World III up in this bitch!" India snapped, walking into her closet and grabbing her black Juicy Couture tracksuit. She really wasn't up for the bullshit. She was leaving.

"So you 'bout to go with that nigga you was talking to all night?"

"You'd like to know huh? Bitch, don't worry about me," India spewed.

"Stop playin' man. Where you going, bra?"

"Somewhere you're not!"

"India what the fuck is you saying, B?"

"Nigga I said that shit clear enough for you to hear me clearly."

"Word to my mutha, son!" fumed Sump.

"Shid, don't swear son this way cause you ain't got no sons 'member?" she said sarcastically.

"Yeah, I got sons." Sump was being funny. "I should just break your fucking face."

"Oh, now you wanna fuck up my face. I dare you to touch me again Sumpter, and I swear on everything somebody going to be leaving this mu'fucka by the paramedics."

"I see you talkin' all greasy cause you pregnant and you know I won't beat your muthafuckin' ass. But keep tryin' me if you want to India. Don't get shit fucked up now, I'm up and off this bullshit, real talk!!" He slipped into his clothes and slid on his shoes, grabbed his keys and walked out.

India followed behind him down the staircase. "So, you going to leave nigga?" she yelled, mushing him in the back of his head over and over again.

"Indy, you better gon' with the wack bullshit ma. I'm not even playin'!"

"I just hate you so much you sicken me. Just stay the fuck away from me forever, pleasssse."

"That's what's up. I'm out." He walked out the door.

"Where are you going?"

"Somewhere you're not," he yelled, climbing into his car.

"I see you like playing games but I can play the same ones. Believe that," she sneered in exasperation.

"Do you, baby girl." He cranked up the ignition, reversed and skidded off into the night.

Chapter Nine

*B*eing pissed was an understatement; India was beyond
infuriated. *Oh Sump, wanna play games with the queen?*
Well, she was very much up for it and glad to bring her childish
character back to life. If that's how Sump really wanted to play the
game, she was willing to do so. She figured; why not give his ass
a dose of his own medicine? India didn't think twice about calling
him, staying up crying, and could have truthfully given two fucks
where he was.

As soon as he left, she packed up a few outfits, heels, tennis
shoes, undergarments, toiletries and her burner. She phoned Kyra
since Sump didn't have a clue where she resided and after the
fourth time calling her she finally answered. India informed her of
what was going on because of her ass dishing out her number for
some extra money. Kyra laughed and couldn't believe that Sump
was trippin' over a hang up and assured her cousin her stay would
be comfortable. One thing India thanked God for was that Sump
hadn't gone through her text messages to find Scrappy's mess. She
knew hell would have been raised in their abode if he would have
seen it.

For the next few days, Sump called constantly, filling up her
voicemail and texting her back to back. India would simply crack
up laughing and not answer. Sump thought he would get the last
laugh but India was definitely proving him wrong. He thought she
would be the one blowing his phone up, but India turned the tables

on him this time. The first day he went without her phoning him, but after that he couldn't take it any longer.

India wasn't answering the phone, he couldn't find her over none of her peoples house, and most importantly she hadn't contacted Nana ... or so he thought. India explained to Nana what was going on and begged her not to tell. Nana agreed to stay out of their business. Sump was sick out of his wits worrying himself half too death. He didn't have any clue where she could be. He just knew India would be calling by morning.

*****

The night Sump left home, he made his way back over to Lilly's crib. Although Lilly was smart, she was also a sucker for Sump's love so he knew it wouldn't take too much to reel her back in. She was always an easy grab. Unlike India she was drama free, obedient and just loved to be in his presence. Sump was her weakness. He knew deep in his heart that no matter what, Lilly was going to stick around. The only way they would separate was by him leaving her alone.

Sump reached her crib around a quarter till 5:00 in the morning, finding Lilly still out partying. At first he was pissed because he wondered if she was really out trying to seek a new lover, but erased the thought quickly.

Pulling up in front of her house 20 minutes after Sump arrived, she wondered what his ass was up to. The night was already a disaster because all she thought about was him. As much as she tried lying to herself that it was officially over between the two, she knew it wasn't and knew she couldn't resist him. It was something about him that she couldn't let go of. She loathed that he was married to India but she thought if she stuck it out with him that maybe her day could come.

Lilly had to come to a realization: if waiting was what she had to do then that's what she had to do. In all her years on God's green earth, she never loved a nigga like she did Sump. Although she played as if she didn't care, Lilly cared deeply and knew it would hurt worse allowing him to walk out of her life than to be second. The thought of losing him made her dizzy. Hell, she'd been trapped this long ... what would it hurt to continue on as long as he made her happy? Blanking India out as if she was nonexistent like before was her way of escaping the anguish.

She walked in, noticing the reflection of Sump's sleeping frame. Sump was lying on the couch and the light emanating from the Sony plasma television screen danced on the walls. She turned off the TV, which awakened Sump, and ascended the steps towards her bedroom. Sump followed right behind her, not saying a word. Neither of them spoke. They both got undressed and got into bed. As much as Lilly wanted to play hard to get she couldn't ignore his touch; the way he pulled her into his chest filled her world up with ecstasy.

Opting to finally fill the air with words, Sump voiced first, "So baby girl, did you enjoy your night out?"

"Being honest, I didn't because you were sitting on my skull so hard the entire night."

"Damn, don't blame that shit on me."

"Oh, so now a nigga got amnesia?"

"Nah, look though ma. Real talk ... I apologize for blocking you out like I've been doing. I'ma man so I'll admit I was wrong for playin' you down ... but it won't be like that for now on, baby."

"Oh really?"

"Really though boo, 'cause fo' real you got respect for a nigga. I see you changed into some more appropriate gear. I dig how you respect a nigga no matter what we go through."

"Hmm, I guess."

"Don't guess. A nigga serious, yo."

"Sump, I'm just saying you be confusing me with your actions. One minute you loving me and the next all we share together is our sons. Sometimes I think you're just using me to get back at India, making yourself feel good after y'all done beefed or something."

"Lilly ... I came to spend time with you, not to talk about India. If I wanted to talk to India I would be lying beside her right now. So please let's just chill. I done had enough for one day, a'ight ma."

"I'm sorry for upsetting you baby; I just wanna make you happy. Sump, I love you baby."

"I love you too, now make me happy." Sump demanded attention as he cupped her chin, kissing her passionately on the lips.

Lilly was gonna make him happy alright. She quickly pulled his long pole out from the slit of his boxers and gave him a splendid blow job. She sucked his dick as if it was the last penis on earth. Lilly surely earned points for her neck dinners, being that she could slob him for long periods of time without stopping. After awhile she put her pussy game on him and they fucked into the sunlight comfortably settled in. To Lilly's surprise, once he woke up he wasn't in any rush to take off. They actually got dressed together, kicked it for the entire day and made a couple of moves. Once they got home they replayed the performances from the prior night over again. Lilly was happy because this was the Sump she remembered.

The following morning was when he noticed that India hadn't tried to get in contact with him. That's when he flipped and began blowing her phone up. Continuously reaching the voicemail, he was furious because he wasn't pissing India off ... instead she had him heated. Lilly knew he couldn't stay with her forever and it was time for him to depart. She desperately wondered where he was going, but she knew her position and knew it wasn't her concern. She hugged and kissed him fervently and then he headed out.

*****

The days that passed were freezing cold and the girls knew it wouldn't get any warmer. So India, Kyra, Nala, and Vanessa decided to go on a winter shopping spree. The girls woke up early in the morning, hitting up every mall in New York's perimeter. They had shopped all day, and that the fact that Willie Stacks, a popular party promoter was throwing a *Help for Haiti* boat party placed the icing on India's cake. India was sure he would be there; he and Willie Stacks went way back. She knew Sump hated for her to attend any party while she was pregnant. The thought of him spazzing out once he saw her had her anxiously excited. Everybody decided to get dressed at Kyra's place since she stayed in a brownstone close to downtown Manhattan near Pier 40.

India had to get extra sexy tonight. She opted to rock one of her newly purchased outfits too. She dressed stylishly in a sequined black tunic blouse, a pair of designer leather leggings and stiletto ankle boots. To complete her look, she wore her hair bone straight and huge diamond chandelier earrings gleamed from her ears.

Once fully clad, India checked out her reflection in the mirror and laughed, knowing she was the shit with a little stomach bulge and all. She heard her phone ringing, playing her oldest daughter's customized ring tone. She answered, "What up Summer?"

"Hey, momma. Where you at?"

India paused momentarily because she knew Summer was a true daddy's girl and she didn't put it past his ass to involve their daughter as if it would make any difference. "Why, what up baby girl? You cool, princess?"

"Yeah, I was thinking maybe we can go out to the movies to-morrow. Where you at?"

I know Sumpter ugly ass prolly on the phone or in front of her little ass. Trick no good nigga, she laughed to herself, *he about to be pissed.* "I'm over Nala's house, baby. Why you act like you working for the feds? What up, bay?"

"Oh, Daddy wants you." India could hear her passing him the phone, but she quickly hung up.

A minute later, a text message came through her Sidekick, reading:

From Hubby (718-555-0743)   Message:
India ok stop da games U win. Call me now dis shit ain't 4 play you gon'
make me fuck U up!!
Received on: Nov 15 11:33pm
REPLY   OPTIONS

India laughed at the text.

25 minutes later, they arrived to the loading dock, where bright lights shone from the massive yacht. The parking lot was nearly full but India wasn't worried about that. She utilized the VIP parking section and also skimmed the area for one of Sump's whips, but she didn't see any of the five.

"Oh, what's up India? I'm surprised you ain't come attached

at the hip with your husband," Big Rell, the huge security guard, teased. "Just pull through here," he said, directing her to a parking spot near the water.

India spotted all of Sump's boy's rides. She surmised he either rode with one of them or he would make his grand entrance shortly.

They made their way up to the yacht, paid their admission and walked up the ladder to enter the interior of the boat. Once inside, they headed straight to the restroom to make sure they were all looking fierce. India applied a hint of Chanel lip gloss to her pouty lips and they quickly headed to the top where the beautiful bi-level dance floor was.

The party drew in everybody that was somebody. India knew she shouldn't have been at nobody's damn party all pregnant. Sump thought he won the game and didn't because she was surely in the lead. It was certainly game time.

As she and her family of girls sauntered atop the glass floor, India bumped right into her fantasy, which she knew could never become a reality, but made sure she stopped to speak. The sexy man that stood before her was Meek, looking sexier and sexier by the second. The Gucci reader frames gave off a cocky but intelligent look, perfectly complimenting his D-boy stance.

"Yo, what up big head?" He hugged her.

"Oh, hey Meek. You good?

"Yeah and you looking good as always," he complimented her.

"Thanks. You do too, fam."

"Yeah, do yo husband know your ass in here?"

"Nope!" she burbled. "And don't even mention that you seen me."

"Y'all mu'fuckas crazy ... but let me get over here, ma. I'll see you." He walked away.

Skimming the boat, India found her girls seated at the bar. She made her way through the crowd and slid onto a barstool herself. She ordered a bottle of Fiji water and sat back sipping on her drink, surveying the crowd and waiting for a certain somebody to show up.

As time moved, India could see Meek grooving with his

champagne bottle in the air, eyeballing her lustfully. She couldn't do nothing but chuckle at the thought of his silly ass 'cause he always threw subtle signs that he wanted her super bad.

45 minutes later, the devil was sure enough ready to start a war. She didn't know how Sump's ass managed to slip passed her, but his ass was parlaying on the second level.

"Oh, Kyra look at this nigga bottle poppin' in the VIP. He gonna be mad once he notice I'm in this bitch," India guffawed.

"India, you so childish. What you 'bout to do?" Vanessa asked.

"Aww, nothing, too outta my league. I'm just 'bout to over-enjoy myself. That's it, my dude."

"India, Sump going to fuck your ass up," Nala added.

"Shuuutt up, c'mon Kyra." India glanced once more and saw Sump throwing a wad of money from the top, making it rain for real. *This nigga clowning throwing money and shit, what bitch he showing out for now.* Soon as the thought appeared, she noticed the same Asian chick she stole on the night she and Sump got into their dispute watching Sump's every move. *Oh, maybe I need to scope out the scene cause if this nigga fuckin' with this bitch it's over and I'm cool as AC, man.* She thought to profile the two, but elected against it. *Fuck it, if he even be near that broad we gonna have a serious problem.* She locked eyes with the chick, turning up her nose and rolling her eyes.

Being that she was polished, she didn't start beef when it didn't need to be and took her focus off the girl. Yo Gotti's smash hit, *We Can Get It On,* was thumping loudly out the sub woofers. While making her way amidst the dance floor, India noticed Scrappy and his small entourage coming through the entryway. *Damn ... am I bugging or is niggas looking sexier these days?* India thought to herself, laughing. Scrappy was looking fine. His long braids hung loose, framing his face. Covering his body was a gray Ralph Lauren jogging suit with matching Air Max 95s, and his jewelry game was amazing.

India couldn't worry about him though, she was on a serious mission and shaking her ass on the dance floor was it. She continued slithering through the horde to hit the dance floor. As soon as she hit the center, the song changed. She began swirling her body rhythmically to the hypnotic sounds, having almost every man's attention on her. The girl was dancing her butt off as she sang along with Lil' Boosie.

"I miss kissing on you ... you know I miss kissing on you ... I miss touching on you baby ... I can't stop thinking about you." India was in her own world.

Scrappy was observing her body swaying seductively to the hip-hop track. He was entranced by how precisely she rocked her hips and loving the suggestive words ... because he did miss kissing on her southern lips. He could vividly recall the sexual encounters they indulged in years earlier. He couldn't divert his eyes from her twisting and winding body for shit. He couldn't believe what he had done to her because of the envy he held. All he knew was he wanted India like never before. The girl was absolutely beautiful and if he could have made love to her in the club, he would.

Upstairs in VIP, Sump was having himself a marvelous time. Poppin' bottles and throwing money, he admired the fine honey from below shaking her booty. He was envisioning the peanut butter-skinned honey with her fat ass in the air as he beat the pussy up from behind. He was gonna make it his business to hop on shorty tonight. Sump couldn't get a clear picture of her face. But what he had seen he could tell she was bad. Long black hair with honey blonde streaks and a banging body to match.

Before he could think any further, Sump noticed his rival Scrappy approaching her. He laughed and knew dude didn't have a chance once he stepped to the chick. He'd snag her the same way he took his first love and Lilly. Suddenly, Gene came out of nowhere fully charged, not wanting to hate, but he was Sump's right hand man.

"Ay, son ain't that yo wife face Scrap all in and shit?" Sump had been so busy surveying her body; he had failed to realize that it was his wife poppin' her ass like she wasn't married or three months pregnant. Stunned, he wanted to see what type of shit India was really on and posted behind the scenes, scrutinizing them for a second. The sighting made him sick with disdain. Mac C didn't make the situation any better, adding fuel to the intense fire.

"B, that nigga really got the fucking audacity to be talking to your wife dawg. I been wanna whack this lame-ass nigga. You wanna handle this kid, son!" Sump didn't know where this dude grew the balls to approach his wife, but what had him livid was India was actually carrying on a conversation with homie. He didn't know the motive behind this shit, but the buzz he had seconds prior quickly vanished and he was going to continue to peep out the scene before he caused any chaos.

India knew Sump could be possibly observing her so she kept the conversation short and simple. She wasn't trying to lead the issue any further, knowing that would only add accusations to her case. She quickly told him she would holler at him later, grabbed Kyra and disappeared through the crowd, making her way back to where her girls were seated. She slid onto a barstool beside Vanessa, unknowingly with Sump already on her heels. His eyes were blood-shot red and India knew that dude was incensed, with flames streaming out of his ass and smoke steaming from his eyes.

"India. I just know my eyes playing tricks on me, correct ma?" he inquired, trying to remain imperturbable.

India acted as if his presence wasn't known, sipping on her bottled water and swaying her head to the beat.

"Aww, so you don't hear me speaking to you, India?"

"Do y'all hear anything? 'Cause I don't." She turned to her girls.

Not wanting to intervene in their business, Nala and Kyra got up and walked to the restroom. Vanessa on the other hand didn't care too much for Sump; she knew about the numerous flings he had with all sorts of chicks. "Shit, I don't hear nothin' either cuz," she replied.

"So you wanna be funny 'cause you in front of Vanessa, huh?"

"Sump, please. You wanna act funny ... leavin' my house in the middle of the night like I'm some secondhand bitch or something."

"Indy, I hope you know how dumb you look in here pregnant."

"Sump, how in the hell she look dumb barely showing?" Vanessa asked snottily.

"Sweetheart ... I'm discussing matters with my wife, not you, baby."

"Bye, boy I was just asking your whorish ass a damn question, fuck you!"

"You'd love that!" He focused in back on India, ignoring the riffraff Vanessa was talking. "So, what you're telling me is that you don't wanna be with me, right?"

India wasn't prepared for those words to escape his mouth with that much certainty. Vanessa smirked, sliding off the barstool. Before she walked off she said, "Sump, you truly disgust me talking like that. You bugging about her carrying on a conversation with Kyra, but she never trips on your ass fucking all these nasty bitches. It's just a shame nigga; you'll never change and that is sad to say. I'll be over here, India." She walked away.

"So, India ... you got co-signers now, huh? You don't know how to speak for yourself now days? You trippin' and I really want you to know that shit."

"Nigga, please! You know how she acts. The thing is, why in the fuck you just gon' leave like you just got it like that? Who do you think I am? 'Cause I'm far from your lame-ass groupie hoes!"

"Just how you got dressed and were talkin' about leaving, India. And did you quickly forget the secret-ass conversation you had for damn near an hour and that you just had this Scrappy nigga all in your fuckin' face?" He ice-grilled her. "Don't you know shit can get real drastic just by simply chitchatting with the nigga? What is your problem, seriously?"

"First off, I don't have a problem. What's *your* problem is the concern. Just because you beef and don't like the nigga because of y'all run-ins don't mean I can't speak." India rolled her eyes. "Damn, the nigga went to school with me and we hadn't seen each other in awhile so he was simply speaking. That's it, that's all."

"Oh, so that's how we playing the game now?" He shot her the oddest look. "Because if we're simply talking to old schoolmates that means I can be in all these hoes' faces laughing and giggling while you right in here? Correct me if I'm wrong!"

India sighed heavily. "Sump, you do what you wanna do anyway so what's the difference? Just 'cause dude was talkin' to me shit gon' get drastic? Are you serious?"

"You know what, you so hotheaded its crazy. I'ma drop all that other shit and just ask you do you know how desperate you look in the club shaking your pregnant ass?"

"If you say so ... a'ight. Whatever, dude!" She waved him off.

"So you just came out to make a fool of yourself?"

"Sump, look, lets discuss where you went when you left my muthafuckin' house. How 'bout that?"

"Oh, so you ready to explain to me what sucka nigga you were on the phone with then, right ma?"

"I'm not even going there with you, boy. Like I said, you know who I was talking to and that's all that matters. I ain't gonna kept explaining a muthafuckin' thang."

"You know what, you're right and I think we must need to be separated."

"Excuse me!" India didn't know what was going on, but she felt their marriage crumbling. She couldn't believe Sump insisted on threatening her like she was the adulterer. Hurt by his words, tears formed her in vision, but she was too gangsta to be caught crying in public and hastily choked them back. She rose to walk around, but he blocked her path.

"What, you don't wanna discuss our problems?"

"Fuck you and those problems!" she spewed. "You keep screaming 'bout gettin' separated and a divorce and shit like that! It's evident that you wanna run around here like a bachelor and I'm not gonna be the only fool blind behind reality. If I'm becoming old news then fine ... we can get whatever you like, Sumpter!"

"India, what are you talking 'bout! You crazy fo' real. A nigga didn't even say nothing about splitting up." He was fucking with her mind.

"Oh, so you just didn't say I think we must need to be separated or something."

"India you trippin', baby. We at this party and we both just need to have a good time." He pulled India into his chest and kissed her on the lips.

It didn't take India too much to fall back into his trap. "I love you so much baby," she admitted. "Just please don't leave out on me like that again," India implored.

"I promise you I'll never leave you, boo, and hopefully you'll never leave me." He planted a kiss on her forehead.

Neither of them knew, but Lilly was watching them the entire time. In the beginning, she was gaining happiness by the minute, then the contentment quickly evaporated once she noticed the argument had ceased. Next thing she knew, they kissed and exited the party early. At that moment, Lilly knew Sump wouldn't be back over her house for some weeks.

Chapter Ten

As the weeks passed by, life was normal again for everyone. India was now four-and-a-half months pregnant and their relationship was still going strong. She woke up at 4:00 in the morning to a white Christmas Eve to find a couple pink boxes wrapped in white ribbons. Since she had Italy, the duo agreed to always exchange their gifts on Christmas Eve, allowing Christmas Day to be Italy's and Summer's time of bliss. Inside the boxes, she found a winter white waist-length chinchilla coat that she was dying to have, along with the matching knee-boots.

Another box held a cuff bracelet filled with pink diamonds and an overpriced crocodile Zagliani handle bag that she implied she desperately wanted for the past month. It was the exact one she saw sitting beautifully in Bergdorf Goodman. *The nigga surely know what a chick likes,* India thought to herself, slipping on her furry slippers and heading downstairs where her husband was concentrating on his PlayStation 3.

"Hey baby, I love all my nice things. Thanks bay." She bent down and kissed his lips.

"Oh, you already know how I do it."

"Yeah, but you know how I do it too. Wait a minute." India excused herself and retrieved two silver boxes with black bows wrapped around them from the computer room. She reentered the living room and handed him his gifts.

He'd paused the game to open up the boxes. Smiling, he said,

"Aww, ma ... this is fly shit and I love it and certainly you." She had given him a brown leather jacket, a pair of boots to match, a presidential black face Rolex, and a pair of designer penny slippers with matching pajamas.

After India showered and threw on her ruby red Victoria's Secret jogging set and white- and-red Moschino sneakers, she headed downstairs to hook her husband up a big breakfast. She cooked him cheese eggs, blueberry waffles, grits, potatoes and steak with onions.

"Damn ma, that shit smells good!" Sump cooed, entering the kitchen.

"Why wouldn't it? I got skills, babes," India giggled. She sat their plates on the table while Sump poured two glasses of orange juice and joined her for breakfast.

"So what's on your agenda for the day?" she asked.

"I'ma head out and do some last minute Christmas shopping, then I gotta do a few rounds. Later on I'ma head to the city to meet my connect. I'll be back around seven in the morning after hitting everybody off with that work. You can just meet me over Nana's house 'round that time."

"Okay, I gotta head out with Nala today too. I messed around and forgot Summer wanted a mink coat. I'ma grab her that and a few gift cards for the family."

After they ate and allowed their food to digest, both of them were on their way out. Sump went into town and shopped for his sons and Lilly. He waited last minute because he couldn't risk India finding unusual gifts. For the past two years, Lilly and Sump celebrated Christmas Eve as a family because it was tradition that everyone have Christmas Day at Nana's place. Lilly could understand that completely.

Three hours later, Sump was falling through Lilly's door with too many presents for his boys to be under three.

"Oooh, Daddy! Wat dat?" an excited Sumpter Jr. asked his father.

"Li'l man, that's your presents I got you and it's a lot more!" He rushed back out to the car and retrieved the rest of the gifts.

His two boys were already rumbling through their presents.

Wrapping paper and boxes were everywhere. It was ridiculous how much stuff these kids had. He copped his sons toys that they wouldn't even be able to play with. At almost one and two years old, these little boys had two-carat diamond earrings, bracelets, chains, two leather coats apiece, and shoes and boots to match nearly every outfit. He purchased Lilly a pink suede jacket, thigh-high boots, and a handbag to match. He even purchased her the same Zagliani bag he bought his wife, just in a different color.

Sump and Lilly seemed so happy helping their kids open up gifts, but all Sump could think about was how wrong he was. If India was to ever find out about his secret life, double life, he knew there wouldn't be anything he could do. He was beginning to loathe himself for being in too deep. He was starting to believe that his life was cursed ... why and how could this happen? What was God's purpose for involving him with Lilly?

His dreams of becoming a hustler had come true beyond his wildest imagination, but lately things weren't right in his eyes. He felt a sign but didn't know what it was. Was someone trying to kill him? Maybe he was just tripping. He didn't know, but he had a funny feeling ... and he knew it was from the Holy Spirit, but he constantly blocked it out. Instead, he allowed himself to believe he was tripping and needed to lay off of all the marijuana. All he knew was there was no turning back from the drug game and he was too much of a man to turn his back on his kids.

*****

Snow flurries were falling from the sky lightly as India stared out of the window expressionlessly. She had decided to stay at Nana's house overnight and wait for Sump to come in the morning. As each car passed by, she hoped it was Sump so they could began the present - opening process. Here it was going on 9:00 and Sump wasn't anywhere in sight. India knew he was a late person who said one time but wouldn't arrive until an hour later. But two hours had passed and he hadn't called and wasn't answering his phone. By this time, India began panicking. She just hoped he wasn't spending his time with a bitch on their daughters' Christmas Day.

Glancing at her watch, she noticed that twenty more minutes

had passed. It was now 9:21 a.m. and he still wasn't there. India picked up the phone and dialed his number again, only to be met with his voicemail. *"Yo, this Sump nigga, leave a message if it's about money."*

India was shitty because now it seemed like he had turned his phone completely off. As soon as it beeped India went loco. "You crab-ass nigga. What kinda shit you on? I just know the pussy you lying in isn't that good where you wanna play my kids on their Christmas. But it's so cool, black-ass muthafucka. Because I'm here to see them enjoy their presents. I purchased enough shit for them to be just as excited as if you were here. Oh, and that shit you copped them ... Please. They good, my nigga. Take all that shit to that bitch you fucking and ..." she couldn't say any more because the voicemail time ran out.

India was like a ticking bomb but she had to hold her composure for the sake of her daughters. As she was going to the kitchen Italy said, "Mommy, where is Daddy? Dang, he taking too long. Can we just open up the gifts that's here and when Daddy come later we'll open his?"

"Yes, Italy. Tell Summer, Brianna, T'ionna, and the rest of the kids y'all can begin opening up y'all gifts." Italy ran upstairs hurriedly to inform the kids and India continued moseying on to the kitchen, furious.

India plopped down onto the barstool in a fury, propping her elbow up on the breakfast bar. She tilted her head to rest on her hand and let out a huge sigh. Nana was sliding her homemade cornbread inside the oven when she noticed something was troubling India.

"Darling what's on your mind? Why I read stress behind those big beautiful eyes?"

"Nana, you know it's your grandson stressing me out once again." She swayed her head shamefully.

"Oh, India I done told you as long as you allow that boy to do you wrong, he'll continue to do it. Sweetie, don't go stressing on something that you accepts."

"But Nana ..."

Nana interrupted. It was her time to speak because she was growing impatient with the young married couple and was tired of biting her tongue. "But Nana, nothing. I know you don't wanna hear ole Nana talking and you know I don't like involving myself in you guys' business, but I'm just gonna tell you, child. You and Sumpter play so many games with each other it's crazy. Y'all have two little girls and y'all are good parents, I'm not going to deny you that. But the way y'all living out here isn't right and Summer growing up. She is able to see how y'all are living. By no way are y'all showing her the correct way of living, not the real way of life." She paused to sit in the chair beside India. "Honey, you are a registered nurse, and Sumpter has plenty of money for you guys to finally settle down and be the parents that I know you both can be. Y'all need to leave that street lifestyle alone and live as a married couple. Not meaning to speak upon this India, but you lost your sister to these streets, or the 'dope game' as you kids would say. Does it ever get old too you, baby? And don't think I'm blaming everything on you. Sumpter is to blame just as well as you are, if not more."

India stared at Nana as if to say, *how am I to blame 'cause I don't sell nor cheat on your grandson! What are you saying Nana?*

Nana replied as if she'd read her thoughts. "I know what you're thinking, child. And like I said both of you all are to blame because just as Sumpter is out here hustling, killing, and sleeping around, you still accepts his dirty laundry and most certainly accepts all the gifts, India. You all's lifestyle is that of a celebrity. It just isn't right. You have daughters."

"Nana, I see where you coming from but Summer is only turning 13. She doesn't know anything about what Sump does."

For a moment Nana didn't speak. Instead, she wondered if India was as stupid as she just sounded. "I'ma be the one to tell you this darling. If you think Summer doesn't know where she receives all these expensive things from, you're lying to yourself. Even ole Italy knows her father is the dopeman, a drug dealer, a crack cocaine and heroin distributor. The other day, she told me 'Nana Pooh, my daddy is a baller!' So if Italy knows, Summer certainly knows." Nana paused. "And all the things you all buy that child are only showing

Triple Crown Publications presents... *Wife*

this young girl a different route. Heck, all of the girls for that matter."

"But Nana, all kids like nice things."

"You are right, sweetie. All children do like nice things. But, for her to attend her seventh grade ballroom bash in a dress with diamond detail and diamond incrusted heels makes no sense." Nana inhaled heavily and shook her head. "India, please. She still has prom ... what will she wear then?" She flashed India a quizzical glance.

"Aww, Nana. That's the type of things they wear out there. Besides, that's what Summer picked out. She said all of her school friends were wearing designer gowns. We felt it was okay to get her that gown," she reasoned.

"That doesn't matter. She could have easily worn a nice dress from Macy's or Sears and you could've gotten her some nice shoes from there too. But y'all are spoiling this child rotten and that's what she'll be used to. Summer don't need to be accustomed to this lifestyle because it can easily turn sour."

"That's what she like though, Nana."

"I understand that sweetie, but once she gets of age what do you expect out of her?"

"I don't understand what you're saying Nana," India said.

"Once she gets of age nothing will be exciting to her. She'll be ungrateful. She won't appreciate nice gifts because y'all shower her with too much now."

"Nana, that's what she likes and I can't help that she wants that sort of stuff. I feel if the parents are shopping in Barney's and Neiman Marcus, children should also receive nice things instead of settling for Macy's."

"India, you're not understanding the moral of the story."

"Nana, yes I am. But I think they deserve the good life just like the white kids do at their school."

"Here you go with that black and white stuff. It's time to stop using that, baby. There's a new president in office so that color stuff should be dead now. Like I said before, you can have all the same things India. All I'm saying is work for it. You're Sump's wife and I'm pretty sure if y'all was to ever sit down and discuss it for the sake of your girls and soon to be boys he'll understand."

"Nana, that boy won't leave the streets alone. That's all he knows. Besides, I can barely talk to him about leaving chicks alone."

"You children will never understand. I guess the saying is true ... let every soul learn from their own mistakes."

To India, Nana was tripping. She didn't know where the conversation was going, but she listened until Nana finished. India still didn't want to believe that she wasn't showing a good example for her the girls.

Shortly after the children opened up their gifts, the rest of the family began to arrive. It was 12:55 and nobody had received a call from Sump. Each time India heard the doorbell she prayed that it was Sump, only to be disappointed. By 2:00 Nana's house was full and everyone in attendance wondered where Sump was.

As soon as India gave up on his whereabouts, her cell phone rang and an unavailable number popped up on her screen. She waited briefly and figured it probably was her mother, then answered, "Merry Christmas."

"What a fucked up one for me."

"Who is this?" she asked, not recognizing the low voice.

"India, I'm sorry, but I'm in jail. Baby, they got me."

At that instant India heart fell to the pit of her stomach. She realized it was Sump.

"Oh my God, Sumpter! Are you serious? What they got you for?"

"You'll be better off asking what they don't got me with. It's not looking good at all and my lawyer out of town for the holidays. I can't get in touch with him for shit."

"So how did you get caught, baby? And when do you go to court?"

"Boo, you know I can't discuss the facts over the phone and I don't get arraigned till Monday because of the holiday. Just make sure you keep calling Gibson. Vacation or not, I don't pay that nigga by the hour for nothing. Call him till you contact him. I haven't been talking to Meek much, but still call and tell him and Mac C what's going on." He paused and continued. "Just tell the girls I'm sorry, but I'm out of town and the flight was cancelled or something. Oh, and

Gene in here with me. I think he already called Nala."

"Oh my God! Are you serious? What happened?"

"Didn't I just tell your retarded ass I can't talk over these phones? I'll tell you another time, damn."

"Muthafucka, don't get no fucking attitude with me because your dumb ass locked up. I'm just concerned. I won't ask no more. Okay!"

"This is certainly the wrong time for you to be yapping that bullshit and getting smart over the phone. I'm in jail facing serious time and you're try'na argue. Please call my attorney and inform my peoples on my current status. Be at my court date, bring some bond money in case they grant me bail and get that money from my safe from the house in the Estates. I'll holla at you." He quickly hung up, steaming hot. *I'm not going to allow India to stress me more than I already am. This some bullshit,* he thought.

*****

Christmas was dismal for everyone because Sump was the family's star and it felt weird to eat Christmas dinner without him. Monday came around quickly and India finally got in contact with Gibson. He called her early that morning and made arrangements to meet to discuss the matter.

India scooped Nala up and they headed into the city, grabbed some breakfast and then headed for Gibson's office.

She signed in and five minutes later, he called them to the back. Gibson had been Sump's attorney for the past eight years and was one of the best attorneys on the east coast. "Hello, India and Nala. You girls have a seat."

"Gib, what's going on? What they got Sumpter and Gene charged with?"

"Mrs. Jones, it seems as if Sumpter and Gene have gotten caught up in a terrible situation. I just rescheduled their court date for 6:30 so I can get further information on the accusations and the matters of their cases. What I have so far is the Feds did a drug bust on them late Christmas Eve. There was a lot of money and lots of drugs confiscated from the scene. There is strong evidence in this case. Federal agents had been watching Sumpter for a year and once they gained enough evidence on the guys, they took action. I feel this will be a very hard case to win because they caught them in the act."

"So will they be granted bail?" Nala asked.

"I'm working on that now. Judge Renton works with me sometimes on drug cases and if my client is willing to pay him, he'll accept fifty thousand to get the time at its least. The more money the more he'll do and more time he'll knock off."

"So, how much time are they facing?"

"India, it's very hard to give an exact amount of time because I don't have all the files and updates on their cases. I can say this is a federal case."

"So, it's not looking good at all?" Nala inquired, worried.

"I'm afraid not. But I promise, I'll try and push it until they both get the least amount of time. One more thing. Federal officials are talking about confiscating eight cars and four homes between the both of them. I'm almost sure the possessions will not be seized because everything is accounted for."

"Right. That's the least of my worries 'cause everything is in his Nana's name. And Gene's things are in his grandfather's name. Plus they both have proved income being that Nana's husband had a huge insurance policy and left lots of ends behind. And Gene's grandfather still has businesses. So how much will this cost, Gib?"

"Since Sumpter has been paying me by the hour for eight years and only had me in the courts for traffic tickets, of course it is already paid in full. But to take on Gene's case it'll be $50,000. I'll take 30 percent now. Once the case is over, I will receive the other 70 percent."

"Alright," Nala replied, pulling out her checkbook.

"Okay, thanks Gib. I appreciate you handling all this mess. And you said the court hearing begins at 6:30 tonight?"

"Correct. I'll talk to them both before court begins. You girls be there twenty minutes before time. I can inform you on any further developments."

"Thanks again Gib and I'll see you later." He walked the girls out and they immediately went to Sump's crib in Jamaica Estates to grab some dough.

Triple Crown Publications presents... *Wife*

As soon as she walked inside the house her cell phone rang. Of course it was Sump.

"Hello," she answered, plopping down on the ottoman,

"What up, you got any word yet?" He sounded dry.

"Yes, I just left him. You have court at six tonight."

"What did he say?"

"Basically that he'll have to look over all the paperwork and see from there."

"Okay. You grabbed that paper yet?" Sump asked.

"I'm at the Estates grabbing it right now. I'll be there later on."

"A'ight, I'll see you then." They exchanged 'I love you's' as India's line beeped. She answered, "What's up?"

"What's good? Where you at?" Kyra asked.

"At the crib in Jamaica, why what up?"

"What's going on with Sump and Gene?"

"Court is at 6:30 tonight. I'll have to see then."

"Well, you know I'ma keep y'all in my prayers. What you gon' be doing till then?"

"Attending a yoga session downtown. I need to meditate and clear my mind. I'm stressing out, man," India said, feeling every bit of defeat. "This case is not looking good."

"Just stay strong for your family. You can't fold, India. You gotta stand tall. You a soldier. I love you and I will make sure to be at court for you."

"Thanks cousin. Love you too." India hung up the phone. Her cousin's words touched her heart. India knew she couldn't fold, so she forced forced the aching pain of losing her husband to the system out.

India dashed upstairs and retrieved several stacks of hundred dollar bills out the safe. She put them into two separate envelopes, placed them into her oversized tortoise bag and they were out the door.

Later on that evening, the girls arrived to the federal court building and ran right into Gibson. He called India and Nala into a small conference room and began discussing the matters of the case. "I'd like to say first that this is worse than I thought. We are in a corner here. We're operating with hard evidence. The D.A. isn't letting up on the cases because it is still on file that Sumpter's father killed several police officers. He's using that against him. They may be appointed to the same prosecutor handling their cases back then because they never got anything out of the case but dead bodies. So he's certainly coming hard this time. If the guys decide to take this to trial, he'll definitely bring a tough battle."

"I can't believe it's that bad."

"It would've been much easier for the guys, but their connect ratted them out. Not any ordinary fish but a big fish ... the top Colombian man. He had been under surveillance for many years and the Feds finally caught up with the dealer as well as the layout of their business meetings. Feds busted his drug ring and many more operations. He told on a lot of guys underneath him. He gave the police information on Sumpter and Gene. They had been watching them for a year. Now the guy is willing to testify in court and not face any jail time."

"Oh my God ... are you serious, Gib?" India's voice cracked.

"I'm afraid so, honey. I'm very sorry."

"So, what are they saying, Gibson? How much time are they really facing?" Nala asked.

"It depends. They have Sumpter and Gene in photographs, on audio, and most certainly at the scene of the drug bust. As of now they're accused of conspiracy, drug trafficking, carrying a concealed weapon, money laundering, tax evasion and Sumpter is also charged with operating a criminal enterprise."

"Oh my God! You have to be kidding me, Gibson. Just say you're joking." India wished she'd wake up from the horrible nightmare.

"I'll try my best to get them the least amount of time, I promise," he assured.

"How much time are they looking at?"

"To be totally honest with you girls, these charges carry a life sentence, but ..."

Nala interrupted. "A life sentence? Hell nah, my husband can't get life."

"I have talked to the Judge that's going to be handling the case.

With the right money involved he has offered a plea bargain of a maximum of ten years served."

"Ten years? My daughter will be 22 in ten years. She loves her father dearly. Gibson, you mean to tell me they will get all of that time?"

"I'm thinking if they take it to trial they will likely be found guilty and serve twenty years or better."

"So you mean to tell me that with all the money you get paid you can't find a way outta this? Man what will it cost? I know all you crooks allow the money to talk and if it's the right amount of money offered y'all gon' be it. So what up Gibson ... what can you do?"

"Nala, I'm sorry but I talked to Sumpter and Gene before I came here. They want to take the case to trial. If they win they are free to go. But if they lose the case then it's terrible."

India sighed as vomit tickled her throat. She was sick to her stomach. "Oh, hell no! Sumpter will not be taking it to trial. He knows that these white fuckers are dishing out that ten and fifteen years like it's applesauce. Nah, Gibson. I know he can't win this case because it's too many charges and way too much evidence," she said sadly.

"I have told the both of them that. I also said they would only end up sentenced to about five years once it's all said and done. Federal time is always lessened. Taking the cases to trial is certainly not smart. India, you know I love Sumpter like family. I will never steer him wrong. If he will plead guilty until I can get my sources together, I can almost guarantee that they just might be out in less than five years."

"Tell Sumpter he better listen to what you're saying. You attended law school, not him because, life." She swayed her head, not able to digest it. "I can't be married to someone serving life. I know any chick can relate to that. These chicks can barely hold they dude down for six months. I know no broad going to hold a nigga down for life. No matter how much they love one another."

"I understand, and I'm going to talk to them one more time before they make their final plea."

"Okay. And here is another 20 percent. I'll just owe you the $25 G's when this is all over with." Nala slid him an envelope filled with fifties.

"Girls, it's time to go inside the courtroom. I will try my best."

"Thank you, Gib." India stood and hugged his neck. He walked out of the small room and they followed closely behind him. They sat their bottoms in the first row beside Vanessa and Kyra. They didn't wind up calling Sump and Gene's case till 8:20.

All the girls wanted to beat the hell out of the young prosecutor bitch. She flaunted around like she was the head bitch in charge, with long blonde hair, blue eyes and dressed in a Versace business suit. She was truly an asshole, and wasn't letting up on either of the men.

When it was Sump's turn, it seemed as if everything went in slow motion. "The State of New York versus Sumpter Jones. His charges are conspiracy, drug trafficking, carrying a concealed weapon, money laundering, tax evasion and operating a criminal enterprise," the clerk announced.

"Attorney Gibson, how does your client plea?" Judge Renton asked.

"Guilty on all charges discussed in the plea bargain."

"Are you aware of all charges claimed against you?"

Sump nodded his heads and replied. "Yes, your Honor."

"Okay, Gibson. The sentencing will be held one week and one day from today."

"Your Honor, I was wondering could there be bail set until their sentencing day, taking into consideration that Sumpter's wife is pregnant ..." Gibson asked as the prosecutor interjected.

"Your Honor, I don't think that should be taken into consideration. He is dangerous to the outside world. They will be able to keep the drug enterprise still running as they please."

Judge Robert Renton didn't have any other choice. And although he wanted to play hardball, he also knew that he'd gain $50,000 just by allowing bail. "I am going to set both bails at $25,000 apiece. Your clients are scheduled to be in my courtroom one week and a day from today."

Nala was relieved; Gene's case had been held first. Yet India's face fell flat. India was very happy that she would be able to spend one more week with her husband. But, Sump had always been there to carry her through her pregnancies and see her give birth to both of their children ... what was she to do now? Things were slowly following apart in India's life again. How was she supposed to go on without him with her? Sump was all she knew and even one seemed much too long.

Chapter Eleven

The next few days flew by swiftly, allowing Sump to put his business intact, fuck quite a few chicks, spend time with his second family and kick it in New York's city streets like never before. But on Thursday night India, Nala, Sump, Gene, Nana and the four girls were all off to the Caribbean Islands. They all decided to spend the weekend in Aruba since it was Sump and Gene's last weekend to enjoy life on the outside for a very long while.

It was the beginning of the year and Sump opted to renew him and India's vows now. The two decided they would have a small ceremony on the beach, unlike the huge wedding that took place in a church in downtown New York City.

The pair had chosen to have their service the day after they arrived, as the sun was setting. The emerald colored water was beautiful and the orange-hued sunlight illuminated everyone's skin gracefully.

India donned a white tent-style knee-length dress and white Emilio Pucci slide-in sandals, wearing her hair pinned up.

India couldn't wait until she could sex the shit out of her husband because homeboy was looking dapper, like a true boss. He wore white linen shorts, a white Versace button-up shirt and

They both exchanged their vows with a charming speech, conveying their true emotions. To Sump's surprise, India slid a six-carat diamond ring on his finger. Their love was deemed unconditional, as they sported wedding rings on both hands.

Triple Crown Publications presents... *Wife*

Afterwards they had their gala at Waterfront Crab House, ordering everything. They ate lobster tails, shrimp scampi drowned in garlic sauce, crab legs, baked potatoes, biscuits, and salad. Champagne, wine and liquor were overflowing their table. Everyone danced the night away, enjoying themselves. Sump and Gene were so fucked up, they could barely move and continued to stagger all over the place all night.

Their night ended at 2:00 in the morning and everyone went their separate ways. Sump had been so horny he was only halfway through the door when he took over India's body. In their ocean-front villa they made passionate love as if it was the end of the world. India knew she was going to miss this man. It was almost crazy because she had never been apart from him since she could remember for more than two weeks. The love they made never felt so good.

The next day they woke up at 1:00 to a beautiful blue afternoon with the sun spilling into their hotel. Once they made love in the Jacuzzi, the couple showered and made their way out to the beach in their swimwear. Soon as they hit the outdoors, they were met with a light breeze kissing their skin.

India loved jet skiing and was an expert at navigating the jet skis on top of that beautiful blue water. India cracked up laughing because Sump couldn't keep from falling off to save his damn life. He was from the hood and didn't know how to drive anything other than cool whips. After awhile, he relinquished trying to cruise on the jet skis and ended up hopping on the back with India as she whipped it through the ocean. She forced lots of gas, professionally though, going at least fifty miles per hour, bouncing over ocean waves without losing control or falling off.

Once that grew old, it was about time for them to head out to their romantic cruise. It was a huge cruise ship that took them around the surrounding islands. Gene and Nala attended but everyone had private rooms. Sump wasn't able to be in a secluded place with India for one second without touching her and went straight into lovemaking once more; he knew he would miss that tight pussy for sure.

By nightfall, the four of them were departing the cruise ship along with hundreds of passengers. They arrived to the downtown casino via limo. Sump didn't want to go because he was never one to win at gambling. He never had luck with that kinda stuff. Yet out of all the many times he visited the islands and lost stacks of dead presidents, this time he won $40,000 playing black jack.

Later on that night, they all attended Jazz Fest and enjoyed the live entertainment. Sump noticed that India had gotten up and walked outside. India needed some fresh air because reality was hitting her hard and no matter how hard she tried to fake it, she was hurting like hell. Sump promptly headed in her direction. He wanted to know what was wrong with her. He spotted her walking along the beach and jogged to catch up with her. Seeing the agony in her eyes caused a sharp pain to run through his body. He cupped her chin and said, "India baby, can you please be strong for me?

Tears formed in her eyes. Those words caused her to lose the air in her lungs and she couldn't help but to allow the angst to fall from her obscured vision. "I'm sorry Sumpter ... but it really hurts me knowing that you're about to be in prison for ten years. Your daughters gonna be 22 and 14, and our sons going to be 10. I mean what I'm supposed to do? I can't help but to cry. You leaving me." She turned around. Sump pulled her into his arms and eased down onto the sand.

Sump felt beyond stupid. With all his heart and soul he wished he didn't have to leave India's side, especially because she was carrying his kids. At that moment, he wanted to execute his connect tortuously. He couldn't believe that the muthafucka he had been dealing with for many years snitched him out. In all this time, he thought he was too careful to get caught dealing drugs. There had been many times when the Feds tried to plant shit on him because of his father's history. But they never could take action because they couldn't prove anything.

Although Sump wanted to murder his connect, Contis, he also knew it wouldn't happen ... those damn Colombians stuck together. Didn't care who they killed either. Wives, kids, or grandmothers. Sump heart didn't pump fear, he just had to use his brain. Needless to say, Sump knew the enemy went after ones who were close to their foe: the family they loved dearly. By no means was he involving India and his family in some street bullshit again so a street war was out of the question.

As he continued to wipe the tears that were falling from her eyes, he thought, *the dope game is definitely reaching its demise. Got the connects getting caught and snitching. What part of the game is that?* He kissed her on the lips savoring the salty taste from her tears. "Bay, you gon' have to stop crying. You gon' have me out here whining like a li'l bitch. You know I hate to see you hurting, girl. It's all gonna be okay, believe that."

"I know it will be. We'll get through this together and I know everyone is going to help me with the boys. I just wish you didn't have to go," she sniffled.

"I wish I didn't have to go either ma." He rested his chin atop her shoulder, rubbing her belly soothingly. "But I have to. But I know Gib going to make sure he work on the case a sap. Daddy will be home before muthafuckas realize I'm gone." He paused and continued on. "I should just go on the run and shit. Fuck it, they'll never find me out here," he said jokingly.

India hit him across the chest. "Now you try'na add more time to your sentence. Don't play." She chuckled.

"Nah, I'm just fucking with you, baby," he said. "But on some real life shit, I want you to be good while a nigga away for awhile. Please. I just beg that you hold a nigga down and don't be on no club hopping shit once you drop just because I'm not gonna be around. You know I still got eyes and ears everywhere."

"I know bay, I'ma hold you down. You already know how I do."

"A'ight, now don't let me hear no bullshit India or I'ma fuck you up, fo' real. I want you to be ready for me once I come home. We're really gonna be a loving family. Fuck everything, you already know. It is going to be me, you and our kids."

"Yeah, well don't talk my ear off about it because I'll just see when you come home," India said, serious. "Now, what you want me to do about money?"

"That won't be hard. I already hooked Mac C and Ronnie up

with a connect from Miami. So money's not going to be a problem. Plus, the safes in our cribs got plenty paper. I'm just gonna need you to back up on your splurging. Just shop a few times outta the month and you'll be straight."

"Oh, my ... a few times a month? I can't go once a week?"

"No, India. Try once every two weeks."

"Oh, well once I drop I'ma have to get a job. I cannot go without shopping."

He laughed lightly, shaking his head. "You really have a bad shopping habit. I don't even think you wear half of that shit you already have."

"Whatever, nigga." India blushed, leaned back on him and buried her hands in the sand. "Ay, Sump. I'm really happy that you're my husband. Wouldn't live life without you, bay."

"Yo, same here ma." He pulled her up and he took her to a secluded area where they could make love on the beach near the water.

He slid her dress over her shoulders and she assisted with stripping him down to the nude. India lay on her back and he inserted his manhood deep inside her juice box, hitting her with slow and mild strokes only. The squishing sounds each time he entered her wet entry caused him to come prematurely. Once he got that one off Sump thrust harder, watching India buck and moan. Caressing her breast, he leaned in and softly bit down on the bottom of her lips, slipping his tongue inside her mouth and kissing her with much intensity.

"Damn, I'ma miss fucking this pussy," he whispered.

"Ooh me too. I love this dick!" India moaned, knowing that she had to hit her man off with one night to remember while he served his prison time. She swiftly landed on top and eased down on his penis. She glided up and down, gaining speed by the second. Observing India ride his dick at her best, all he could do was hold on for the joyful ride. His wife looked so good with beads of sweat all over her body. He admired the way she moved with so much precision. Twirling her hips with her ass plopping down on his thighs, India's creamy juices squirted out of her opening as she screamed in sheer gratification.

The following day was a family day so Sump, India, Nana and the girls were up at the crack of dawn and their first stop was at the breakfast club. Once the family ate, the girls wanted to shop before they did anything else. Sump wound up purchasing everyone designer sneakers and outfits; ticket prices were hefty.

After the family finished shopping, they all opted to partake in the island's activities and participated in everything possible, from horseback riding which was Italy's favorite, to jet skiing. Nana and Sump sat out and conversed.

"Ma, look at my family. I'm very disappointed in myself." Sump sounded dismal.

"Baby, you know that I've been telling you this for a long while now... all good things come to an end. I just hope and pray that you've learned from your mistakes. You know the first time you mess up it's a mistake that you learn from, but the second time you're just a fool. So I just hope this is a lesson learned."

"Oh Momma, stop preaching. I'll retire one day. That's my promise to you," Sump said as India walked Italy over to them.

"Your daughter don't wanna ride on here with me anymore."

"C'mon baby, sit here with your Daddy. I don't like those stupid thangs either." She sat on her father's lap.

"Y'all weak! Bye, 'cause I love them thangs." India took off.

"Daddy, so is you really going to jail?" Her long black hair had curled up into a wavy 'fro.

"Baby, Daddy has to go away to an all boys school to learn. You know how you go to preschool? I have to go to adult school."

"So why Mommy don't have to go to adult school?"

He knew it would be hard for him to break things down to Italy's little butt 'cause she always questioned him as if she were interrogating a witness. His li'l mama wouldn't give up until she felt she understood the situation completely. Sump looked at his beautiful daughter, and the thought of leaving her caused his heart to ache and it weakened him. He felt like a failure. He allowed the streets to take him away from his family; he let down the only people he trusted.

Glancing out to shore, Sump noticed that his princess Summer was growing up and he couldn't believe that he wasn't gonna be able to teach her about the streets. She was on her way to becoming a beautiful teenager and he probably wouldn't be around to see her grow. That was his little girl; his first-born. The way she was spouting out scared him. She was petite just like her mother, with a slim waist and too much butt for a preteen. Her rich caramel complexion and long silky hair with his sleepy eyes made her flawless. He knew his baby was going to have the little niggas flocking all around her. Summer was absolutely gorgeous. He gazed at her little cousins and hoped they wouldn't become victims to the streets. They had already spouted out and looked stunning. He knew they probably already had little dudes scoping them out. He just prayed that they wouldn't get introduced to that dope boy lifestyle.

He looked back at Italy and saw the same thing in her. He couldn't believe how gorgeous their kids looked. The way Italy stared at him with her head tilted to the side waiting on his response caused him to double over into laughter. "Because babe, your mother have to take care of you girls and plus girls can't go."

"Okay, Daddy. I think you're tricking me," Italy put one hand on her tiny hip and squinted her eyes. "Because sissy was saying that you have to go to jail because you getting money and the police hate to see black people ballin' out of control."

Not wanting to continue on with their conversation, Sump looked at his Nana whose eyebrow were raised in the air as if to say, *I told you so.*

"No, sweetheart. Don't believe everything you hear and let's not talk about me because I think somebody might wanna get a snow cone," he sang, tickling her tummy.

"Daddy, Daddy ... stop it, stop it!" Italy laughed, squirming out of his arms. For the rest of the day, they all had a tremendous time. That Monday was their last day in town so India and Nala knew it had to be the best of all. They had planned for their men to have the time of their lives. They partied until midnight and then got ready to indulge in some adult entertainment.

The fellas didn't have any idea that their wives found two

island girls, twins named Ruby and Emerald, to entertain them until the sun rose. India and Nala both held onto their husbands' hands and led them into the room.

By no means would the girls have done such thing under normal circumstances. But since their husbands was going away for Lord knows how long, the girls decided they were finally going to allow their fantasies to become reality. They weren't going to indulge in the sexual performance because they didn't get down like that. But the twins were going to make sure the guys had an awesome time.

While they were out they had the twins set up the room beautifully. They had white rose petals trailing the floor and all the lights were turned off, allowing scented candles to send off a dim glow. Nasty slow jams were playing on low in the background. The guys were knocked into a trance once they entered the room; they didn't know what was going on. To India's and Nala's surprise they weren't only the twins in attendance. The twins had gotten two other girls to perform sexual stunts with them, making sure it was one party to remember. There were two queen-sized beds in the room, one against the right wall and the other one on the opposite side. Two girls lay butt naked on each of the beds, already fondling on each other.

"Wow, what's going on people?" Gene said, eyeing the nude chicks.

"This is y'all going away present. Now c'mon." India and Nala both grabbed their men by the hands and led them to the beds. "Baby, enjoy yourself," India said. "I'ma sit right here and watch." India placed herself in the chair that was positioned in front of the bed while Nala did the same, their backs to each other.

It didn't take these hood niggas a second longer and they stripped out of their clothes, hopping straight into the performance with the island honeys. Those chicks were wilding out, on some straight freaky shit. They were sucking the skin off dicks and penises were going in every hole there was. India was actually learning moves from the girls because they were spinning and twirling in positions that she never tried. The thought of being with a chick never crossed her mind, but the way these chicks was moving had her wanting to join in. But she elected not to; it wasn't her steelo at all. So she just began toying with her pussy.

She glanced over her shoulders and saw Nala ahead of her with her eyes glued to the show that stood before her, softly moaning. She was playing with her kitty also. Focusing back in on her sexy chocolate husband, she played with herself until she exploded.

After hours of mind-blowing sex and constant finger fucking, the sun was seeping through the blinds and the show was finally over. The two cousins thanked the girls for the night they arranged and all parties separated.

Sump thanked India and they headed straight to the bathroom. They showered together, gave one another messages in the Jacuzzi and reminisced on the old days. Once they reentered their room, the duo cuddled and fell into a pleasant slumber in each other's arms.

Tuesday arrived quickly, and the courtroom was packed with Sump's family members. This was going to be a short hearing. He had already pleaded guilty and the Judge already had the sentence set. After a few minutes the bailiff walked in and announced, "Will all rise for the Honorable Judge Robert Renton?"

The judge sat in his chair peering over his glasses as he read, "We the court are sentencing Sumpter Jones for attempt to distribute a controlled substance, two counts of drug trafficking, and two counts of conspiracy charges to five years in the federal penitentiary. After two years served parole is available. Court is adjourned." The judge banged his gavel and it was finally over. India couldn't believe what the government would do for money. Sump understood, shit, Sump and Gene had paid Judge Renton a quarter of a million to drop a lot of the charges and to give them the least amount of prison time possible. Sump still felt as if he had been fucked raw.

India was left with a few minutes to holler at her husband and they kissed, wishing it could last forever. Surprisingly, India remained calm, cool, and collected as the bailiff came and slapped the cuffs around Sump's wrists and took him away from her.

Chapter Twelve

*I*ndia missed her husband dearly. It was still hard to believe that he was gone; India had never been so depressed or lonely. It had been two weeks since the sentencing, but to India it felt like eternity.

To be closer to the city, she stayed in their crib in the Estates. Sleeping, crying and eating had become her best friends again. India knew it wasn't healthy for her sons, so after that stage she collected herself and cleared her mind. She had to learn how to cope.

As the weeks continued to pass by, she was growing accustomed to the visits, letters, and several calls throughout the day. It was a tough situation but everyone was showing India much attention, allowing her to feel extremely comfortable during her time of need. India was finally getting through the problematic times or at least she believed she was.

One day in particular, India was making her way to see Dr. Osmanski because for the past week she had been enduring an uncomfortable feeling in her vagina with a mild odor. She knew it had to be bacteria or yeast infection. So she scheduled an appointment and luckily, she took the spot of a patient who cancelled that same day.

When India arrived to the deserted clinic she was called back right away. "Hello India, where is my guy?" Dr. Osmanski was friendly as usual.

"Oh, he wasn't able to make it today. He's out of town." She

lied because it wasn't professional to have the doctor all up in her personal business.

"Okay, so what brings you in today?"

"I think I have a yeast infection." Dr. Osmanski instructed India to strip from the wrist down and she examined her, exited the room and returned shortly after.

"Oh, India ... it looks like you are infected with gonorrhea and Chlamydia."

"Excuse me, gono who, Chlamydia what?" India inquired, shocked.

"Yes, I'm afraid so. But the good thing is these STDs can be treated."

India began contemplating. If Sump was there she could have just strangled him to death. Then the thought of the event that occurred in Aruba appeared.

Nasty-ass island bitches, she thought and then pondered further into that night. *Hell nah ... Sump wore a condom and plus I didn't have sex with him after that. We just cuddled. Nasty dick bitch.* India was beyond incensed. She couldn't believe out of all times to give her a sexually transmitted disease it'd be while she was pregnant. How could Sump do this? India was running very low on tolerance.

Dr. Osmanski explained the treatment, gave her the prescriptions and India left mortified. She whisked through traffic and dropped her scripts off to the nearby Walgreens. As soon as she climbed back inside her car, her phone rang. Of course it was Sump. She pressed ignore and continued to ignore the calls until she reached her house.

India pulled into the driveway and hopped out. She immediately un-transferred her calls from her cellular phone and turned the house phone ringer off. She didn't have anything to say to him. She was already in a messed up situation and she learned that she'd contracted two diseases at once. How trifling!

To come down off of her fury she popped in Kevin Hart's "Seriously Funny" and couldn't stop laughing. After she replayed the DVD for the third time, she headed back out. She picked up her medicines and headed into town to do what she loved to do best: shop.

After finding a parking space in the parking garage on the lower level, India made her way inside Palisades Center Mall. Her first stop was in Armani Exchange. She was only going in there to get a comfortable tracksuit and wound up spending close to one thousand dollars. She departed that store and made her way up to Bloomingdales. As soon as she entered the department store her phone rang. She groped through her handbag to retrieve her Sidekick. India was happy that it wasn't anybody trying to call her for Sump. It was Vanessa.

"'Sup wit it Nessa?"

"Shit, chillin'. I was seeing if you wanted to go eat at Justin's around seven tonight. We all going."

"You know it."

"A'ight, see you then cuz."

India sat down onto the bench and tried matching up boots with the three outfits she had picked out. The saleswoman came over to assist her and India held up a pair of Chloe ankle boots and asked, "Do y'all have these in royal blue? If so can you get me a seven-and-a-half?" Not even a minute later some guy called out her name and when she looked up, it was Scappy.

"Oh, hey. What up Scrap?"

"Shit ... but what up with you, ma'?" he asked, licking his lips.

"Nothing, out shopping," she answered.

"I see you still doing you while yo nigga in jail."

"You know that li'l shit ain't stopped a diva like myself," she giggled.

The saleswoman reappeared. "Will you like me to get you anything else, ma'am?"

"No thanks, I'll just take all of these things here."

"Alrighty." The saleswoman helped her gather her items. Scrappy followed her to the cash register.

As the saleswoman rang up the items they talked casually. The saleswoman said, "That'll be $2,723.00 even. Will that be cash or credit?"

India began fumbling through her purse for her wallet but

Scrappy told her, "I got this ma." He retrieved a knot out of his back pocket and peeled off thirty crispy hundred-dollar bills. He felt that was the least he could do. He owed it to her.

"That's what's up. Thanks."

"You know it. But you can keep the change and I'ma holla at you later."

*****

When India arrived to Justin's soul food restaurant, her cousins were sitting down and had placed their orders already.

"Dang, y'all couldn't wait on me?" India joked, sliding inside the booth.

"Shut up fatty, I ordered you your favorite. Don't even trip fam-fam," Nala said.

"Well, thanks." India immediately wanted to go into conversation with her cousins on how to handle her current situation. The four cousins were so close that India wasn't worried about none of them judging or talking about her once she left. They had all discussed worse things than this. Hell, it was actually a normal thing for Kyra and Vanessa; they stayed in the clinic getting cured for a venereal disease. So, in front of them she wasn't at all embarrassed and really wanted their opinion. "Y'all, why when I went to get a checkup today I found out that I got gonorrhea and Chlamydia."

"Are you serious, India?" Nala asked, stunned.

"Yup, and I am very upset. Sump ain't never gave me anything except for trick. I was like 17 the first time and 21 the last time."

"Damn cuz trippin'. I can't believe he did you like that."

"That's what I'm saying, fam. So what should I do?"

"Girl bye, at least you got something curable. It could have been worse," Kyra said.

"I know that but Sumpter grimy. Evidently he's been fucking whomever cause the nigga gave me two diseases at once. How trifling is that?"

"You know it's nasty ... but y'all 'member that one time when I was fucking Bird from uptown? That nigga gave me both of what you got, plus trick and crabs. Now that's nasty."

All the girls doubled over into laughter. "Fo' real y'all that shit ain't even fucking funny. Who in the hell still gets crabs? C'mon now!"

"Sorry Nessa. But I do 'member Bird nasty ass giving you all that. You fucked up all four of his cars, bleached all his gear and stole what, ten racks from the nigga?" India asked in between laughter.

"Certainly did. And ain't fucked with that dead dick nigga since."

"You're a fool, ma." India shook her head, coming down off her laugh. "But fo' real y'all I haven't told Sump yet. What should I do? I haven't answered none of his calls all day and I really am mad because it is disgusting as shit."

"Yeah, and he gotta know. They thoroughly check them niggas when they first arrive to the prison," Vanessa said.

"You ain't never lied about that," Kyra added.

"I'm so mad at him. And if he knows he got that monkey ... man. I just don't know, y'all." She tried choking back the tears. "Things between the two of us seem like they have been drowning for a minute now and we're just holding on just because." She paused and continued. "Keeping it one hunnet, I don't think our love is as strong as it should be. For some reason I feel he's hiding something from me. I don't know what, but I do know it's something," India expressed, feasting her eyes on something approaching. "Oh yeah, this must be ours." India quickly dropped the discussion and danced around happily in her seat, famished.

India continued to mull over the fact that Sump had been dealing with other chicks unprotected. To her that was completely disrespecting the G code. A cold feeling ran down her spine and the thought of leaving him for a minute while he was in jail would give him the heartache that she had been enduring from jump. Sump wouldn't like that at all. India knew he wouldn't. She had something for his ass and she wasn't going to answer any of his calls. India surely wasn't going to visit him until she was ready to. It really sickened her and to keep from crying her bleeding heart out, India just didn't want anything to do with him for a while. Not until she got over the fact that he'd played her in the worst way. For now,

India was in the state of mind of: Sumpter Jones Who?

"Ay, y'all know Willie Stacks having his annual party tonight at Club Rosé," Kyra, the party info specialist, broke out.

"Oh yeah, I'm in there," India said.

"Gurl, your pregnant ass gon' get a fuckin' beat down, try'na hit the club. You know that shit gon' get back to Sump," Nala said.

"And! Who cares?" Vanessa screwed her face up. "Sump's ass is serving time. What can he possibly do to her?"

"Right! That's my whole point. I want it to get back to him. The nigga didn't care about passing down this shit, so fuck 'em."

"You're pregnant though, India."

"You act like she's big and pregnant. Nala you can barely even tell. She just got a little pouch, babes."

Nala really didn't feel like debating with them, not today she didn't. "Yeah, a'ight. Let's be out."

*****

It was a couple of minutes after midnight when the four girls strutted through the club doors. They briskly made their way upstairs to the VIP room and found themselves a table. Bottles were ordered as soon as the girls sat down. Vanessa and Kyra instantly began taking shots to the head, chasing the Patron down with Red Bull. Within thirty minutes, VIP was jam-packed with the celebs of the dope game. A couple of upcoming music industry cats were in attendance too.

Luckily for Vanessa and Kyra they were single, mingling and receiving mad hollers while India and Nala were turning down more hollers. Everyone was bopping to the Jay-Z track as India sat bobbin' her head to the beat. That's when she noticed a girl had the same Japanese symbol that she had behind her ear. The girl's was on her neckline. India waited for the chick to turn around, and it was Lilly. Oh, Vanessa did tell me that bitch had that tat. India was pissed and wanted to know what this chick and Sump really had going on. She gently sat her bottled water on the table and approached the chick. "Yes, I know you know me but I have no clue who you are. But what is it that you and Sumpter have going on? Like really?" India asked, sizing the girl up.

"Did he tell you that we have anything going on?"

"Aye, my dude. Cut that fly shit out," India said, bossy. "You and I both know that nigga ain't nearly that fucking stupid!"

"My point. Dude ain't that crazy to cheat on you, right?" Lilly said, sarcastic.

"Nah, he better not be. But why you have the tat on your neck that says Sump in Japanese? That's all I'm saying."

"Listen here. I don't have to keep explaining myself but I'ma tell you this, me and Sump is nothing and never will be." She didn't wait for India to respond and walked off as if nothing had just happened.

Instantaneously, India's hood instincts kicked in, but she quickly had to calm herself. If India wasn't nearly five months pregnant she would have embarrassed Lilly in front of everybody, but since she was she decided against it.

"What was that all about, girlie?" Vanessa asked as India walked back over towards them.

"Oh, nah. I was asking that girl about Sumpter. I really wanna know why she got that tat, fo' real."

"Y'all crazy." Vanessa didn't want to hear anything about Sump's no good ass. She brushed it off and continued getting her dance on.

As India sipped on her Fiji water, she leaned up against the couch watching her girls get low and observing the crowd below. Suddenly a tipsy Scrappy pulled her towards him out of nowhere.

"What up ma? I know you missing a nigga fo' real though. I miss you. Please come with me for tonight ma." He paused weirdly. "Please, I need you."

"C'mon now. You know I'm married, Scrap."

"India, that nigga in jail. I ain't try'na fuck ... I just want you to lie with me. That's it, ma." He ran the back of his hand down her cheek, which caused her pleasure box to become wet. India was so horny she could have just burst a nut by that simple touch.

"Scrap you know all Sump's people is in here. Please back up. I don't need anything getting back to him, please."

"Fuck them India. I just wanna hold you, shorty I know you wanna be held." He surely wasn't lying. India was in desperate need for her body to be snuggled up against a nigga. Plus, she was still angry with Sump. After a second thought, India accepted his offer. "Okay, Scrap. I'ma meet you after this over with. Just call my phone, a'ight?"

"You know it's on, boo." He tried to lean in and kiss her on the lips but she dodged it.

"Hold on now, Scrap. We in the club and people is watching."

"You right, my bad. You just so fucking sexy ma." He stared at her, glossy eyed, and rejoined his small entourage.

Nala strolled over to her instantly. "C'mon now India, Mac C in here prolly watching us. That wasn't a good look, family."

"I know, Nala he is just drunk though. And fuck Mac C fat ass! He probably going to tell we was in here anyway." India shrugged, really not caring if he saw her or not.

"Yeah ... I just don't want it to be any bullshit. That's why every time a nigga come in my face I scurry off. I ain't try'na hear Gene's mouth." India ignored Nala and ambled off.

After two hours of dancing with herself and pondering on the Asian chick that eye fucked her, she wanted to leave with Scrappy that night even more. Looking at Lilly made India extra livid. India couldn't deny that she wanted to cry a river, but what would that accomplish? Nothing. Because it wasn't anything she could do about the fucked up situation. All she knew was that she was hurt and angry by his careless actions. Each time she glared at the chick, it seemed to remind India of her problems. The facial expression plastered on Lilly's face said she had a thing or two to get off her chest, too.

Resentment panged her heart — and the thought of Scrappy's strong hands caressing her body had a tingle in her vagina. Honestly, India was emotionally drained and just needed some affection — and the only man she truly loved couldn't be there to explain to her that everything would be alright. He'd actually cheated and brought something back to her. He'd promised her that he wouldn't bring diseases home anymore. How could he be so selfish, knowing she was carrying his seeds? It was starting to hit her that Sump really didn't give a fuck. At this moment, she didn't care either.

The DJ called out the last song and announced that the club was about to close. India rushed and told her girls that she was leaving. Trying to beat the crowd outside, India hugged them and told them she would holler at them tomorrow.

Once inside her car, India called Scrappy and informed him that she was out front, and demanded he hurry up before someone started probing the scene. After a few minutes, he walked out. He hopped in his truck and directed India to follow him to his crib in Coram.

Entering a gated community, Scrappy curved in front of the condo's office and hopped out to check his mailbox. He jumped back inside, hit the garage opener and pulled his truck in. India parked her car alongside of his.

"I can't believe I got you to finally kick it with me."

India laughed because she couldn't believe it either and followed him inside. She scrutinized his abode as she perched on the French sofa. It was a nice two-bedroom condo but it was too plain for her sense. She thought it was just like an ordinary nigga to have everything black and gold. "So you want me to grab you a pillow and blanket or you sleeping with me?"

This nigga already trying to game me, now he know he want me to lie with him, India laughed to herself.

"Boy, don't even game. You know I'm not sleeping on nobody couch ... you can though."

Scrappy cracked a smile, admiring India's beauty. Pregnant and all, she was still adorable. The way her thick thighs crossed over each other screamed sexuality. He ambled over to India, tugging her up from the sofa and led her to his bedroom. Lying India on the bed, he took her shoes off and covered her up with his plush comforter. *How cute,* India thought. She watched as he undressed down to his boxers and climbed into bed. Getting underneath the covers, Scrappy pulled her warm body close to his and she nestled comfortably against his frame. Scrappy caressed her body and soothed her mind, silently expressing his feelings were still there.

Although Scrappy really wanted to cuddle up with India, he still wanted to feel her. Her warm juices were the sweets and he loved

getting freaky with India. Slowly, he forced his hands up her shirt and gently planted kisses all over her face. As much as India wanted to resist she couldn't, and allowed him to toy with her nipples. "India, I just want you baby," he whispered into her ear. "I'm glad you're here. I just want you so bad."

"No," India purred.

He paused momentarily to gaze into her eyes and noticed that her eyes were shut. He eased up, slid her shirt over her head, pulled her bra over her breasts and began sucking around her dark nipples. "Open your eyes," he commanded. She ignored him because she was afraid if she reopened her tears would instantly fall. He slowly removed his mouth from her breast and worked his way up to her face again. He placed his lips onto hers and gently forced his tongue inside her month, grasping hungrily onto the sensation of their lips intertwining.

"Scrappy, I can't," India moaned. She knew that she was pregnant, and that was totally disrespecting Sump. And on top of that she carried two STDs. She didn't want to infect him.

"Yes we can, baby. I love you." Scrappy continued savoring her sweetness and played with her tongue devouringly. India's pussy was so wet. His touch was warm but his tongue was even warmer. With each motion India quivered. Numbness filled her body as she basked in the moment. All she could do was tremble and squeal because she was surely gratified.

She rubbed her hands through his single braids as he began nibbling on her earlobes. All the while she relished the way Scrappy tantalized her body's interior with his tongue. Circling his tongue inside her ear, he knew that he needed to feel India's place of warmness after massaging her firm ass. He tugged at her belt loops.

Snapped out of sexual pleasure, India was brought back to reality by Scrappy caressing her stomach and fondling to unbutton her pants. "Uh-uh Scrap. We can't do this," she said in between moans.

"Why, baby? You want it and I certainly want it."

India sighed. Being the real chick she was and knowing the uncommon bond that they shared, she didn't mind keeping things funky with Scrap. "'Cause Sump gave me two STDs and I don't want you to come in contact."

He sat there and thought momentarily. Just the sexual effect India had over him caused him not to care what she had. "Baby, we can use a condom. I just want you badly."

"Nah, Scrap that's nasty and some mo' shit," she hissed.

"India just let me do me, please," he pleaded.

India said no more because he piqued her curiosity. Under normal circumstances she wouldn't have dared to act upon his nasty intentions. But she marveled at him. Was he actually disgusting enough to engage in sexual activities with her knowing she was infected? India was speechless.

Busily, he slid her pants and thong off and threw them to the floor. He began holding her thighs and fondly trailed kisses down her neck to her wrist line, leading to her secret place. Gyrating his tongue around her swollen clitoris, she moaned in pure ecstasy. He then freakily traced his wet tongue to her asshole in a lizard-like motion, tantalizing and teasingly. *I can't believe this nigga doing this*, she thought as she begged to come all over his face. To arouse India with further intensity, he slid his finger in her storming pussy all the while gliding his tongue in and out of her butthole. Scrappy desperately wanted to send her to her heavenly place of an orgasmic bliss so he aggressively pulled her closer to his mouth and roughly buried his tongue inside her.

"Damn, I'm fenna come, shiitt," India squealed.

India's body jolted up as her warm juices stormed out of her slit. After meeting her needs, it was his turn. He promptly placed the condom on his manhood and inserted it inside India. *Damn I forgot this is the mere reason why I never fucked with this nigga like that*, India laughed inside. This would be a short process and India was willing to fake it to speed it up. This dude already was four inches short on hard, but that wasn't the worst part. He didn't know how to work it and came in sixty seconds. *This nigga stroke number sure is twelve*, India thought as she counted each time he thrust his hips and grinded like he knew what he was doing, whimpering like a bitch. "Gotdamn, I knew I missed this pussy for something."

"Mmmm Mmmm!" India moaned, fake, lifting her butt off the

bed and rotating her hips to rush his orgasm.

"Ohh, shit, ohh India mama, yo shit is so fuckin' tight!" His body jerked as he quickly propelled his small man inside her hot box. After the twelve strokes, as anticipated, he collapsed beside her.

India lie wondering if that was her only solution to gain vengeance against her husband. Her heart dropped to the pit of her stomach. She realized that she had actually cheated on Sump and that wasn't normal. She had been faithful for years and she engaged in the ultimate betrayal. Instead of feeling better, she felt worse.

Without saying one word, India climbed out of bed and threw her clothes back on. Scrappy tried asking what was wrong but she ignored him and left feeling like a complete whore.

Chapter Thirteen

India opened her eyes, wondering if she was dreaming. After scrolling through her missed calls she realized it was all true. Scrappy had called nine times. India smothered her head in the pillow as if doing so would prevent her from remembering her state of affairs. Gazing at the family picture displayed on her mantelpiece was enough to send her back to the previous night. India felt she didn't have any other choice but to forgive Sump because she was just as wrong as he was. India climbed out of bed to fix some breakfast, only to vomit all the food back up.

Feeling disgusted, India ran some hot bath water and poured in pear-scented bubble bath. She went inside the linen closet, grabbed her oversized towel, and placed it on the rack. She groped through the CDs displayed underneath her stereo system and popped in Pleasure P's album. His smooth and soulful voice pacified her solemn mood. She flicked the steam switch on low and eased her body inside the warm water.

I ain't try'na waste your time ... and, I ain't try'na waste my time ... there ain't no need to waste no time ...'cause we done put in too much time ..."

India looked back on her life and she felt deep in her heart that the good outweighed the bad and the happiness overshadowed the sad. Upset with herself, all she wanted to know was what allowed her to step out of character. It wasn't like she had sex with some stranger, but still, it was the fact that she committed an affair. It seriously hurt her heart because no matter what Sump did, he was still the one taking care of her and he was a nigga. Besides, it wasn't like none of this shit was new! He gave her STDs before. India was so confused; she didn't know if she was to blame or if he was to blame for her sexual encounter. All she knew was that she couldn't take it back and wanted to forget about the whole ordeal.

After washing up, she stepped out of the whirlpool, wrapped herself into a towel, and trudged to her bedroom. Patted dry, she applied Christian Clive body lotion to her skin and squirted Light Blue fragrance into its needed areas. Next, she searched for some pajamas. Deciding on her colorful robe and pink ankle leggings, she slipped them on and slid into her furry pink slippers. She made her way downstairs to watch she and Sump's favorite movie, *Jason's Lyric*.

It was more of the movie watching her than she watching it because all she did was cry. She balled up on the couch in her knitted quilt and after awhile she fell into a deep slumber. She planned to get a nice siesta in but wounded up sleeping through the evening and night and into the next afternoon.

When she finally woke, it was 2:00 in the afternoon so she opted to watch her favorite soap opera. Hearing the piercing sounds of her house phone ringing, she answered. It was Nala. "Hello?"

"Bitch, damn! I haven't talked to yo' ass all yesterday. What up wit that, fam?"

"Gurl, if you just knew the half ... I'm really messed up."

"Well, tell me all about 'cause I'm outside. So open the door."

India hopped up to unlock the door and returned back to the couch. Not even a second later, Vanessa and Nala entered the living room. "Now, what the hell is wrong with my family? You look terrible!" Nala said, eyeing India's tearstained face.

"Right, what's wrong baby?" Vanessa asked, taking a seat on the couch beside her.

India sighed. "Y'all, this is really crazy."

"India I know you still ain't trippin' about that STD?" Nala sucked her teeth. "'Cause I done talked to Sump and he begged me, talkin' bout cuz tell me what's going on. So I told him. He was really concerned about you not answering his calls. He knows that ain't like you."

"I know, but what did he say?"

"He kept apologizing."

"Oh my God, y'all! Why did I cheat on him?" India confessed and burst into tears.

"What, when, and with who?" Nala screamed.

"The other night when I left the club, I left with Scrap and we did it."

"Oh wow, did y'all use protection?" Vanessa asked.

"Yeah, and I told him what I had. That's not the problem 'cause he didn't care but the thing is I feel so bad," she replied in between sniffles.

Vanessa smacked her lips. "Gurl, I thought you was trippin' on something else." She paused briefly. "And so the fuck what? That nigga cheated on you millions of times." Vanessa shrugged, rubbing her cousin's thigh.

"No Nessa, don't tell her that. But India don't be stressing about it either because what's done is done and you acting like Sump gon' find out. Stop trippin', B," Nala said.

"But still, it's wrong and I don't know what to do."

"First off, off stop crying like you a weak-ass bitch instead of a gangster chick and just chop that shit up. Sump's ass got five years. What the fuck can he do to you?"

"Vanessa, shut up," Nala snapped. She positioned herself on the floor beside India. "Now, you already know what you gotta do so stop stressing yo' self out. We all make mistakes. Hell, at least you fucked up while the nigga was in jail." Nala tried making the situation better. "I cheated on Gene twice and he was out and it was while we were married. So sometimes things just occur. But I tell you this   I don't go sobbing over it because it's done. Now pick your ass up and leave that shit behind and do this li'l time with your husband and that's that."

"I do feel you on that Nala. Let it go, India." Vanessa laughed. "But what up with Scrap nasty ass? You told him and he still fucked you?"

India didn't want to laugh but she couldn't help herself. "Yo, I was just as shocked as you man. The nigga ate it and licked the hell out of my ass," she replied while cracking up.

"That's one disgusting nigga when it comes to you, on the real."

Nala's celly rang, startling the girls.

"Tell Gene to stop calling, damn," Vanessa yelled. "He done called your ass ten times!"

"Yo' fam-fam, bring it down just a notch." Nala scooped up her phone from the round glass table and answered. "Hello?" It was a collect call from the federal prison and as soon as Nala pressed zero she was met with Sump's voice. "What up, Nala? Have you talked to her yet?"

"Yeah, she right here. Hold on." Nala handed India the phone.

"Hello?" India voiced in a low tone.

"Baby, I'm so sorry and I know you mad but I promise I'ma make it up to you when I get outta here. You know I talked to Gib and he saying we might have to serve a year and then we can get out since we never been in trouble with the law prior to this offense."

"Oh bay, that's great and I know you're sorry. I just wish you had fucked the bitch with a condom. This could have been worse."

"I know baby and I'm really sorry. When you coming to see me?"

The operator said they had sixty seconds left and she informed him that she would be to see him the next day. They ended the call.

*****

For the next couple of weeks, India was up and down the highway as much as possible, visiting her man. She was happy about it. A few of the times she carried her daughters along, but the girls really didn't like seeing their father in prison, knowing they would have to depart without him. That was the reason why India and Sump decided that India would enjoy shopping and receiving pampering services on Valentine's Day with the girls instead of visiting him.

India wasn't having that though. She had never, since Summer was born, gone a year without spending Valentine's Day with her husband. And she was damned if she'd allow prison to stand in between not only Valentine's Day, but their five year anniversary.

She scheduled her surprise visit for 10:00 that morning and then she planned to arrive back in the city to scoop her daughters up by 4:00. She was going to take pleasure in spending time with the three very special people in her life. Seeing her husband and chilling with her daughters in the same day thrilled her. It was the best of both worlds.

All the while India traveled up the highway, she found herself on a journey down memory lane to their wedding day. To India it couldn't have gotten any better than her wedding. Her wedding was phat. All the who's who of the hip-hop industry, the major niggas in the dope game, and the boss chicks in the city were in attendance. Even folk they didn't even know were outside posted.

The huge church, which seated one thousand, was crammed even with it being invitation only. The two of them separately had a vast family and connecting them as one enlarged their numbers drastically. Not to mention their popularity together.

India's favorite R&B singer Keyshia Cole and male R&B artist Avant sang at her wedding ceremony. India hired the best wedding planner the east coast had to offer, Lisa Dun. Homegirl had the entire church looking superb. She decorated the church in white roses, meaning loyalty, and red, for the love the duo shared. Hanging from the ceiling were heart-shaped chandeliers.

India's gown cost well over 50 grand. It was a handmade beaded white dress with a long train by Vera Wang. Diamonds covered the front and half of her back was revealed. The high heels that she wore were diamond-encrusted and she accessorized with galore diamonds too. Sump was high maintenance in a white Armani tuxedo with a red vest, tie, a handkerchief that peeked from the breast pocket and red Mauri gators. India could remember that day vividly; indeed, it was one of the best days of her life.

Before India took notice she was pulling inside the prison's parking lot. She parked and hated the process of traveling on the bus to the facility. After applying gloss to her lips, she grabbed her car keys and peach Express pea coat, and hopped out looking so-phisticated.

India signed in and patiently waited to be called to the visiting station. Surveying the crowd, India noticed that the room was heaving with too many broads from the hood. Some spoke while others didn't. A few chicks even had the audacity to stare at her funny. She could'nt have cared less; she was able to understand their motive. They were the ones starving from their men's lack of savvy in the streets and they could tell India was lacking in absolutely nothing. It wasn't her fault that she was able to maintain her fabulous status and they couldn't. One girl couldn't seem to fixate her stares elsewhere and observed India like she'd recognized her from some place.

The guard finally called out "India Jones." She popped up, glanced at the girl from the corner of her eyes and for some reason the girl's eyes were damn near fucking her. So India being the chick she was, asked: "Do you know me or something? 'Cause you staring a bitch up and down like you do."

The girl ignored her sarcasm and simply sniggered with a huge smirk plastered on her face. "Bitches, I just feel so sorry for, ugh." India twisted her face up and proceeded to the front desk.

"Jones, were you scheduled to be here at the 9:00 visit along with someone else?"

India squinted her eyes. "No such, why you ask?"

"Because there are visitors back there now, his mother and a friend."

"Okay, well I'm his wife. So will it be a problem if I go to the back? Or will I have to wait?"

"Go ahead."

Damn, I gotta put up with Ronnie ignorant ass, ugh, India thought to herself as she walked through the metal detector. India lingered around the sealed front door until everyone got through and the guard ushered everyone via the corridor and into the room filled with blue uniforms. In search for Sump's seating area, she spotted Ronnie with a baby on her hip at the vending machine. Confused, she shifted her eyes around and landed on the far right corner.

Then she noticed that Sump had a little boy on his lap.

Not even a second later, she discovered the same Asian chick that Sump claimed to not having any dealings with engaged in a good conversation. The chick's head was moving happily and he was laughing and gazing at her like he would do with her.

The ligaments in her knees weakened and her stomach performed somersaults. Her head spun beyond control. The pit of her abdomen was hollow and all India wanted to do was hurl, but she refused and tried to regain control. She couldn't believe that Sump lied to her. What part of the game was this? She didn't know. She stood background posted by the door as jealousy ran down her spine. *How could Ronnie like her and not me and I'm the one who been here from jump?* India watched Ronnie pass Lilly and Sump some chicken wings.

India eyed the two little boys' attire and hatred filled her heart. Both boys were dressed in Jordans, designer jeans, and jackets with matching T-shirts. She knew both of the boys were Sump's because they were damn near identical to the nigga, except their skin color was a shade or two darker than the children Sump and India shared. The boys both possessed the same good hair of her girls and both of their eyes were sleepy-slanted. As much as India wanted to tell herself that they were ugly, she couldn't. The boys resembled the images that she envisioned her sons to be.

India frantically walked over in their direction with her heels stabbing the floor. Everybody was too deep in the conversation to notice her coming. Once India approached them, everyone's eyes widened, including the inmate's that sat beside Sump. He knew exactly who she was. India placed herself into the empty seat in between Ronnie and Lilly and shook her head, disgusted. Everyone sat in astonishment.

Thirty seconds passed, and India voiced first. "Oh, I see. Nobody has shit to discuss now, huh?" She continued on. "Sumpter ... so basically you lied to me the entire time. You been fucking this bitch. You have kids with the bitch, and she here visiting you like she's your family with Ronnie, though!"

"Don't bring my damn name in it."

"Fuck you and your name, Ronnie. Do it look like I give a fuck 'bout you or yo' name?"

"Mu'fucka it ain't my fault. You better blame this nigga right here."

"Ronnie c'mon now, fo' real," Sump reasoned.

"No, no your mother is so right, Sumpter. I can't blame anybody but you. Me and you have a commitment. Not anyone else, Sumpter." She glared demonically into his eyes, her arms crossed over her chest. "And you got me out here carrying two sons for your raggedy, trifling ass and you already got two sons! I tried to give you the benefit of doubt, but you really fooled the fuck up outta me. When were you going to tell me, Sumpter?"

"Tell you what, India?"

"Bitch, I swear if we weren't in this place I would spit on you!" She clenched her jaws together, furiously. "Don't play dumb now you retarded, cheating bastard! I just want you to know I hate you and I'm filing for a divorce first thing Monday morning. Don't ever in your life say anything to me, again." India stood intensely, choking back on her tears. She wasn't about to allow them to see her get played and play herself in the same token. She slid both rings off her fingers and tossed them onto Lilly's lap.

Lilly said nothing. She gazed into Sump's eyes and tried to feel bad for him, but all she could do was feel relieved. Never in a million years did she think that Sump's secret to India would come out in this way.

"That's what you want Sump? That's fine with me. You cheated on me with this bitch. Now you got this same bitch."

"Yo ... stop callin' my daughter-in-law out of her name," Ronnie declared.

"I'll call you a bitch too, Bitch. You're so lucky we're in here because on my life I would take yo big fat ass," she said, calm enough to throw off the guard's attention but also firm enough to let them know she wasn't bullshitting. "I never got too out of control with you because of Sumpter. But now that nigga ain't shit to me, but the father of my daughters."

"India, don't entertain yourself because you know I'll

manhandle yo' li'l ass down."

"Picture that!" India giggled in anger. "Don't let the small size fool you, my nigga. Better ask your son about me." India focused back in on Sump with a stare. "So the cat got your tongue and big mouth? Sump ain't got shit to say, huh?"

"Baby, look. All this shit is not what it looks like ..."

She interrupted him. "I might have been blind from what I didn't see then. But the shit can't become any clearer than this. I'm cool." India turned her back to walk off, but Sump tugged at her arm.

"Ma, you know I love you, this li'l shit is nothing. I told you I used to fuck with her and now she cool with Ronnie. I didn't even know she was coming up here," he lied. Lilly had visited him just as much as India had.

"You must really think I'm very dumb because you have this girl here and she has two sons that look just like you. Shit, fuck the visit that shit is nothing. Explaining these kids is the real problem. I'm pretty sure lots of hoes visit you. But carrying along kids that look like you is another story, nigga!"

"Yo, India, you can ask her. These ain't my kids."

India's entire facial expression contorted into a scowl. It was one thing to lie, but another thing to get caught and still lie about his DNA. India could no longer take the charade. "I feel so sorry for you, girl. For a nigga to play not only you, but your kids, is really sickening. But hey, if that's what y'all like ..." India didn't wait for any response and walked away from a long-lived marriage.

Before India walked out of the prison, the same chick who was studying her earlier was still in the waiting area. It dawned on her that she was obviously with Lilly, and basically trying to warn her before she walked in. India felt so stupid; she could have crashed into the damn prison wall. She knew that would never occur; she had too much dignity to allow Sump to provoke her into killing herself.

Once India hit the cold wintry breeze she whizzed to the bus and held her tears. She allowed the heavy drops to downpour from her eyes and cheeks the second she stepped off the bus and slid inside her car.

At that moment, India felt as though Sump had stabbed her numerous times in the heart with a scalpel. Pain filled not only her heart, but her mind and soul. There was nothing else for her to do because the damage was done. There was no excuse in the world that would be able to reel India back in. India was so stubborn and had too much pride to allow him to have not just one, but two kids on her. Nothing could've eased her pain. She had already forgiven him for the ultimate betrayal of fucking nasty-ass hoes, but a baby? Fuck nah ... she was tired of playing the fool for Sump over and over and over again and he was idiotic to think he had her that open.

Staring out of the window, India busily watched as the light snowflakes fell to the ground. In all India's time with Sump, she had never been so hurt and heartbroken. *I trusted Sump. How could he play me... me though? We were in love. What made him step out on me like this? Was I not good enough for him?* Those were the questions she continuously asked herself. She couldn't have imagined how time consuming it was to manage two families and surmised that Lilly had to be connected closely to him for some time now, for her to be still lingering around.

Resentment and jealousy consumed her as she thought about the family moments that Sump and Lilly shared. Lilly was intimate with her husband in a way that India felt only she should be. She knew his likes and dislikes. She knew how he liked to get down in bed and more heart crushing, Lilly knew how it felt to lay in his arms lovingly. She knew his affectionate touch and above all, that was something that he was only supposed to share with India ... his wife.

India had allowed so much, from fights to his consistent cheating ways and diseases. But now that this shit was dead smack and firmly in her face there was nothing left for her to do but to let it go. She had dragged out being his dummy far too long and India would have rather lost her life than to accept him having kids with another chick. She finally understood what Keyshia meant by those man-bashing songs.

Needing some music to calm her nerves and soothe her mind, she placed an R&B mix CD in the disc changer and turned to "Deuces" because she was chucking up her two and it was over. India really couldn't believe that Sump had killed her heart like he had. He'd promised that he would never step outside their marriage and produce kids. Tears continued to fall from her face as she listened to the inspiring lyrics.

"I hate liars ... Fuck love ... I'm tired of trying ... my heart big, but it beat quiet..."

What really messed India's mind up most was that this muthafucka was literally carrying on an affair with the damn girl. *How could he have love for somebody else?* She didn't know, but knew that she wasn't able to allow him to play her in the way that he had been any longer. Their marriage was over.

Trembling, she dabbed the tears from her face and retrieved her Sidekick from her handbag. Dancing in her mind at that moment, were the thoughts of her being finished, and to complete the process she had to get rid of the nigga's seeds. She already had enough ties to him and adding an additional two would have caused serious problems. India wasn't having it and speedily dialed the abortion clinic.

After she scheduled her emergency termination for the following Tuesday, she called Vanessa. She wanted to phone Nala, but knew that she would try to coax her to forgive Sump, because Gene had quite a few children on her.

"What up wit it," Vanessa answered, amped up.

"Let me tell you!" India exclaimed. "First off, you were right about this clown-ass nigga after all. So I don't wanna hear *I told you so.*" She paused because it hurt to speak upon it. "Why I was just at the visit and Sumpter had that little Asian bitch in there with two muthafuckin kids looking like his twins, man!"

"Swear to God?"

"Man, on my sister, Nessa. This nigga had the bitch there with his two kids and Ronnie, yo."

Vanessa tried her best not to laugh, but found it very hard and doubled over into laughter.

"That shit ain't funny. This shit is serious."

"My bad but India, you act like you didn't know this shit. I specifically told your ass what the damn girl said. Then you see the hoe in his face ironically the very same day that I told you, ma. That was a sign right there. Then this chick got a tat with his name. India, you're a hood bitch. I just didn't know you was that stupid and blind."

"But it wasn't clear to me, Vanessa."

"I guess you are just as dumb as these hoes! How much clearer can it become? The nigga is a dawg. Will always be a dawg, and that's why I fuck and leave these dawg-ass niggas like they do us."

"But Nessa, how can he do me wrong though?"

"India what makes you different from the next chick? Niggas get tired of the same bitches. I can just imagine how tired the nigga got of you. Y'all been fuckin' since middle school." Vanessa sighed. "I tried to tell your hardheaded ass but to you, everybody a hater and they can't tell you nothing. I've never been able to understand how a chick of your caliber be fucking with his lame ass anyway for so long, knowing that he cheats."

"I know, now. But enough is enough. I just scheduled to get these babies terminated. I'm filing for a divorce Monday and I'm cool on dude. Real talk."

"Bitch, how in the hell is you getting an abortion and you due in four months?"

"What you mean? You can get 'em till you six months. I don't turn six months for two weeks."

"Oooh, India. You foul ma. That's fucked up. You should just have 'em. You done made it this far," she tried reasoning. Vanessa didn't believe in abortions because some people were lucky enough to have kids, and unfortunately, she wasn't able to.

"Oh well, cause I'm there a-sap Tuesday morning," she voiced with much attitude.

"Gurl, you raw. But how much that shit going to cost you anyway?"

"$2800 since I'm carrying twins."

"Hoe, you crazy! That's a new Gucci bag. Don't do that, fam."

"Vanessa, I'm doing it!" India screamed, annoyed. "You're starting to get on my nerves. I'll call you when I get home." India's voice cracked as she hung up because in reality she was attached to the babies. Bur there was no way she could continue to live her life attending to all Sump's needs. She just couldn't live her life as a lie any longer. They were finished, done, finito.

*****

Months moved by quickly for Sump. He knew the less he was in contact with the outside world, the shorter his time seemed. The only person he was communicating with every other day was his attorney, Gibson. Sump had mad love for Gibson because he wasn't procrastinating. He began scrambling through the evidence right away to see if there were any glitches, so that he could get his client out as soon as possible. Sump chatted a few times with Lilly, who was still pissed that he denied their kids in the presence of India again. He apologized to her but he was really fucked up because India wasn't his anymore. That was the reason he rarely conversed with people on the outside. Sump knew the longer he was incarcerated the more time he was losing so he needed to focus. Sump was more than certain that there was no way he could gain India back behind bars. His chances of getting her back outside of prison walls under these circumstances were slim to none. The mere thought of him calling to get back with her over the phone only enraged him. So to prevent from killing somebody in prison out of anger, he didn't even attempt to phone India. He knew she would reject him and rejection wasn't an option. He was in desperate need to get out of that hellhole and reclaim his wife.

Chapter Fourteen

The afternoon sunlight shined brightly through India's blinds; she half-smiled, being the sun-infatuated girl she was. Plus, the near 90-degree weather was rare because May had just begun. India fixed a fruit salad and headed upstairs. She switched on the stereo system and out to her bedroom balcony she went. The sunrays danced gracefully upon her spa-tanned skin as she sat in her recliner chair dressed simply in a white negligee, scrutinizing the houses and hills that surrounded her peaceful, prestigious community. Monica's soothing voice explained to her from her classic hit "Why Her" that basically he did what he did and it is what it is and now the relationship was over.

India knew that and also knew that things had been growing old prior to this situation. They both were just holding onto something that they thought was there. India really had herself believing that he was her everything. She never envisioned spending life without Sump. She tried to block out her feelings towards Sump's love and for awhile she did just that. But now that it was proving evident that she was cool and love didn't live within her for the two of them anymore.

She really thought she loved him unconditionally, only realizing that it was the material things that captured her heart from day one. She constantly made herself believe that she was madly in love with Sump but frankly she was in love with the things he blinded her with. The many years that he provided for her needs

Triple Crown Publications presents... *Wife*

and supplied her every wants was a beautiful distraction in her life. Sump's standard of livings was stalling India's purpose in life.

India just knew it was till death do they part. Truth be told, she was loyal and he could have done anything else to India but have two kids. Dude would've had a better chance giving her AIDS than having a long-term affair with some random chick. Although she felt that their love was dwindling for a while, India also knew if it was something other than this maybe it would be a sign for them to take a break from one another. Unfortunately, it wasn't and there was no way she could forgive him. Hell nah, India wasn't accepting any babies she hadn't birthed herself.

India had persuaded herself that she had to live by Sump's commands. Everything she did was because of Sump. She never dreamed of nursing school after high school but Sump insisted that she went. She never expressed that she despised it. Caught up in Sump's glamorous lifestyle from a very young age, she never got the chance to explore what it was that she wanted in life.

Here she was, 27 years old and the only thing she had done with her life was follow behind the ghetto-fabulous American Dream. She was so young and stupid that she allowed herself to follow in her mother's footsteps. But that was what India was equipped to do. It wasn't like Sump introduced India to the good life because her father spoiled her rotten. She was used to rocking high-end designer threads. To keep her extravagant lifestyle after her father went into protective custody, India was prepared to gain a boss and snagged Sump up. She accepted everything that came along with him, stupidly.

People constantly told her that a situation like this would occur in time and being the wife wasn't all that it was cracked up to be. And sadly, India had to admit to herself that it wasn't. She felt bad that it was actually soaking in her head while he was incarcerated, but to India it was the best time to get over him. She was beyond tired of the stares and glares she'd received in the streets for years from women. Times were changing and before she looked up and found herself to be 30, she had to find herself.

For starters, she was finally going to read the letter Sump sent weeks after the altercation. India didn't want to hold a grudge any longer. For the past few months she mended her heart so that she could forgive. In order to move on with her life she knew she had to forgive Sump and now she was able to do just that. She jumped up, dashing to her drawer to retrieve the letter.

My Dear Wife,

India baby, I know you don't want to hear anything I have to say but I received the divorce papers yesterday and I can't blame you for wanting to leave me. Before I go any further in this letter I just thank you for all the delightful memories and experiences that we've shared throughout our years together. I really enjoyed our good days and I thank you for being a true wife and the love and affection that you suffocated me with during the time we shared. And don't go thinking it was you India, it wasn't at all. You were all I ever needed but it was my set ways that allowed me to do extra shit in the streets. India you were in full throttle and always kept our family afloat but I want you to know no matter what happens you will remain the only chick that could ever have my heart like this. I apologize baby, and for what it's worth I'm very sorry for stepping out on you and having two kids with another chick and even sorrier for loving someone other than you. Don't misconstrue the facts because although I love Lilly (that's her name) I'm in love with you and I want us to be together. I promise this time India if you can forgive me a lot of things will change. I'm not saying you have to be with me now but I just want you to think about it and maybe once I come home we can start over. Baby, we're each other's soul mates and there's no way we can end it here. I have been sitting up here unable to sleep and realized that life without you is like the moon without the sun or the sky without earth or cars without an engine. Life just wouldn't be the same. India I know you get what I'm saying baby, I'm pleading for your forgiveness please. I just can't imagine life without you in it. I'm even thinking about once this prison shit is over maybe we should move down south together. Hell, anywhere you wanna go so we can get away from the drama in New York. One last thing, you know I got a few ends in the Estates and in the Islands but Mac C got my real dough so he will be expecting your

call. He got 15 bans for you and you can blow that on whatever you like. Just think about what I said.

Forever and Ever,

Sumpter

"Fuckin' bullshit." India was reeling from the letter at first, but luckily she was smart enough to look past his manipulative ways. It was something. Just a few months ago he would have screamed at the thought of her splurging $15 G's at the mall, but this really proved that Sump thought he could buy her off each and every time he did something wrong.

She didn't totally blame him because she was just as to blame for allowing him to do her wrong from the beginning for so long. Although India never cheated on him while things were optimistic, she still felt that she was to blame. Flashbacks of their years together popped up in her mind. India had realized that she and Sump were entirely too much alike and different at the same to carry on a long lasting relationship. It should've never gone past their puppy love dealings. They both held the same stubborn attitude and India wasn't with obeying any nigga like Sump had preferred. She listened sometimes to prevent disputes but in reality she loathed it.

Wrapped up in the lavish life and teen sexing she birthed her daughter, which India didn't regret having her at all. She just wished she would have delayed it and figured if she would've waited then just maybe her and Sump wouldn't have furthered their relationship into a more serious one. She felt that just because they shared a baby they had to be with each other forever. Needless to say, their girls were the glue holding them together for so long with the help of his currency.

India knew life wasn't life without mistakes and even though her mistakes dragged on for so many years, she still knew it was never too late to start over. *Where will I begin?* That was the question that played over and over in her mind. That, she didn't know because she was so adapted to Sump's being the sole breadwinner that she never had to grind hard for anything. She knew life would be very different, being in the past, her least worries were her finances. She never had to budget or have any form of financial limitation when she hit the streets. He took good care of her, purchasing her nothing but the best of things. And when she looked over it all, she realized that she'd looked at Sump as a father. She was so used to her father lavishing her, she automatically expected the same in Sump and never thought things would come to this matter.

Even though India didn't like her current degree, she knew that she couldn't and wouldn't sit around and wait on something to come through for her. From the moment she stepped out of the federal prison she knew Sump and his finances were finished. India could have easily gotten money from the safes in either of their two abodes. But she didn't and only dipped in them to pay the bills at their two homes. She had a few thousand in her bank account, but it wasn't enough for her to survive on, being that she used to spend money like it was water, whenever she got it into her hands. It wasn't nearly enough funds for India so for the past three months she worked full time at the hospital downtown. She stayed overtime, gaining over fifty hours a week, working twelve hour shifts, four days per week.

Homegirl's checks were fat, bringing home close to two thousand dollars a week after taxes. She hated that she was previously stupid and didn't stack much money. But after working her ass off for three months straight, her papa called, informing her that the insurance company had finally found Ton'na's policy. Papa split the money with his wife, India, and Marla, leaving them each with 25 grand a piece. *What a coincidence*, she thought.

As much as India didn't want to accept Sump's money, she was no fool and had to let her pride die and do what was in her best interest. So she'd be straight for the time being. Thanking God for the blessings upon her life, India gazed around her living room and wondered what was next in line for her. Before she decided to leave and meet her peoples at the spa, she wanted to reply to Sump's letter and drop it off at the post office. Once she finished she scanned the letter and decided to read over it aloud. She read:

What up fam,

 I know you already tripping that I begun this letter with "what

up" because I'd usually begin by saying I miss you hubby, but that's true and I still miss you Sump; it's just that this marriage can't continue going on. I feel that our entire time spent together was built upon a lie. Don't get me wrong — I had a pleasant time throughout the years with you also, but let's be honest here Sumpter: you showered me with gift after gift to shut me up and that I allowed. I'm not saying everything is your fault and I'm not totally blaming you because I should've stepped up as a strong black woman and not accepted your street life just because you financed my expensive tastes; and like I said it's not all your fault, I just simply shouldn't have allowed you to blind my intelligence. But you know you're wrong for this stunt and deep down you know I'll never forgive you for it. That's wrong, because I have already forgiven you but I'll never forget it and that's why I can no longer be with you because that is a permanent fixture in your life and by no means do I want you to put me before your children. And before I go any further I had an abortion because there was no way I could bring kids into such a fucked up situation. I'm very sorry for that but I think you'll enjoy the two sons that you already have with ole girl Lilly. Yeah, but enough of that, things are going to be different without you I know, but I have to move on with my life. You'll never understand how bad you hurt me and the pain I feel inside. You done played me many times but none can amount up to this here. You may think I'm wrong for playing you while you're in prison but that's not the case 'cause I will continue to keep you updated with your daughters and even bring them to visit sometimes, but me and you are finished. I know you love me but not enough to leave the bitches alone. So like I said it was good while it long lasted but it's over Sumpter and nothing else matters now because what's done is done and I hope your case goes well and I wish you the best in the future.

    I'll always love you,
      India Jones

India almost cried after she reread the letter because now it was officially over. There was no turning back. She had to find and love herself. She was moving on with her life and hoped he'd do the same. Lost in the moment, she was knocked out by her Sidekick ringing. She answered, "Yo, what up?"

"You on your way down to the spa yet?" Kyra asked.

"Nah, I'm 'bout to get dressed and I'll be down there. What everybody rocking, kicks or heels?"

"Heels hoe. Do you see the beautiful day, hon? I'm positive I'll be kickin' it all day long. So we must look posh." Once India hung up she whizzed to her walk-in closet.

"What the hell am I 'bout to put on?" she asked herself, sighing. After contemplating she laid her clothes out on the bed.

After she showered and dressed for a girl's day out, she grabbed her orange Lauren Merkin clutch and headed out. India was looking cute because she hadn't gotten dressed in a while, and it felt really good to be out of scrubs and nursing clogs. She wore an orange and yellow pinstriped puff button-up blouse with ruffle detail in the front, Haute Hippie orange suspender shorts and pinstriped peep-toes that matched perfectly with her blouse. Shielding her eyes were a pair of oversized Bvlgari frames, and long link diamond danglies accentuated her unique look. Her beautician tried something new on her, cutting her hair slightly under shoulder length.

Three hours later, after receiving facials, full body massages, and Brazilian waxes, India and her girls were stationed in the mani-pedi area to receive their last treatment.

"Damn, India. That's crazy ... I can't believe you and Sumpter ain't together. That's fucked up," Nala said.

"Gurl, I had to let him be. He wanted the streets so that's exactly what I gave his ass." India shrugged.

"What's so fucked up about it?" Vanessa asked as she twisted her nose up.

"Ay, Vanessa, I wasn't even talking to you." Nala threw her hands up. "Now like I was saying India ..."

Vanessa cut her off. "I don't give a damn who you're talkin' to. I just asked your ass what was so fucked up about it. Shid, unlike some people, smart muthafuckas get tired of the constant bullshit. So today Nala we're not try'na hear the bull ma. Just 'cause you accepts Gene's player ass don't mean India gotta live in misery with Sumpter."

"Gurl, muthafuckin' bye. I'm just saying the shit crazy. But seems to me that somebody real happy about their breakup, though."

"Because I am. You know I'ma keep it one hunnid with all you clowns. Shid, the nigga was a dawg and your nigga is still an infested dawg," Vanessa said snottily. "If you were some kinda real bitch you'd be happy for your family, too. But I guess since they're both your cousins you really can't choose sides or some shit." She flashed Nala the "you a clown" stare.

"Okay they both my fam, and what? I treat them both the same."

"I know Sump is your first cousin! Fuck that, wrong is wrong no matter what the situation is."

"You are a real fuckin' hater so I expect shit like this from you. But fuck all the bullshit. Let's just be real since you try'na be real and take it there," Nala said sarcastically. "I just think you're just jealous because me and India married some true bosses and you didn't, flat out my nigga."

That enraged Vanessa. "Bitch, you gotta be fuckin' smoking that shit. First off, the nigga Gene ain't even caking like you try'na make it baby girl. And for your info the nigga done tried to pay me 5 G's to fuck plenty of times. So who's the fool?" She cocked her head back. "'Cause trust and believe me baby, my mack hand so ill I can have your husband or any nigga for that matter precisely where I want 'em." She furrowed her eyebrow in certainty. "The nigga got ya head so fucked up you're thinkin' outside the fucking world. Clown-ass girl."

"Oh, so now Gene tried to pay for the pussy?" Nala laughed, far away from angry. "You know what I tell hoes like yourself? If you fucking and sucking you better be getting something out the deal. But I know no hoe going to be pushing that six series joint like I am. By Gene's expense, they won't. How you love that fam?" She puckered her lips. "So if 5 G's was the low class amount he offered, okay! Was I supposed to be mad, my dude?"

India and Kyra continued looking back and forth in between their cousins. They didn't say anything because this was normal for the two of them.

"It's fuckin' sad that you really are that open over this nigga. But I tell you this Nala, I'm not getting paid to debate with you. So if your ass like it, I love it, family."

"Y'all are fuckin' retarded." Kyra was cracking up.

"Nah, that's this hatin'-ass chick," Nala said, giggly. "Hoe need to be a contestant on a game show called *Who's Nala's Biggest Hater?*" She roared with guffaws.

"Naw tramp, you need to be starring on a reality show ... *Who Wants to Wake Nala Up From Her Fucking Fairytale-Ass Dream?*"

India doubled over into laughter. "You both really need to try out to be comedians 'cause y'all is comical. Now anyways, what's been jumpin' with you Kyra? These broads been bickering since we got here?"

"Gurl, nothing much. You know I been working with Willie Stacks."

"Working doing what?" India frowned.

"Oh honey, nothin' relating to that world you're assuming. You know dude promote parties and I been helping him out. That's my boo, too." She beamed.

"Bitch, get the fuck outta here. Why you didn't tell me you'd been fucking with Willie Stacks?" Vanessa said.

"Why you all up in her business, Vanessa?" Nala loved to get underneath her skin.

She knew Nala well and was done feeding into her trap for one day. "Fo'real though ... when y'all start, Kyra?"

"That night we all went out and you left with that one dude that looked like new money."

"Oh okay, yeah. That li'l nigga a go getta. I need to keep him logged all the way in," Vanessa said. "But damn, you got over on that Willie Stacks dude though fo' real?"

"Y'all, he is so nice! A couple of weeks ago he took me shopping and then we went on a private jet and just talked about everything. He nasty but y'all know I'm lovin' it."

"What you mean he nasty?" India wanted to know.

"Let me tell y'all. Y'all know I'm a fuckin' freak. But when I say

I'm no match for this cat, I mean don't stand a chance. This dude must have a doctoral degree in sex," Kyra burbled in amusement.

"You're such a fuckin' sex addict."

"Both of these bitches are whores," Nala said.

"We be paid hoes though. Best believe that," Vanessa countered.

"But fo'real though, Willie like that wild sex. Seriously, that white people, kinky, wild partying type fucking." Kyra giggled. "Why, the nigga like me dressing up in nurse outfits, doll baby costumes with a fuckin' lollipop and officer uniforms. He loves that X-rated sex. I mean dude like the cuffs. Even whips and lashes in the bedroom."

"Oh my God, K! What the fuck? Y'all be in there inventing sex?" India asked, covering her mouth.

"Creating, honey ... hell yeah ... we making new shit in sexual performances. I bullshit y'all not, this dude had me hanging from the ceiling off this rope ..."

India quickly interrupted, "Hanging from the ceiling!"

"Yo, listen. I was literally hanging from the ceiling by a rope and the nigga was eating the fuck outta my pussy. I swear to y'all I came five times back to back. No bullshit."

"True story?" India inquired.

"On my lungs, son."

"Damn, babes. I need to be turned out in that way fo' sho," Vanessa declared.

"You look like you wanna get turned out," Nala teased.

"Sure do! And ya husband going to be the one turning me out."

"Like I was saying," Kyra continued. "He loves fuckin' in the booty. He even made up this sex game called Fuck-It."

"Fuck-It," Vanessa hissed.

"What you mean Fuck-It?" India wanted to know.

"Yeah, it means no holds barred. We gets down. I mean Willie got me sucking his dick, licking his toes, he comes all over my body, and he licks me everywhere. It's just saying fuck it. We going all the way in and doing whatever."

"Now you taking that too far. Ain't nobody coming all over me," Nala said in disgust.

 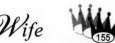

"Gurl, I'm sure you swallowing Gene kids. So you just oughta allow him to bust on yo body and face, hell," Kyra stated frankly.

"Girl, you got me totally fucked up. I barely suck the nigga dick let alone swallow his damn nut, ew, disgusting."

"You still on that childish shit honey. We're grown as hell now. I just don't understand how you barely suck your husband's dick. No wonder why he wanted to pay! He knows I'ma get the nigga all the way together," Vanessa stated snottily.

"Yeah, that's what I allow all the hoes to do while I'm spending all the dough and receiving his good art work. Y'all desperate chicks necking it out, eating his dick and all that is certainly fine and dandy with me. Leaves me with nothing to do but get fucked."

"I'ma have to agree with them on this one Nala," India said. "Sorry, but you gotta get down in the bedroom in order to satisfy your man's every needs."

"Fuck that. I get mines off and if he wants all that extra shit, he can get it from them extra lame-ass hoes in the streets," Nala exclaimed.

"Well, better you than me because the shit turns me on just by giving my niggas pleasure," Kyra said.

"I know that's right K. I can't wait till I get another nigga that can put it down on me real good." India laughed lightly.

"What happened to Scrap?" Vanessa asked.

"Gurl, I haven't been talkin' to him but we're cool. He just don't know how to have good sex. I need a dude that can eat it up and beat it up like Kyra would say ... professionally." India laughed.

"I feel you on that India, and I know you miss getting dicked down by Sump."

"Gurl, yeah I do. I'm not even going to tell a lie 'cause I miss that."

"Yo, you better find you some soon for your pussy goes into dick depression, hon."

India swayed her head, cracking up. "You and K are so dumb, always coming up with odd language for sex."

"We're the sex masters, babes. I was thinking about coming out with a DVD on sex. Good sex, rather."

Triple Crown Publications presents... *Wife*

"Yo we should do that for real. That'll sell like crack, especially once the niggas hear about my sexy ass on there," Vanessa gushed, dancing freakily around in the chair.

"You retarded Vanessa." Kyra laughed at her. "Now ... do y'all wanna run with me down to Club Envy? I gotta discuss some matters with my boo."

"I wish I could but I gotta handle something for Gene."

"And I have to go handle my little girl."

"What little girl, Nessa?"

"My bitch. Y'all know I cannot discuss all this shit about sex without getting horny. So I gotta fix her."

"I forgot your nympho ass can't go without sex for one day." India cracked up.

"Sure can't and won't," Vanessa declared.

"You're crazy. But I'm go with you, K. Ain't nothing else to do."

"Well let's be up and out of this piece."

Chapter Fifteen

After spending the entire afternoon with their peoples, India and Kyra finally headed over to the club. As soon as the girls stepped foot in Club Envy, dudes were drooling over the fine honeys strutting through. India always soaked up attention that she received from the opposite sex, but none of them were too appealing. So she paid the fellas no mind and headed over to the bar while Kyra went to handle business in the back.

India wound up ordering a cran-apple and Patrón cosmopolitan along with a red bull. She handed the bartender a twenty-dollar bill and allowed her to keep the change. Then she walked over to the booth near the stage and nestled in to roll up her cigarillo. Overfilling it with kush, she swayed her head to the R&B melody and sparked up. For some odd reason India felt good and relieved. She couldn't remember the last time she felt this good. It was as if a burden was lifted from her chest. She realized it was because she had never been free to do as she pleased without Sump trippin' on her all the damn time.

Blowing smoke through her nostrils in a trance, she was snapped out by a familiar voice. "Long time, no see."

India glanced up and found Meek standing before her, looking fine as ever.

"Oh, hey! What's good, Meek?" India stood to greet him.

"Nothing special. But what's good with you, big head?" He hugged her longer than necessary.

"I'm sure you done heard by now." India briskly hugged him back and released, because nothing needed to lead into any lustful thoughts.

"Nah, heard what? What you talkin' bout, ma?"

India contorted a sly smile and thought he was trying to fool her so she could speak upon the situation at hand first. "Don't play Meek. I know you know me and Sumpter ain't together."

"Fuck outta here. Stop bullshitting. What you mad at the nigga for that got you not claiming him?" he asked, laughing.

"Oh, you must've really not heard." India motioned for him to sit down and took her seat also.

"Me and Sump aren't together. I filed for a divorce. Where you been?"

"Hell nah, that's mad crazy ma. What the nigga do?" He was shocked beyond belief.

India went on and explained what had occurred. Meek was absolutely thunderstruck. He couldn't believe that the rumors floating around for some time now were actually true. Sump really played and had kids on India? That he didn't understand. He used to always ask Sump why he cheated on India because it wasn't like she was ugly or snotty. She was rather cool and down to earth, unlike other hustlers' wives. Let Sump tell it, she had the best performances in the bedroom. She wasn't a whore like most chicks they knew either. Meek knew for a fact that India could count on one hand how many dudes she slept with and that was very seldom for cute girls around their way. He really couldn't believe India and Sump had finally called it quits.

"Yo, I ain't heard nothing about y'all splitting, shit's wild."

"So you didn't know about Sump and that girl?" she asked, peering over her frames.

"Nah, I ain't know." Meek knew but didn't want to get in their business.

"If you would've known would you have told me?" India wanted to see where his head was.

"C'mon India, my name Da'Meek Dillard ... not a lame-ass nigga. I'ma man and I don't be on that li'l boy shit. That's why I barely

fuck with niggas now unless it's business affiliated."

She sucked her teeth. "Yo, I thought you were my good friend. You would've just left me in the dirt, knowing that I was looking like a damn fool and shit?"

"You silly ma. But you know a real nigga don't get in all that..." He slowly shook his head and said modestly, "Nah. You found out anyway though, baby."

"Yeah, you ain't my friend anymore." She took a sip of her drink and folded her arms, playfully pouting.

"So we're not cool?"

"Just fuckin' with you. You going to always be my nigga for life." India blushed.

"I better be." He rubbed his hands together.

"Yo, I'm still trippin' though. I can't believe Mac C big mouth ass ain't tell you what was going on," India said.

"Nah, I haven't talked to that nigga in a minute so he ain't even had a chance to."

"Damn, what's up with that? Ain't that your people?"

"I'm mean, yeah. I got mad love for all them niggas but our heads ain't focusing on the same thing right now."

"Oh, so you must not be doing business with them no more. You done got a major connect and left them niggas, huh?" She chuckled.

"India where you been? I haven't sold dope in over a year now. That don't have nothing to do with it, sweetheart."

"Are you serious?" That was very hard for India to believe. Hell, he was still maintaining his appearance and she didn't see any signs of him being stressed out from being broke. She could detect that from anywhere because broke dudes had a stressed-out look and all the niggas who had money had that getting money appeal to them. Meek definitely still had his and even appeared superior and refined.

"Yeah, baby girl. I stopped pushing weight before '09 even hit."

"Shows what kinda friend you are. I done talked to you a few times by myself and you ain't told me anything."

"Maybe because I was only hearing you out, ma?"

"Forget you, Da'Meek," she cooed, "But that's what's up ... I didn't know but that's real good though. So what have you been doing to keep up on the world's latest?"

"I got a few underground projects. Right now I'm in here 'bout to meet up with Willie Stacks nigga. You know dude?"

"Who don't know that nigga?"

"Right, but me and the kid just put our money together. We about to debut a club here downtown and one out in Cali. You know dude got mad clout ma. The clubs are for the elite like yourself." He smiled. "With a hip hop vibe."

"Wow, Meek. You been meaning business, huh?"

"We all know this dope money ain't going to be here forever. I'm no fool, ma."

"I sure wish my kids' father thought like that. Dude thinks the dope game is forever — even I realized it's not."

"Every man lives and thinks differently and more than anything for themselves."

"I know that's right. So you don't even fuck with none of them anymore huh?"

"Yeah, I told you them my people and I love them niggas. Matter of fact Sump just called me a few weeks ago and had me drop of some dough to Gib for 'em 'cause Mac C was out of town. Gene just called me a couple days ago just to talk, and I put money on their books just out of respect."

"That's what's up. Y'all just don't deal with each other on an 'I fucks with you hard' basis anymore?"

"Exactly ma. I'm doing my own thang and ain't none of them ready to put the drugs down. I'm try'na turn all this drug money legit, feel me?"

"I know precisely and you're doing it smart."

"Yeah and I got many other projects I'm working on now as we're speaking."

"Okay, I see you doing the damn thang." India chuckled.

At that moment Kyra and Willie Stacks emerged from the back office and approached them. "Hey, what's up man? You ready?"

"Yeah, Stacks. I was just chatting with India."

"I see ... What it do India? You straight ma? You need anything?" he asked good-naturedly.

"I'm fine, but thanks."

"You got it," Willie Stacks said graciously.

"You know if you need anything India I'm only one phone call away. Don't be afraid to hit me up for anything you need ma," Meek assured her. "But I'll see you around. I'ma be out a'ight?" He stood and hugged her again.

"Okay, I'll see you. Bye, Stacks." India waved them goodbye. She and Kyra conversed for a little while longer and after India finished her drink they were up and out.

*****

After the pair left the club they prepared to hit up the Italian restaurant a few blocks away. En route they conversed, reminiscing on the old times. Suddenly a dark Denali truck pulled up alongside them. The driver blew the horn, causing the twosome to stop. India looked at Kyra as if to say, *You know what cat drive this?* Kyra flashed back the same awkward stare, implying that she didn't have a clue who it was. At times she was still jittery from her previous kidnapping experience, so she placed her hand inside her bag and firmly gripped her gun.

Finally the window came rolling down, and a sign of relief washed upon her face when the driver yelled out, "So you just gon' keep walking on a nigga?"

"Oh, Scrap, don't play like that. You gon' fuck 'round and get shot pulling down on me, son," India laughed.

"Look at you ma ... what up? I ain't talked to your ass since ..." He threw his head back. "Umm ... since you left my damn house that night. You don't fuck witcha boy no mo'?"

"Nah, it ain't like that."

Scrappy scrunched up his face and hopped out the truck. "I can't tell you don't fuck with the boy."

"I just been busy, that's all." India smiled.

"Well, I'm glad to see you still lookin' fine as ever," he complimented, barely able to look in her eyes. "I like the new look."

"Oh, you know I ain't gon' play with 'em." India struck a few poses for him, being silly.

"You crazy, India. I'ma run inside this wireless store real quick." Kyra laughed at her cousin and went in the store.

"Oh, I know you're not bay ... but hold on. Something ain't right." He skimmed her up and down. "Ay, you had 'dem kids already?"

"Oh ... now that's another story."

He cocked his head back and checked his watch. "Ain't got nothing but time, sweetie."

"Well, I got an abortion 'cause me and Sump are no longer one."

"Bullshit." He looked down at her hand. "Hell nah! You don't have yo rings on. You fo' real?" He sounded excited.

"Dead ass serious."

"Damn, what the nigga do?"

"To make a long story short he been carrying on an affair with some broad and they share two sons."

"Fuck outta here, I can't believe you found out." He stumbled back, slightly shaking his head. "I told you that nigga wasn't shit. But you ain't wanna listen."

"That was then and this is now, so whatever." India rolled her eyes.

"Yo, you wrong though ma."

"How in the fuck I'm wrong?" She figured he was about to bring up their affair.

"You free and I been free and you ain't fucked witcha boy. That's real fucked up, India."

"Nigga, I was just getting myself together, it was a lot going on. But all that is behind me."

"So that's what's up. Since you ain't with the sucka nigga no more maybe we can make some real shit happen."

India laughed. "Yo, you crazy boy."

"Real talk. We should kick it. Now we ain't gotta hide from the public eye because you're a free agent now." He winked.

"And you're so right." India felt she did need a male companion. "I guess we can kick it sometimes."

Scrappy was beyond thrilled. He couldn't believe that he would

finally be able to work his way in on India without any disruptions. He thought by the time Sump got out of jail India would be his and they would be married with children. Revenge was finally settling in and life couldn't get any better than this. Back then, Scrappy figured by him fucking India and being able to laugh in Sump's face was payback. But nothing was amounting up to this.

The beef between Sump and Scrappy dated many years before, when Sump and Mac C were only 15 years old. The cousins dared Scrappy's crack head momma to suck Mac C's dog's dick for a piece of crack in front of the entire hood. That caused a skirmish amongst their crews.

After that, Sump fucked Scrappy's high school sweetheart Denise. That fracas lasted for a minute and because he and India were both hurt behind it, they hit it off secretly. But the serious problems came along when the crews were battling about who was getting the most paper in the streets. They began a street war, leaving three of Scrappy's partners dead in a massacre not too far from 21st Street-Queensbridge.

The beef ceased and then resurfaced when Scrappy caught Sump with Lilly whom he had been dating five months prior. It seemed like these dudes were born to clash. Scrappy knew he could cause a serious war by engaging in the ultimate no-no with Sump's wife. But the temptation to repay Sump for all their battles over the years, especially for fucking his only true love Denise, was too thrilling to decline.

"You know it's on, ma."

*****

Over the course of several weeks she and Scrappy had drawn closer. Although he wasn't the greatest man piping, he made up for that with his tricky tongue performances. Scrappy found himself developing strong feelings towards India. The two had been inseparable. They weren't together because India wasn't ready. India made it clear to Scrappy that he didn't have to buy her anything because she was over that phase in her life. But that was hard for him to do and he wined and dined her just as Sump did. He even copped for her daughters when they were out together.

India was truly enjoying his company, but there was something missing. She didn't know what, but it was something. Almost two months had passed since they ran into each other and India still wasn't physically attracted to Scrappy. He was just super cool and she cherished the friendship they shared, but she knew their relationship wouldn't go further.

It was a beautiful Saturday afternoon and she was preparing to scoop up the girls from Nana's so they could meet up with her cousins at the salon.

Once she arrived, she spotted an unfamiliar car parked outside. Instead of blowing the horn for the kids to emerge, India walked in and was bewildered.

"What up, Ronetta?" She spoke and flared her nose up at Lilly who was sitting on the sofa next to Ronnie. Her heartbeat quickened a notch. *Is this chick really kicking it with the family now though?* India was confused that her daughters had failed to mention this shit. Beads of sweat started to form her forehead and her body tensed up. She quickly collected herself because there wasn't any true animosity between the women.

"What it do India, you looking mighty fly girl."

"You know one thang don't stop a fly diva show like mines, baby!" She smirked at the pair on the sofa.

"You came to grab the girls?" Ronetta perched up instantaneously. She already knew what India was capable of doing and had witnessed India perform in plenty fights over Sump. She always went in like a beast. But India was far over those days though and wouldn't have given them the satisfaction.

"Yeah. I'm about to take 'em to get their hair done. Where the girls and Nana at?"

"The girls still getting ready and Nana's in the kitchen. Let's go in there." Ronetta motioned her into the kitchen where Nana was preparing dinner.

"Hey Nana. What's going on?" India pecked her on the cheek.

"Don't be hey-ing me. I done told y'all hey is for horses," she joked. "Now, hello India! What's been going on, Nana's baby?"

"Nana you're crazy." India shifted her weight to one leg. "I

haven't been doing too much of nothing. How you?"

"Well, I'm glad you finally came in to ask instead of blowing for the girls to come outside. You know how you been doing me recently." Nana gave her the look.

"Nana, it's not like that. You know I love you, I just ..."

She interrupted India. "I don't wanna here none of the non-sense. I know it's because you been having problems with my grandson. But like I told you before, I don't care if that's my grandson or not. I'ma always love you like a granddaughter. So you never have to distance yourself from me," she told her.

"'That's right, Momma," Ronetta chimed in.

"I know and I'm sorry. I love y'all just as much as y'all love me."

"We know." Nana beamed. "Now do you want any of these cookies I just made, India?"

"Oooh Nana, tell me you ain't home make none of them sugar cookies now!"

"You know she did gurl."

"Now y'all know I want some and some to go." India eagerly retrieved a few cookies from the stove and took a seat at the break-fast bar.

"So how's life treating you? You look splendid."

"Don't she Momma? She don't look stressed or anything."

"Gurl, I'm not ... I finally don't have to be worried about a man that's not thinking twice about me. Life feels good to be free from Sumpter's world."

"I know exactly what you mean. After leaving my girls' father I finally felt free and could breathe again."

"Net, I know exactly what you mean. I mean, life gets lonely sometimes because I do miss talkin' to Sump all the time. This new guy I've been seeing for a few months just ain't really me. So that's making me miss him even more. I mean, dude cool I just think we're really not good mates."

"Well India, if you not feeling a guy don't do like girls and get with one dude just to get over another. I can tell you from expe-riences that will slow up your goals and possibly mess up your future. You see me now, thinking that I had to settle for anybody to get over my kids' father. That's not the case, baby. You better correct those problems now and just allow that guy to be your friend until the right one surface. Once you get comfortable with yourself everything will fall into place and things might happen that you never thought would happen."

"She's right, India. You better make sure you search for the right guy. I promise you he's out there waiting for you to come along," Nana said assuredly.

"I know, but sometimes life just gets so confusing to me. I don't know what I'm going to do with myself." India sighed.

"Well, I can tell you that time waits for no man. So why don't you try to go back to school to upgrade your RN?

"Nana, I've been thinking about going back to school but it surely won't be nursing."

"Ain't that what you like India? You went to school for it."

"No. That was just something that Sump wanted me to do. And I guess I was the fool that went along with it."

"Although I just knew you was my grandsons soul mate I have to admit – y'all are better off apart." Nana said, removing the cornbread from the oven. "I can tell that you were living for Sumpter and not India. To see you sitting here not knowing what you want in life is kind of odd. And it's sad to say but Sumpter really had you in one place. Your mind never expanded for development and growth."

"I know. But God is good 'cause he finally opened up my eyes. I don't know what he really has in store for me right now, but I'm patiently waiting."

"He is indeed the greatest darling. As long as you believe it you can achieve anything you want in life. Believe me, India."

At that moment, Lilly appeared in the kitchen with her handsome son on her hip and handed Nana the phone. "Nana, Sumpter wants to talk to you," she said in her screeching voice.

Nana wiped her hands on the apron and grabbed the cell phone. "Hello, son. How are you doing?"

"Ma, put India on the phone please."

"Now, Sumpter ... I'm not trying to get in between your mess.

Lilly is right here."

"Okay, just put her on Mother. Please."

"Alright." Nana looked over at Lilly then said. "India, Sumpter wants you."

She scrunched up her face. "What he want me for?"

"Just get on the phone and see." Nana shoved the phone to India.

"Yo, what up wit it?" India cradled the phone to her ear.

"Yeah, I received your letter. I guess you was serious ... you ain't fuckin' with a nigga?"

"That's all you want?" she inquired snottily. She was disgusted that he was blatantly disrespectful while his woman was in her presence.

"Nah. You ain't came to see me like you said you was. What up with that?"

She huffed in frustration. "Oh, that's all you wanted?"

"Mmm ... you must be fuckin' some nigga cause you shooting a nigga down. Who you fucking with?"

"Sumpter, your girl right here. Please question her and not me because I'm not trying to hear it. I'm 'bout to pass her the phone." India stood up and handed Lilly back her phone. "He's all yours, hon," she said with much sarcasm. "Nana, that's my cue. But I will be back to talk to y'all when I drop the girls off. I promise." With that said, India darted upstairs and informed the girls that she was ready to go.

*****

Leslie's Celebrity Styles was buzzing with people prepping themselves for the grand opening of Willie Stacks and Meek's new club premiere. Hot 97 played throughout the salon speakers while the flat screen televisions on the floor and in the waiting area were tuned to BET. Nonstop women were coming and going. Shampoo or perm, under the dryer, then style ... everyone was out in record-breaking time. That was one thing India loved about Leslie. She had her shop well organized and you were sure to be in and out, even though it was always crammed.

Within 15 minutes, all of the girls were underneath the

hairdryer gossiping.

"Here's your Pepsi, Momma." Summer handed her mother a soda and took her seat in the chair, pulled the dryer atop her head and crossed her legs over each other.

"So why wasn't y'all little chickens going to tell me about your daddy's li'l girlfriend?" India eyed in between the youngsters.

"Mommy, that is not my Daddy girl." Italy hissed, frowning. "You buggin'."

"Well, okay. When was y'all going to tell me about y'all new brothers?"

"Momma, please. You know you couldn't take the heat and how you know anyway?"

"What don't I know Summer? And believe me it ain't the heat for me to be taking. I'm far from hot over the fact."

"India, quit actin'. You know you in love with cuz, don't front," T'ionna chimed in, laughing.

"Was, baby girl. That's old news to me," she said quite frankly.

"Mommy ... so you don't love Daddy anymore?" Italy asked, sipping on her juice pouch.

"Italy, you know I'ma always love your father. But like I already explained to you when we were at your skating party last month ... me and your dad have problems that can't be fixed and although I know you and your sister would be happy if we got back together, it just can't go back."

"Why, because he has kids with Lilly now? That's what Summer said," she snitched.

"Something like that, baby. But we're friends and will remain friends forever."

"So when he come home y'all won't be living together? He'll be with Lilly?"

"That Italy I don't kn ..."

Vanessa quickly interrupted. She couldn't believe India was actually carrying on this conversation with her 5-year-old daughter. To Vanessa it was sad. These little girls knew far too much than they should have in her eyes.

"Girl, why is you up here talkin' to them like they grown?"

"Vanessa, you know I don't hide anything from my girls. Better hearing it from me than the streets."

"Right, but you carrying on a conversation like they your cats."

"A mother has to have a friendship with her daughters. Besides, they already know what it is. These kids are far from dumb and know what goes on no matter if it supposed to be a secret or not. Their Nana keeps them updated. Believe me."

"Right, so shut up Vanessa. What you want her to be a mean and a distant mother?" Nala asked.

"I haven't said anything like that. I'm just saying Italy too grown for my likings. What 5-year-old know all this stuff? She too grown and worrying about the wrong things at such a young age."

"No it's not. Italy just was here before or something. And her knowing the real won't stop her from learning in school. That's good. She is already being taught how to be street and book smart. That is great in this damn world we're living in. At least we know she won't be stupid and naïve when she grows up," Nala said.

"Right Vanessa, Italy is smart and she be around us so much sometimes she knows more than she need to know," Brianna declared.

"Mommy, I think Auntie Vanessa just hatin' on me because I'm cuter than she is," Italy kidded, giggling.

They all exploded into laughter because no matter what, Italy was gonna speak her mind. She was indeed too grown.

"Little girl bye, and you better stop 'fore I take off my belt. You know I whoop kids."

"Yeah, but not me because my Mommy right here." She rolled her neck smiling, knowing her mother would protect her.

"India, get your bad-ass daughter 'fore I hurt her."

"Vanessa, stop picking with them kids girl. Now is you going out with us tonight or what?" Kyra inquired.

"Right," India said. "That place gonna be jumping."

"Momma, can I go out with y'all?"

"Now Summer, you takin' it too far. Don't play."

"That's exactly what I'm talkin' about." Vanessa shook her head.

"Gurl, shut up. She was only kidding."

"Yeah, that's what you think her little young ass was doing."

"Y'all, guess who I saw yesterday while I was out shopping with Stacks," Kyra said.

"Who?" They all questioned at the same time.

"Denise, honey." Kyra shook her head. "The broad working in the mall as a cashier for Foot Locker."

"Fuck outta here," Vanessa said.

"Girl, what happened to her baby daddy? Wasn't they still messing around?"

"Yeah, but his connect set him up just like they did Sump and Gene. The feds took everything. Unlike Sump and 'dem, the nigga had everything in this broke bitch name. He knows damn well she never worked a day in her life. Stacks told me that the feds got every item down to their underwear."

"You know what?" Nala said. "Gene did just tell me the nigga was in the feds serving that long way sentence. Dude got 20 plus years. Because he ain't have no bread for a lawyer after the feds took his dough. That's fucked up."

"Ain't it though." Kyra shook her head.

"Right even though I don't like the chick ... that's still messed up," India said. "That nigga was eating out here and now it's down the drain. That's why I'm cool on any nigga selling drugs. I mean we might be able to be cool but nothing more, on my kids."

"That's why I'ma stick to Stacks. I'm done with all that other shit too. Been there done that," Kyra said.

"Honey, you? I done been here, there, all the way that way." India laughed. "Fo' real though, I'm gonna find me a good man one day and be happy without the dope man lifestyle."

"Well, I'ma be with Gene forever and I keep enforcing it. He want to quit but he said he need a few more years," Nala explained.

"Look at y'all trying to down the dope boys! Y'all know y'all love that fast drug money," T'ionna exclaimed.

"Yeah, TT ... while it lasts," Kyra told her. "But anyhow, everybody going tonight right?"

"You already know. I haven't been out in a minute, I need to have some fun," India said excitedly.

"I know that's right. It's on then. Everybody dress to impress 'cause we gotta be the flyest on the scene. Shutting bitches straight down."

*****

Club Opulent was jumping and was overflowing with ballers to say the least, but India wasn't paying that shit any mind. It just wasn't appealing to her anymore. It was the same old shit happening. Bitches were wearing their skimpiest clothing, trying to out-dress each other while the niggas rocked their most costly D-boy gear. People were crammed shoulder to shoulder as the crew of cousins squeezed their way to the VIP section.

All the girls were fresh to death in designer dresses and stilettos. But India's sheer multihued mini-dress stood out, complementing her Cesare Paciotti suede booties. Instead of wearing her hair down, her stylist had pinned it up with loose curls draping to the side of her face. She accessorized with a colorless diamond choker, oversized studs and a block-face watch..

Being amongst Willie Stacks and his crew, the bar waitress brought over bottles of everything back to back. Everyone seemed to be enjoying themselves but India. She tried desperately to have fun but felt nothing. Partying didn't live in her anymore. It seemed as if there was another life she was supposed to be living. Her cousins tried everything to get her amped up but nothing seemed to work.

Sitting at the bar while her cousins mingled on the dance floor, she slowly sipped on Patrón and surveyed the crowd miserably. She spotted Ronnie and Lilly together dressed in "Free Sump" T-shirts. It didn't take long for Ronnie to spot her, but she turned around real fast.

Ronnie did see her and only turned around so she could see the picture that lay on the back of her shirt of her, Lilly, Sump and their two boys. Ronnie was once again on one of her childish missions. She only walked past India so she could see that her son and Lilly were official. Little did Ronnie know, India was happy for the two of them because she didn't want him. If she did she could've had him in the blink of an eye.

India didn't feed into her and continued to sway her head with time. She was halfway feeling the Patrón when the DJ switched from fast hip hop to softer hip hop. He was playing "I Can Take Your Girl." That was India's song so she jumped to her feet and slowly wound her body to the beat. Everyone stared as she moved her midsection with precision to the tune.

The next thing India knew out of nowhere, someone wrapped their strong arms around her waist and began to dance along. Caught up in the mood, she didn't even turn around to see who it was. She finally turned around and smiled when she realized it was Scrappy. "Should've known," she mouthed and playfully hit him across the chest.

"Yeah, I love how you movin' these hips like you a video vixen."

"Nah, I move like India ... but thanks," she said and continued to wind, even getting low a few times.

India didn't know it but Ronnie was watching her the entire time, fully disgusted. She despised India and hated that she was able to keep up her stylish appearance and be so happy without her son. Ronnie had been waiting on them to split for what seemed as eternity and now that was here, she still held resentment towards India. She observed quite a few guys staring at her and was even more disgusted. *The li'l ho ain't even cute*, she thought.

"Y'all, I'm fenna go over here and be funny 'cause I don't like her ass."

"Who, Ronnie?" Lilly asked.

"India ... so come on with us," she voiced in a demanding tone.

"Nah, I'm not on that. That is childish. I'm grown Ronnie."

"You a scary mu'fucka." Ronnie smacked her lips.

"We don't fuck with scary bitches, Lilly," Ronnie's feminine girl-friend Redd said.

"I'm not scary. I just don't be on that drama type stuff; that is so unnecessary. What you mad at her for? She's not with Sumpter anymore, I am."

"Yeah, whatever Scary Sherry." Ronnie and her girlfriend laughed and made their way over to India. By the time they made it through the crowd of people, India was walking towards her cousins. Ronnie didn't care and followed right behind her. It was like an addiction to fuck with India.

Slithering through the crowd, India returned to the bar and sat beside her peoples. Seconds later, Ronnie walked by and used the crammed club as an excuse to bump into India's barstool and spill her drink on her heels.

"Damn, bitch," India said with much attitude.

"Oh, my bad ... I'm sure they were paid for by my son's expense anyway," Ronnie replied with a smirk on her face.

"Nah, not these bitch. Don't get that shit fucked up." India shook the liquor off her heels and hopped up. She didn't know what Ronnie would try and wasn't going to give her the perfect advantage over her.

"Yeah maybe not, you probably fucked another nigga for 'em. You are such a gold digging whore."

India had wanted to fight Ronnie's ass forever and it was definitely a long time coming. She was sick and tired of her nit-picking. India never gave Ronnie any reason to disrespect her. Today enough was enough. "You talk so much shit and your big masculine-ass bark is louder than ya bite. If you was a real bitch and not a pussy you would've been 'bout yours. But I'ma be the one that show you." Rearing her fist back swiftly to steal Ronnie, Vanessa and Kyra grabbed her. "Yo, this your kids grandmother! No matter how much y'all hate each other, y'all can't be fighting."

"Man, this dyke-ass bitch got me fucked up, K. She just spilled her drink purposely on my heels, yo. These shits cost almost a thousand dollars."

"Hell nah, Ronnie. Don't be in here starting shit on the grand opening night especially, this ain't even that type of club, baby," Willie Stacks told her as he walked up. "Go to the other side and don't come back over here or you going to have to be escorted out."

"A'ight Willie I'ma be cool. My fault, this is yo club dawg." Ronnie directed her attention back towards India. "I'ma get you though, you little bitch."

"You can try 'cause I'ma be the little bitch that's gonna give yo old ass a run for your money. Believe that."

Willie Stacks signaled the bouncer to guide her to the other side of the club. Nala was just returning from the bathroom when she saw the commotion erupt, only missing it by seconds.

"What just happened?" She was worried.

"Ronnie fat ass gon' spill her drink on me, bitch mad angry and shit." India brushed the light dispute off. "But it ain't nothing though."

"You should've bust that bitch upside her fuckin' head with a Patrón bottle," Nala said sternly.

"Your violent ass stupid," India chuckled. "Forget her though, she won't spoil my night. Actually I'ma give the fat dyke a reason to hate on me."

"Right, fuck her miserable ass," Vanessa added.

"Oooh y'all this is a mean-ass joint right here." India burbled, bobbing her head.

It wasn't long before T.I.'s smash hit "I'm Back" had everybody on the floor dancing. Ronnie already had India extra crunk and she needed to let some steam out. As soon as her feet hit the center of the dance floor, she bopped, pumping her hands through the air. Then the DJ chopped, screwed, and mixed some other hood shit in. India got real amped and went bananas, raising her bottle of Patrón in the air.

By the end of the night, India found herself having a good time after all. It wasn't something that she wanted to do as often as she used to, but the club scene was alright. The club was clearing out, and India decided that it was time to go home. She hugged Kyra and Vanessa goodbye. She and Nala parted from them and headed for their vehicles. Nala bumped into a couple of people she knew and began chopping it up while India waited.

Tap, tap!

She snapped out of her thoughts – the tap on her window scared her shitless. Realizing who it was, India electronically rolled the window down. "Boy, don't be scaring me like that! What up?"

"I think we need to talk," Scrappy said.

"What up, talk about what, fam?"

"Me and you. I think we should take this relationship to a

higher level," he said bluntly, poking his head in the window and gazing into her eyes.

India sat there for a second and tried to find the best way to explain that their relationship could never work out like he wanted it to. She turned and looked at him. "Let me get out." Scrappy opened up her door and closed it behind her. She leaned against the car door and reached for his hand. "Scrap ... you a cool dude no doubt, baby. But you and me have been friends for many years and I just wouldn't feel right taking this thing to the next level. Plus, I'm far from an ignorant-ass bitch. You and Sump are enemies. The last person he would want to hear about me fucking with is you. I love my daughters' father and I just can't disrespect him like that," India said. "And even though we're not together it's still about respecting his gangster and being with you just won't cut it. We'd prolly have to sleep with one eye open because y'all done been in a lot of serious altercations ... I refuse to live like that. I just think we should leave this at a friendship. Anything other than that would be complicated and would cause serious conflict."

"Yo shorty, fuck that nigga. I'll protect you."

India looked at him sternly. "Nah, for real though I'm not gon' do that to him." She knew Sump would lash out if he ever heard about them creeping, let alone being an actual couple. But in reality, that was just her excuse to Scrappy. India knew Sump would probably blow up with anybody that she called herself being with, not just him.

Scrappy understood and didn't want to pressure her. He wasn't happy about her decision but respected her mind. He nodded smoothly. "Yeah, I feel you on that. Guess I don't have no other choice but to respect that. Keeping it one hunnid, Sump and me prolly would have been battling for each other's souls if me and you got together. So I feel you." He sincerely understood.

India walked up close and hugged him. "Thank you, I'm glad you understand." He wrapped his arms around her waist and hugged her back tightly. Then he kissed her softly on the lips. "We'll forever be friends and stay in touch no matter what, right?"

"You know it's always love on my end, fam."

Chapter Sixteen

As the weeks passed by, India was learning India Jones. She stopped everything and focused in on the basics. Getting to the person she wanted to become would be a difficult task, but it was something that she was determined to accomplish. She knew her ambitions would expand because she was done with putting a man first like most chicks do throughout their lives.

There was no more living for a man or the world. India was living for herself and her two daughters. No more thinking she had to be defined by a man's being. No more feeling entrapped, stuck and stagnant because of a nigga. Life was too short to live that way. She had to make herself happy in order to strive for success. No more going back to depending on the drug money. She wanted her own success, her own money, and her own man ... one she didn't have to share with the streets. She was transforming into an independent woman that she was entitled to become. She wanted a clean slate and to possess everything on her own. It was time for her to stand on her own two feet and handle business. She knew that right man would come along, but she had to put herself first.

In only a few months time, India had explored several different things. Culture, antiques and fine arts were intriguing to her. India had started to educate herself. She would sit around and contemplate and contemplate even more. She began attending art and fashion shows, cultural events, and even theatrical plays. She started to visit museums and art galleries and the artistic exhibits entranced her. She began to read inspirational books; and one that caught her attention was Russell Simmons' book *Do You*. That book had her exploring things she never dreamed of. India even started taking sketching classes and painting lessons. She already knew she had an amazing talent in drawing, but had only engaged in that for fun. She looked at that as something to do when she was bored and never wished to become a famous artist. India also knew how to sew her ass off. Nana had taught her when she was bored and pregnant with her first daughter. Being a quick learner, she grasped sewing fast. Every now and then she and Nana would shop at the fabric stores in midtown and make scraps into quilts and unique curtains.

She realized that success was staring her in the face from the beginning. Fashion, that is. Clothes, shoes, and jewelry had always motivated her to be fabulous. She just had realize that fashion was her calling. With that interest, India started fashion design courses online and part time classes on campus at FIT. She occupied her time focusing on school and chilling with her girls.

As summer rose over the city, India dedicated majority of her time to school and her daughters. She had arranged for her girls to stay at Nana's place only two days out of the week so they could bond. She felt she needed spend time with them other than shopping and pampering services. She was trying to show them the simple things in life. She began attending dance rehearsals and ballet lessons with them. She even took them to children's workshops and festivals. It felt really good to have her daughters around. India did miss the days of hanging out on the town with her cousins though.

One balmy summer evening, she dropped her daughters off over to Nana's. Since it was Kyra's birthday, she decided to kick it with them. She and her three cousins went to the movies, ate at La Dolce, and then headed over to the nearby bowling alley. India was ready to call it a night because she had no intentions of hitting up the club, but her cousins insisted that she go since it was Kyra's birthday.

"Girl, I don't see why not. You ain't been out in a few months, just come out," Nala pleaded.

"Right, India. You been very remote lately and plus it's my day," Kyra added.

"Nah, y'all can just drop me off to my car."

"C'mon ... come with us, please," Vanessa implored.

"Y'all, that means I have to go all the way home and change." She sighed.

"Why, what's wrong with the outfit you're wearing? You look cute!" Nala scrunched her face up.

"This simple shit? Girl, bye. I just threw this on to kick it."

"Please girl, you look polished. It'll be fun. I promise we don't have to stay long – I'll drop you off at your car by one o' clock."

"Look at my hair, y'all. I'm really not feeling the club shit tonight."

"Girl you going, so stop tripping. And your hair is just fine. You look straight ma. Don't even trip. So take off the bowling shoes and let's go." Vanessa laughed. After begging and pleading for five straight minutes, India finally agreed to go. Although India was dressed plain, she still looked stunning. Her hair was pulled to the back, a white headband lay atop, and her baby hair was slicked down to perfection. She was clad simply in a white and silver shirt, a pair of ripped jeans, and white leather thong sandals to match her satchel.

The club was packed, as India had anticipated. They met Willie Stacks and his entourage at the door and slithered right through to the lower VIP section. They sat amongst the crew so they didn't have to pay for anything. The waitress catered to the group and brought over bottles of various champagnes and liquor. The DJ was only playing crunk music and India was cool with the hip-hop vibe.

Tired of chilling in VIP, India and her family made their rounds, bumping into people they knew and receiving warm salutations. After hitting the picture man up, they all hit the dance floor. The DJ was surely playing all the megahits. He switched to a new joint and they really started getting it, winding to the fast beat.

"What up, India?" She heard a familiar voice come from behind.

She turned around and beamed, slightly tipsy. "Oh hey! What up

Scrap, what's been good?"

"Shit, chillin' and getting money. That's 'bout it."

"That's what's up. But I see you ain't called me since I said the friend shit." She winked.

He chuckled. "Nah, it ain't even like that. A nigga been out of town handling business, that's all. Shit, you try'na leave with me tonight, ma?"

India smiled thinking about his professional head performances and being tipsy enhanced her thoughts. "Just get with me after this over and we'll work something out."

"Oh yeah, it's on."

Perspiring and out of breath, India and Vanessa made their way over to the bar. "Yo, I'm hot as shit, son."

"Man, I told you it would be fun! Ain't you glad you came?"

"Yeah, it's straight but I think it's 'bout time for us to be up and out."

"Let's just wait till Nala and Kyra come back over here. K having her a good ole time."

"I know. Stacks got her butt glowing." India giggled, eyeing her obviously happy cousin.

Watching Willie Stacks approach her cousin only brought a wider smile to her face. India could tell that she was on some happy-go-lucky shit. Kyra's man was whispering some sweet nothings into her ear. The DJ must've been feeling the way they were and threw on an old school track. Silk's "Freak Me Baby" had them wanting to be on some straight love in the club.   Nobody knew it, but Mac C was upstairs with his small entourage surveying Scrappy's every move. He hit his people on the outside and informed them to stand their positions. He had craved the day to take the nigga out; it was truly a long time coming. Mac C was the crazed psycho out of Sump's prestigious, ruthless organization.

He was the one who didn't have shit to live for and always had an itchy trigger finger. Folk from all surrounding boroughs knew Mac C meant business. He had a reputation for holding niggas up in broad daylight, laying niggas down for good. He was the hit man for the crew when necessary. There had been several occasions over

Triple Crown Publications presents... *Wife*

the years when he had to lay disrespectful ass niggas and make niggas disappear into thin air. Mac C was Sump's problem solver. When he couldn't handle some shit he knew Mac C could, and most likely handle it better than he would.

Sump had put him on game that he needed to take Scrappy out for old and new. He had disrespected Sump in the worst way and although he was locked down, he was to still have all his missions accomplished. Searching high and low for him for the past few months, Mac C had become frustrated. Then he got tipped that he was out of town. Hearing that he was back in the city allowed Mac C to make his appearance that night. He knew chances were Scrappy would be in the club, being that he was one of those ole partying type niggas.

Mac C never gave a fuck who he hurt in the midst of him handling his business. He figured if an innocent person got hit, evidently it was their time to go. Not caring about the thousands in the club he drew his gun, extending, then aiming straight at Scrappy.

Next thing everyone knew, bullets were flying and scattering everywhere. Screaming and hysterical wailing could be heard throughout. People were trying trampling over each other, trying to escape the massive pandemonium. India and Vanessa huddled underneath the nearby table. Taking cover, Scrappy frantically grabbed the girl he was conversing with and used her as a human shield as he escaped to the front entrance. Bullets ripped through the young girl's chest and he tossed her lifeless body before he hit outside.

Once the gunfire ceased, India and Vanessa stood up and hugged each other for dear life. But, they quickly remembered two of their cousins were missing. They prayed and prayed that they would find their cousins safe and sound. Scurrying in search for their cousins, they stumbled over dead bodies of the innocent. Out of nowhere, Nala approached them.

"Oh my God, I'm glad y'all a'ight," Nala said, holding onto them tightly.

"Where is Kyra, Na where is she?" India demanded to know.

"Stacks gotta have her y'all, stop buggin'," Vanessa declared unsurely.

Fearing the worst, they surveyed the bodies. India's body froze, seeing the crimson covered outfit and recognizing the heels. She screamed as she realized she'd found her cousin. At that moment, it was as if they had all lost their breath.

"Why! This just can't be happening to me again!" India yelled with tears streaming down her cheeks. Grabbing India into his soothing arms to console her, Meek looked at Kyra and Willie Stacks lying beside one another lifelessly. Vanessa and Nala kneeled over her body, crying hysterically. More tears stormed out of India's eyes as she saw Stacks' big-framed body sprawled out on the floor in an attempt to cover her baby cousin.

Chapter Seventeen

The weeks had passed by quickly. India made it through both funerals but was still in a state of emotional shock. She was drained and didn't know how much more she could take. A deep grief had engulfed her entire life. India could remember when her life was problem free and she didn't have to worry about anything. She couldn't fathom why everything seemed to be happening to her. She felt her life was falling apart. First her sister and now Kyra. What was she to do? Was she supposed to be the one dead? Why did Kyra's B-day have to be her D-day too? Thoughts ran through her mind unremittingly.

The weeks consisted of her sleeping and when she mustered up the strength, she would do assignments online, but never once went outside. Her daughters were back at Nana's place. India didn't want them to see her in a state of depression. Her two cousins would constantly come and go to make sure she was all right. They wished she would come out of the gloom because they noticed that India was losing weight like a terminally ill cancer patient. She wasn't the same anymore. It was actually worse than the first time. It was all too much to bear, all occurring in such a short time span. They tried everything, but nothing seemed to work.

Meek even stopped through and brought her food. He would stick around for hours at a time, sometimes crashing in the guest bedroom. He could only get a few words out of her. He begged her to open up the mail but she refused. Most were letters from Sump and she really didn't care to hear his words.

Since the shooting, crazy rumors were floating around town. At first Nala and Vanessa figured they were false allegations. But after watching the morning news and reading the newspaper, they knew they were in fact true statements. They didn't want to tell India but they knew she would find out one way or another.

"Ay, India. Open up the door ... we out front ma," Nala spoke through the phone.

She dragged herself to the door to let them in and curled right back onto the couch. They followed and took a seat also. A lull filled the air. The girls didn't know how they would break the news.

Vanessa inhaled heavily and exhaled. "India, I know you fucked up and shit still but they found Scrappy's body in the river. He was shot in the head, burnt up with his hands cut off."

"What? Are you serious?"

"Yeah, India. I didn't want to be the one to tell you but he been missing since the shooting at the nightclub. They said the bullets were supposed to be for Scrappy because he fucks with you. Since he didn't get hit they snatched him up outside the club, kidnapped and tortured him then dumped the body in the river once they were done."

"With me?" Nobody ever knew we talked, who would ..." India didn't bother finishing the question because it was evident that someone was watching her, and informed Sump that she was creeping with Scrappy. But who? India really felt lost. She already felt responsible for Ton'na's death, but now Kyra's, Stacks's and Scrappy's deaths too. Tears instantly fell down her face. She couldn't believe that it was because of her that people's lives were taken. She wanted to die. With each nanosecond that passed it was harder to breathe. How could God put all this on her at once?

"Y'all, all this is my fault. Ton'na, Kyra, Stacks, and Scrappy are dead because of me. If it wasn't for me all them would still be breathing." She cried hysterically, rocking back and forth.

"India, stop blaming yourself," Nala consoled her. "None of this is your fault. It's not up to you or nobody else. It's only according to God who stays on this earth. So stop trippin' and get through this.

India, you have to be strong. You have two daughters and you have to move on with your life."

"I know, but how could this be happening to me? I just don't understand," she said in between sniffs. Tears and snot mixed on her face.

"It's not for you to understand, India. You know God is just sending you through a season but the good thing is that seasons end. After every stormy day there's a very bright one, India. Stop trippin' babe and suck this up. Now, I'ma have to run but do you need anything?" Vanessa inquired.

"No." She knew she would have to stop blaming herself.

"You want me to stay with you?" Nala asked.

"No, I'm fine."

"Are you sure?" Vanessa eyed her suspiciously.

"Yeah, I'll be fine," she said reassuringly.

India walked them to the car and hugged them both. She watched them drive off and collected the stacked mail from her mailbox. She walked back inside and began roaming through, as she tossed all the junk mail in the garbage can. She thumbed through the bills, bills, and more bills and then came across Sump's letter. She was surprised to see that letter because she never replied to all the ones he sent previously. Staring at the letter, she didn't want to read shit his loony ass had to say. Then again, she yearned to know what was said. Opening the letter hurriedly, she took a seat on the couch and began reading:

Indy, Indy, Indy:

It's real fucked up how shit turns up, huh? Yeah we went from happy to horrible in such little time. You were supposed to be that bitch that held on no matter what situation arose. I took care of you. Basically raised you up and taught you the game. You didn't have to do anything India but stay loyal but you played ... me ... out of every breathing human being. First you leave me for having an affair. Come on now. Can you be honest with yourself for once? Because you knew what I did in the streets India ... don't even front slore. You know that comes with the territory. So what the fucks the problem? Where did you fall short at and think playing me was

the key to solve your problems? Problems that we could've easily worked out. Yo, but the silly thing about this, that got me tripping, is how when I was there to lavish you and lay the pipe down things were straight no matter what I did in the streets. You found shit, numbers in my phone, you answered when bitches called my phone, found condoms in my pocket, and different bitches perfume on me often. The proof was there, and even though I lied you still knew deep down inside, so don't play victim here. They say that's how bitches do you when a nigga down and out though. When a nigga unable to touch and treat you to the glamour world you start flipping the game. I guess the nigga was lavishing you some way I couldn't, huh? Since I couldn't be there you had to go out and be a little whore and exchange money for your services. Honestly I couldn't expect you to hold a nigga down for so long without fucking another nigga though. You could've fucked anybody else. But when you go went out and fucked with my archenemy, you fucked up. If there was any chance of us rekindling, you totally blew it baby girl. I just want you to know you allowed this nigga to play you, to pay me back for fucking his bitches over the years and our constant beef in the streets. You were pure bait and this nigga used and abused your ass. But the thing that you don't know is the shit that happened ain't because of you, because I let a hoe be a hoe. It's not because he fucked my bitch, it's because he played me. And remember the shit involving Ton'na? Well, well, well — the man you called yourself playing me for evidently didn't give two shits about you. Yup, all I have to say is some people talks and you know mad shit spreads around these prison walls so just for the record it wasn't for the nigga fucking you, it was about, my sis Ton'na and total disrespect. But hey he played you and you were sleeping with the fucking enemy. Fucking dumb ass broad. It's really sad to say but you're very weak minded.

India quivered as cold chills consumed her body. She couldn't believe her eyes. How could she be so stupid? At that moment, flashbacks of the incident appeared in her head. "Yo, man what the fuck just happened?" She could now clearly hear Scrappy's voice. "Son, that shit wasn't the fuckin' plans, this shit is about Sump ...

you always beefing with bitches, man." The voice echoed in her head again and again. "I can't believe this shit. Always fuckin' some shit up, nigga." The voice screamed, reverberating. "The nigga just made the drop. Let's get India and get the fuck ghost, son." India's heart pumped erratically as she continued to read.

You should feel real big India. You really should. But it's cool though because Lilly my bitch and holding a nigga down well. Ain't that funny how a bitch that I haven't known but three years is down for a nigga and me and you been together for more than fifteen years or at least in each other's life. You were supposed to be that one that held shit down from jump, but you ain't do shit. You didn't stand tall. You just used me for what I could do for your bourgeois ass. I'm glad I kept her around. She's the woman that you'll never become. You played me for a nigga responsible for every loss in your fam, and I surely apologize for Ton'na and Kyra. It wasn't meant for them at all... but you, I feel should suffer in pain. Hell, just say basically you killed y'all people for being so damn naïve. And last, a nigga will be home soon and only thing you can get from me is a beat down, so please don't be in sight. Believe that. And I don't want shit to do with you after this and you're free to be with any nigga that'll talk to your jigging bitch ass. And good luck 'cause I know you'll never be able to make it without me! You'll never amount to shit but a usual-ass project chick, ghetto girl, or hood bitch that depends on a nigga to look after you!

P.S. – I'm finished with your tired ass, HOE.

India sat there stunned. She couldn't believe that he was trying to flip the tables on her. How could he be so cruel and say that she needed to suffer? Sump struck a nerve and India felt that he was right; she was responsible for the deaths of her loved ones. Not directly, but she did feel guilty indirectly. All sorts of "ifs" jumbled across her mind and maybe she did need to suffer. Maybe she meant nothing to the world after all. Maybe it was her time to go.

How could Scrappy use me as revenge to get back at Sump?

She felt there wasn't any need to breathe life's air any longer. Tears pouring from her eyes, India retrieved her satchel and grabbed her gun out. She didn't want to live any more. She wanted to visit her sister and cousin and tell them how sorry she was. She wanted to confess that it was her fault. There was nothing else for her to do but pray aloud.

"God, I just ask that you forgive me for all my sins. I repent of all my wrongdoings, Heavenly Father. Please forgive me for what I'm about to do. I know you don't believe in this, but Lord I just ask that you accept my soul through the heavenly gates. Lord, I want to see my family and tell them that I'm sorry for everything that happened. I know it's my fault and I no longer want to live. This is a huge burden for little ole me to carry Lord. I love and hope you accept me through it all. In Jesus' name I pray. Amen." As India cradled the gun to her temple to pull the trigger, she heard the door bell ringing and repeated knocking at the door.

It had to be fate because deep down inside she didn't want to do it. She placed the gun back inside her bag and went to open up the door. When she opened up, Ronnie and her little girlfriend were standing on the porch.

She looked at her, face twisted up. "What is it?"

"Well, hey to you too," Ronnie said. Bypassing India, she walked into the living room.

"Yo, what the fuck is up Redd?" India asked Ronnie's girlfriend snottily.

"She just asked me to come here with her. I don't know," she replied, shrugging her shoulders. India motioned her to come in and she followed her into the living room.

"Ronnie what up, what's the problem?" India asked.

Ronnie didn't have any time to waste. She wanted her out and got straight to the point, no small talk. She had craved this day for many years and was ready to enjoy it. She looked at India and broke shit down to the tee without one blink.

"Well, I have to tell you since you're no longer my son's wife and the divorce is final, there's no need for you to be living in his house. So you have to get your shit and bounce."

"Ronnie, you sound like a mothafuckin' fool." India cocked her head back. "This is my house just as well as it's his house. So if you think I'm leaving outta here, you must be out yo' rabbit-ass wits."

"You're leaving, trust me."

"And how do you plan on getting me out of here Ronnie? I'm not just gon' leave. Then on top of that when did you ever have any authority over any assets this way, my nigga?"

"Shows how much you know and care. Last night Nana slipped into a coma and as we all know, everything is in her name. I'm her power of attorney, so like I said you gotta mothafuckin' go. You ain't gotta go home but you gotta get the hell up out of here!"

"Nana's in a coma?" India was dumbfounded.

"Yes, I'm afraid so India," Redd said, amiably.

"Where are my daughters?" India jumped up and grasped her phone.

Redd answered, "India, they're with Ronetta. She picked them all up late last night."

"Shut the fuck up," Ronnie told her girlfriend. "Enough of that because you haven't been worried about them this long so please don't start. Like I said, everything is now in my hands and this and the house in the Islands you are no longer welcome in. Hell, you shouldn't want to stay here knowing you played my son for his enemy. Partying in the club with a nigga that done did dirt to you and your family ... and you allow him to fuck you. I just hope you never had the nigga in this house."

India glared at Ronnie and it immediately dawned on her that Ronnie was the one who informed Sump about on Scrappy. Nobody else knew about the casual relationship they once shared. It could have only been her; she saw them at the club conversing that night. Instinctively, India went for her purse and pulled out her burner.

"No India, you have kids," Redd screamed. She really admired India but she knew never to let Ronnie know that. "Please put the gun down."

Ronnie smirked sinisterly. "Oh, so you big and bad now? Girl, put that gun down. You know you won't kill your kids' grandmother." Ronnie tried walking up closer to her but was stopped by India cocking the hammer back.

"Bitch, you must not know me that well." India waved the gun in her direction. "It would be my honor to blast your dyke ass. Now back your big ass the fuck up."

"India." Redd had tears in her eyes; she didn't wanna see this pretty young girl fall victim to the judicial system. She knew India had potential. "Please don't do it," she begged.

"Yo, quit crying like a little bitch. This hoe ain't gon' pull the trigger." She walked up on India again. This time the sounds of a gunshot's blast erupted and barely missed her head.

"Bitch, next time I won't miss."

"It's not my fault that you ..." Ronnie spoke many words, but India blanked them all out. She couldn't even think any longer. She was going to beat this big bitch once and for all. She lunged at Ronnie and cracked her upside the head with the pistol repeatedly. The powerful blows sent blood flying from her mouth and she fell straight to the floor. India towered over her body and continuously whopped her with the pistol, mentally checked out.

Next thing India knew, she was in the air being aggressively escorted out by the cops, gore covering her tracksuit and hands.

Chapter Eighteen

pending the entire weekend in that filthy county jail made India disgusted. She was pissed that it was Friday when the event unfolded and had to get comfortable until Monday morning came around, which seemed to take an eternity. To India's surprise, when she finally attended court all charges were dismissed. Ronnie hadn't shown up to testify. Luckily, India's gun was registered, so the state didn't pick it up and she was free to go.

While in the county jail, she phoned Nala and Vanessa and informed them on her status. They were both in court that Monday morning and assured her that one of them would be waiting on her once she was released. After she collected her belongings, she emerged from the jailhouse and surveyed the cars lined up alongside of the curb. She spotted Nala's silver S550 Benz parked across the street. As she waited for the cars to pass by, she diverted her attention to the pearl Cadillac that was easing up in front of her.

She peered into the light tinted windows, not recognizing the truck. Rolling down the window, she smiled seeing it was Meek. "Damn, you act a fool, get in trouble with the law and don't hit a nigga up. Where they do that at? We 'posed to be cool, big head."

"Boy, how did you know I was down here?" She puckered her lips, hand on hip.

"Resources, ma. But tell Nala I got you from here," Meek extended his hand out the window, handing her his phone.

"Well, how do you know I don't have anything to do?" She

grabbed the phone from his hand.

He jumped out the car. "I'ma take you where you gotta go. Get in." He ushered her to the passenger side and opened up the door.

"Alrighty then, Mr. Commander." India promptly dialed Nala, informing her that she got a ride and was cool.

"So, where to madam?" Meek joked.

"I have to go to the hospital. Nana's in a coma."

"Damn, that's fucked up. How you know that?"

India explained how Ronnie told her.

"Yo, she trippin' like that? Wow ... that's a serious low blow."

"Right. That's why I pistol whooped her fat ass until I couldn't remember no more."

Laughter filled the air and then an awkward silence enveloped. She busied herself staring out of the passenger side window, over-looking the blur. She mulled over on everything that was happen-ing. All the while she was incarcerated it never once dawned on her that she was going to be released homeless. The mere thought of her going from having the whole world in her hands to having her life turned completely upside down caused a cold shiver to race through her entire body. She knew Ronnie despised her but never knew she would be so cruel. India knew the dilemma was only going to get crazier if Nana didn't hurry and wake from her coma. All sorts of crazed thoughts danced around her mind. Thoughts of losing her daughters were the strongest and that caused her heart to beat erratically. She didn't know what Ronnie was capable of do-ing just to hurt her. She thought more rationally. She knew she had family who loved her dearly and wouldn't allow her or her daugh-ters to go homeless for a second.

When Meek pulled up in front of the hospital, he looked at her. "What time you gonna be ready for me to pick you up?"

She furrowed her brow in confusion. "Who said you were pick-ing me back up, Meek?"

"I said it. So what time, ma'am?" He looked at his Franck Muller watch and then at her again.

India sighed. "Since you won't give up, I'll just call you."

"India, don't play now. You gon' call ma?" Meek was skeptical.

"Yes, I'ma call Meek and yes, I'm fine. I'll be straight."

"Well, here. Take one of my phones and just call when you're ready." He gave her his spare phone.

"Okay, thanks. I'll call you in a few." She hopped out, closed the door and Meek watched her plump ass bounce away as she unintentionally swayed her hips and strutted through the glass entryway.

Once India figured where Nana was located, she rushed to the sixth floor and ambled into her room. Ronetta was sleeping in a recliner covered in a baby blue blanket. Nana was resting in the hospital bed with several IVs in her arms and hooked up to a respirator with her vital signs stable. She looked as if she was sleeping in such a peaceful world. India walked up to Nana, took her hand in hers and kissed it.

After she said a silent prayer, she took a seat next to Ronetta and nudged her leg. "Aw, hey girl. Thanks for coming," she said groggily, rising up to hug her.

"You know it's only right. Nana like a grandmother to me," she said. "What's going on? What are they saying?"

"Well, they said she slipped into a coma because of a thrombotic stroke. Topping that, she's been having serious kidney problems."

"Oh, man," she said, choking back her tears. "Where are my daughters? Nala said they been staying at your house."

"Yes. They fine India. Where have you been? I've been trying to call you since Friday to tell you what was goin' on."

Ronnie was so embarrassed that India had gotten one off on her, she didn't even bother to tell her sister about it.

"I bet you have." India filled her in on the details that took place and Ronetta went into a state of total disbelief.

"Girl. Tell me you stuntin'! My sister did that shit?" She covered her mouth in awe.

"On my people's soul." India raised her right hand. "Yup, she's trying to play me like I have to get out of a house that I basically worked for too. I mean, I wasn't selling the dope, but shit I done reaped all the benefits that come with the dope game, not just the good shit either. Chicks get it twisted about being dopemen's wives. The position is overrated. We be the ones sitting home worried half to death, stressing and crying. Getting STDs and losing family to these dumb streets." India sighed, fighting back her tears. "The game so fucked up I wouldn't wish it on my worst foe. Real talk, Net." She shook her head sadly.

"I know baby. But the days will get brighter like I done told you before. I've gone through this stage, India and I can see that you're a lot different from me. Once I left one drug dealer I went on to the next then to the next and on and on after that. You don't want that anymore. I see you been going to school and try'na better yourself. Making something out of your life for you and yours."

"Netta, you don't understand. All my life I been involved in the drug life. All I know is the drug life. I swear I just wanna see what's on the other side. It's gotta be better than this." She cried softly as she slightly rocked back and forth. "I done lost two of the closest people in my life to this cruel-ass dope game. Muthafuckas don't play fair in this game. It's a cold world, especially in this shit. Not to mention my father leaving us at such an early age 'cause of the game. I never tell people, but that shit still hurts, knowing my dad can only send post cards and call to let us know that he's fine. Which, he never calls and I know it's because he feels guilty." India dabbed her face. "I loved my daddy so much. That's mainly why I fell into the hands of another man ... just to feel secure and loved."

Crying along, Ronetta stroked her hair. "I feel you, India. And I never knew you even tripped about yo' pops."

"Girl, I been trippin' since the feds came and got him. That's why it was so easy to involve myself with Sumpter at such a young age. If my daddy was here nothing like that would have ever happened. Mostly because he wouldn't have allowed it to happen, and I know if my dad was around I wouldn't have been trying to find a provider and a nigga to love me. Man, I gave Sumpter my all but all he ever did was hurt me," India sniffled. "I never wanted my marriage to fail but it did. I have so many open wounds. These fresh scars never even let the old ones heal." India murmured, shaking her head. "It's so much that has happened! It'll take forever to explain, but I can say I'm done being everybody's fool."

"India girl, everything will get better. And you know once Sump find out about what Ronnie's doing he gon' curse her out and you gon' be back in your crib."

"The thing is Netta, I don't want to go back. I want to start over. Sumpter thinks I need him and I do not. He think I can't survive without him, but on everything I love I'ma show him better than I can tell him. Net, I don't need him for anything. I have just as much street savvy as he does. If he thinks I'ma fool then he can think again. I'm a strong woman and I know I can make it without him."

"I truly understand. And it's messed up how soon as my mother goes into a coma all Ronnie is worried about is Sumpter's property and assets. Ronnie always been grimy, but believe God don't like ugly. We all know he handles all fools, so you don't even have to worry about her."

"Gurl, trust and believe I'm not. I'll mess around and get a serious case foolin' around with her. I'ma leave it all alone. I'ma have Nala grab my car tomorrow and figure out what I'ma do with myself. It just feels like I'm in crazy competition with my past. I can no longer live like that, Net. I wanna put that life behind me."

"I feel you ... and everything will work out for the better," she declared reassuringly.

After lingering around for a few hours, India retrieved the celly and phoned Meek. He answered, "What up?"

"I'm ready, where you at?"

"On my way."

"Okay, I'll be out front," she told him and stood up, sliding on her jacket. She asked Ronetta, "So TT at yo' crib with the girls?"

"Yeah, they all there chillin'."

"Well, just call and tell her I'm on my way to pick them up."

"India, where are you gonna take them?"

"I'ma just go over to Nala's house and I'ma start searching the web for a place in the morning."

"Girl, just go on. The girls will be straight. I'm 'bout to go to the crib in an hour or so."

"You sure, Netta?"

"I'm positive. They cool," she reassured her.

Glancing at her watch, India noted that twenty minutes had passed and began dialing his number. She smiled and tapped end on the phone when she saw his truck turning into the hospital entrance.

"Took you long enough," she said playfully, sliding inside.

"Nah, I knew you was gonna call soon as I got out of the area. You know how that be."

"Yeah, Meek. I know you was prolly going to see one of yo' chicks in another borough." She was kidding with him.

He chuckled. "You a mess, ma."

He peered off into traffic as India watched him navigate his Cadillac truck. He stopped for a light in front of Burger King and glanced over at her. "You hungry, big head?"

"I'm surprised I'm not dead. I haven't ate since Thursday night." She giggled.

"Oh, I can tell 'cause your stomach growling like lions at a circus."

India playfully mushed him in the face. "Shut up, punk."

He pulled into the drive-thru where they ordered. Hating to eat and drive, he opted to chill in the parking lot. He smiled as he watched prissy India smash on her Tender Crisp, onion rings and lemonade. India tried her hardest not to admire Meek, but he was enticing. Even the way he tilted his head back to take a gulp of Dr. Pepper from his wax cup intrigued her.

He took a handful of French fries and shoveled them into his mouth. Then he took the last bite of his Whopper. Meek finished chewing his food, wiped his mouth with his napkin, and turned to look at India. "So what up, big head? Tell me what's on your mind," he asked, reading the stress on her face and the sorrow filling her eyes. Her once naturally radiant skin now appeared pale, but all in all she still looked beautiful.

"Nothing, why you do you ask?"

"India, you ain't gotta stunt with me ma. It's me, bay."

After a second she spoke. "Meek, what is not wrong? I done lost my sister and cousin because of me." She went on and explained how Scrappy was in fact the one that kidnapped her and Ton'na, how Sump found out in prison and had someone watching Scrappy. Also how he was partially responsible for the massacre at the club. Meek listened attentively.

"Yo, ma, don't blame yourself. You never once pulled a trigger or kidnapped anybody. That shit ain't your fault. Sometimes we don't know why shit occurs, it just does. Even though I know you hurting inside, you gonna have to let that shit cease. Shit, Stacks was my man and we was handling a lot together. He put me onto some shit that I hadn't dreamed of doing and now the nigga gone. But I tell you this ... life goes on. I know life may hit you with some powerful blows but you gotta pick yourself up and keep strutting ma."

"I know, but I miss them both so much. There's not a day that goes by that I don't think about them."

"I can feel that and its okay to miss them. But I know they don't blame you for it. I'm sure they would want you to move on with your life, India."

"I understand." She knew he was telling the truth but quickly changed the subject. "So what up? You ready to take me over Nala's now?"

"Naw ..." he shook his head. "You got too much tension in your body so I already called a masseuse for us out at my place. I'm due for one too." He shrugged his shoulders back and forth.

India sucked her lips. "You would get a woman, huh?" She eyed him funny and playfully rolled her neck.

"You know ain't no nigga coming in my crib, ma," Meek said and turned on the ignition.

She blushed while an awkward, uncomfortable lull followed.

"India, I know you prolly don't want to, but we cool so you can stay at my house. I never really be at this crib because I be handling so much shit. But you're welcome to stay however long you wanna."

India looked at him. "I don't know about that. You know how chicks be stalking you."

Meek smiled at her comment. "You know I don't got no shorty."

"Yeah and why is that?" She knew he was way out of her league. But she desperately wanted to know why his fine ass was still a free agent.

He glanced at her momentarily and then looked back at the road. "All the chicks that I done been with never led to anything. I would just fuck a chick and that'd be it. I never really had time for the nagging. You know how y'all do," he joked.

India burst out laughing. "You know, I was the furthest thing from being a nagger. Keep it real ... the only time I went off was when shit got too out of hand."

"Yeah, that's what your mouth say. What about the time you cracked your mans in the hand with that Alize bottle? You know what ... that ain't even nagging. That's a straight up sucka attack, baby girl." He chuckled. "Yeah, you were wildin' ma."

India sucked her teeth and folded her arms. "Oh, I see you wanna go throwback on me. But you know that nigga deserved that shit. He only slept with my homegirl from around the way," India said sarcastically. "But that shit was tight to y'all, huh? Y'all niggas think getting shit off like that is a good look, huh?"

"You silly, yo."

"Nah nigga, you silly," she countered. "Try'na stunt like you ain't got a tribe full of chickenheads. You know one of these chicks got you open all over them."

Meek wanted to tell her how she had him open, but decided it was inappropriate. Sensing something was on his mind, India hissed. "Speak what's on your mind, pimpin'."

"Oh, so you think you know me, huh?"

"Evidently I do. So just spit it out."

"Okay, I'ma keep it funky with you. I was digging you and maybe still am," he admitted. "But you was my man's girl from way back so I never really tried to get you how I really wanted to."

"That's why you always tried to get at Ton'na ... 'cause we looked alike."

"Tried?" He glanced at her slyly and then back at the traffic ahead. "I messed with her once, but for real I was drunk as shit. But yeah, that's partially way I did, being honest."

India covered her mouth. "Y'all li'l sneaky dawgs. Gon' try to front like y'all ain't never even been in the same room alone," She shook her head laughingly.

"Nah, that was long time ago. I think it was like her second year in school. I ended up telling her I had a thing for you too."

"Now why would you go and do something like that?"

"I'm just a real ass nigga ... you know that."

Silence.

India finally broke the lull. "I already knew that you digged me though. It was the same feelings here for a very long time," she confessed. "That time in the car was wild but the thing was I didn't even feel guilty. I blamed it on that Patrón." She giggled and slightly shook her head. "Knowing it wasn't nearly the liquor because I enjoyed it. And I surely don't feel bad now because turns out the nigga really did have kids on me. Ain't that some shit."

They both began contemplating and for the rest of the time they rode in complete silence, consumed by their own thoughts. Once they reached the mini-mansion in an affluent community in New Jersey, Meek pressed his garage remote and pulled his truck inside.

"This my ducked off crib that nobody know about. You gotta be special to come here."

India smiled and followed him through the downstairs door. She thought her house was breathtaking. But once she scrutinized his place she about fell the hell over. It was absolutely gorgeous. The first thing she noticed was the beautiful leather burnt orange sectional sofa with auburn, brown, orange and crème throw pillows, vast burnt orange leather chair and suede ottoman atop the glossy cherry wood floor. She adored how the flooring complemented the cherry wood brick wall. The rest of the walls were painted a pastel crème. Then she took in the rest of the things that were surrounding her. A glass table sat in the center of the floor above the checkered rug, while expensive paintings by Renoir and Jackson Pollock decorated the walls. She could just imagine the rest of his place.

"Now, Meek ..." India summoned him to come closer.

"What's poppin' ma?"

"Who decorated this for you?"

"C'mon ma. I did this by himself. All niggas don't like plain shit now, big head."

"Uh-huh. You know you had somebody helping."

"On everything ma. I'm ..." Meek was interrupted by the door-bell. To India's surprise, it was two masseuses. Meek wanted them to relax and enjoy themselves together for the two hours he paid, being that he had to make a business run before eight.

Laughing and talking while receiving, massages, India couldn't believe how sincere Meek actually was. She never knew he could be so affectionate and enjoyable. As many years as she had known him, she wouldn't have thought in a million years that he was so charming. He was always the perfect listener but surprisingly was the ideal communicator also. She learned how he had promised his mother before she passed away how he would get out the game and did exactly that. He confided all his secrets to her. Meek wasn't a typical drug dealer; he had plans and dreams. He always had plans of turning his money legit once he had enough paper to be comfortable. Meek didn't allow the streets to define him. He defined the streets and was destined to become a mogul. Although he was straight out of the projects, he had the mentality of an entrepreneur.

He was bringing things out of her that she never knew existed. It seemed as if he knew her so well it almost scared her to death. He spoke to her about where she went wrong in her marriage, and she completely understood where he was coming from. She loved the connection they shared. It seemed as though he had all the answers to her unanswered questions. She enjoyed his company. Towards the end of the massage, he excused himself; he had to get ready to head out for a business meeting.

After the masseuses left India phoned Ronetta and talked to both of her daughters, who were fine. She chatted with them for a few minutes and as usual they rushed her off the phone. Hanging up with them, she dialed Vanessa, who called Nala on three-way.

Triple Crown Publications presents... *Wife*

She conversed with them briefly and assured them that she would call tomorrow.

She was relaxing on the sectional couch when Meek summoned for her to come upstairs. She wondered what he wanted and dashed up the right staircase. He was in the bathroom. "What up?" she asked, breathing a notch harder than normal and not paying attention to her surroundings.

"I figured you might enjoy my hot tub ma."

India thought, *damn, this dude done read my mind*. She had been waiting for him to leave since she got there. She had planned to utilize the tub and indulge in a hot steamy bath, but he was already a few steps ahead of her. He had the lighting set amber dim and the Jacuzzi filled with suds, sending off a delightful scent of peaches. Bordering the Jacuzzi was lit up peach scented candles and a pint of Patrón. After she took in her surroundings she laughed and said in a giggly tone, "Let's not forget about the Patrón."

"Yeah, you know I already knew that was your shit. What could relax you more?" He chuckled, sitting in the crème leather chair. He turned around and retrieved the Bloomingdale's bag that sat behind him and handed it to her. "I swung past the store for some pajamas and a few outfits while you were at the hospital."

"Well, thank you. You are such a good friend, Meek." She ambled over to him like she was a kid and hugged his neck tightly. "I really appreciate this and I will repay you when I get my car tomorrow."

"You straight, ma. It's cool. We peoples," He perched up and before he left he said, "Make yo'self feel at home and get comfortable, big head. I'll be back."

While India was relaxing in the Jacuzzi she thought and thought. She admired Meek for his generosity. She knew it was wrong, but her heart wasn't vetoing the intense emotions springing for Meek. He wasn't anything like Sump ... but he was his boy though. That was certainly playing a deadly game, a death trap for real. She didn't want to deal with that even though she didn't know when Sump was actually dated to come home. But, she did know that his lawyer was paid and had connections so it was bound to be any day soon.

Blocking the world out, India drifted into a daze. She could actually see them together, building a life and living the way she was supposed to. He could tell when something was troubling her. He could just sense it and she knew he could. They were meant for one another. India loved how he checked on her while she was in her depression. She knew he was busy, but he still made time for her when she needed him the most.

She checked herself. India was lost for a second, but remembered that Meek was Sump's longtime friend. It could never work out. Stepping out of the Jacuzzi tub and grabbing the velour towel from the rack, she patted herself dry.

Covered in the plush towel, India made her way into Meek's bedroom. *Damn this nigga really got taste.* She loved how clean and neat he was. Everything was so well organized. It was a really nice-sized and elegant bedroom. The walls were a soft gold, perfectly complementing the gold drapes. A brown silk bedspread covered the beige king-sized bed, which was decorated with taupe, gold and crème pillows of all different shapes and sizes. The rest of the room carried a nice size flat screen television, huge armoire and a taupe chesterfield.

She plopped down onto the bed and removed the items from the department store bag. She opted to throw on the stylish camisole and satin shorts he had purchased her and slipped into the matching slippers. India was famished and wondered what he had inside his fridge, assuming his ass prolly didn't have a lick of groceries. Surprisingly, he had a refrigerator full of goods. She decided to cook smothered pork chops, mac and cheese, green beans and cornbread and for dessert she ate a slice of cheesecake.

It was raining. India adored nature's work so she pulled the wide blinds back and watched out of the oversized bay window as rain poured heavily from the sky. She retrieved a bottle of Hennessey from Meek's mini bar, poured a double shot and drank slowly. She knew better than mixing dark with light liquor, but at that moment all her despair returned and she was lost. She needed the thoughts to disappear, or at least cease. So India took the Hen to the head and gulped it down.

Navigating the streets bumping Jay-Z and thinking about India, Meek headed back to his home. He couldn't believe that India had been on his mind so much lately. He always felt some sort of connection between the two, and discovering what she felt for him had his feelings floating right back. He craved everything about her. For many years he pined for her, but she was Sump's wife and for that reason she was forbidden fruit. But then again, that marital status had been renounced.

Evidently, Sump didn't care for her enough to salvage their marriage. He had her and obviously didn't cherish what they shared. Although that was his boy, he felt that she was supposed to be his. He wanted to pick up the slack and show India the way a man supposed to love and treat someone special. All along, he could tell that India's intelligence was intoxicated by drug money. She had potential, but he knew somewhere along the road she got stuck. But he was ready to be the one that directed her onto the right path. Meek wanted her to become the woman he breathed for.

Several thoughts roamed his mind. Would he be a grimy ass nigga, getting with his boy's ex-wife? Should he just conceal all his feelings and live the single man's life? Meek was tired of the bachelor life. It was cool, but that shit was for the birds. He was tired of fucking all sorts of women. He was 29 years old and it was time for him to settle down and have a stable relationship. After all, he and Sump were doing their own thang now and he couldn't help who he loved.

He tried to collect himself before entering his crib, 'cause it was definitely becoming hard for him to be in her presence without wanting things to escalate further. When Meek walked in the living room, he found her curled up on the sofa, too cute in her sleepwear. He could tell she was tipsy from her glassy eyes.

The aroma of delicious food filled his nose as he placed his keys on the glass end table. "Yo, you just gon' fix you something and forget about your people, huh?"

She slowly shifted her head in his direction. "Now, you know I left you some."

"You better had, big head." He dashed to the kitchen, fixed his plate and returned. "Damn, this shit slamming, ma," he said with a mouth full.

"You, know how I get down in the kitchen. Don't even trip, playa."

"Yeah, right. But I gotta leave out of town for a couple days. You gon' be straight here?"

"Of course I am. Where you going?" She wanted to know.

"Dang, you a bit too nosy for the kid," he said in between bites.

"Boy, boo. Where you going? With one of your hoes?" She furrowed her eyebrow. "You would leave to be with a chick when you got a guest as fly as me that you supposed to be keeping company." India was only kidding, then again she didn't know.

"Nah, I'm messing with you. I gotta meet with some important folk on the West Coast to discuss this soul food restaurant I'm opening up."

"Dang my dude, you really ain't gon' play, huh? Making major moves, I see."

"You know it," he said, taking a swig of his soda.

"When you leaving anyway?"

"My flight leave out tomorrow at nine in the morning but I'ma head outta here 'round like six. You can drive the SRX or the 745 till you get tired of it and wanna jump in yo whip."

"Oh thanks, but I'ma have Nala grab my car tomorrow. Also, I will be out of your hair soon. By the time you come back I should be gone."

"Whoa, whoa, hold on ma. You can stay here till you find you another spot. I barely be here."

"I don't think that would be good. I'm cool staying at one of my peoples."

"Why stay there when you got all this space here damn near to yourself? The girls can come out here and stay too."

India looked at him and realized he was serious. "Well, I guess it wouldn't hurt until I found me another spot. I'ma start looking tomorrow."

"Cool. You don't have to rush it though. You can stay here

however long you want, India. Let me go up here pack and hop in the shower. I'ma come back down and take some drinks to the head witcha."

Twenty minutes later, Meek returned in nothing but a pair of boxer shorts and a towel wrapped around his neck. India had to gasp for air; she was mesmerized by his light brown five-foot-seven stature and chiseled physique. Although he was a little nigga, it seemed as God himself had crafted him. Homeboy was cut in all the right areas.

Small beads of water illuminated his skin. Entranced, India wanted so badly to get up and suck all the water from his glowing body. The sight before her had her panties wet, but she ruled against it for several matters. "Ay, put this lotion on my back ma." He handed her his bottle of lotion and sat on the edge so she could massage it in.

He went into the other room and grabbed a bottle of Grey Goose and a glass of cranberry juice from the kitchen and reentered the living room. Fumbling through a few CDs, he turned on a slow jam mix at the perfect volume. He sat in the chair across from her and took shot after shot to the head. India couldn't help herself. She realized she hadn't had sex in months and by the way her pussy was screaming, she knew anything was liable to happen.

After emptying the bottle he finally felt relaxed and in a state of peace. Now he was absorbing her beautiful body fully. Eyeing India's thick legs tucked underneath her bottom and perky breasts, he slowly licked his lips. Sensing his obsession, she unfolded her legs revealing her bare fat kitty cat. Unable to resist this aphrodisiac, he whispered, "C'mon here, ma."

India sat still, not knowing if she should follow suit. She couldn't resist what her heart was commanding her to do, but she still felt paralyzed. She couldn't move. Not waiting for her, Meek rose up and walked over, pulling her up from the sofa.

He couldn't help himself and softly kissed her on the lips. His dick was already rock hard, bulging out of his boxer shorts. Wanting to show the effect he had on her, India started kissing him on the eyes, nose, neck, and then made her way to his lips. He knew this was real because no chick ever did that shit before.

Without saying a word, Meek picked her petite frame up by her butt and carried her to his bedroom. Positioning her in the center of the bed, he slid her shorts off and tugged her camisole over her head, leaving her nude. Strikes of lighting flickered throughout the room while the heavy sounds of thunder and intense rain vibrated around them. India was in seventh heaven. Meek tantalized her, circling his tongue around her pretty vagina lips. India moaned in bliss. Wanting to taste her fully, he buried his face inside her tunnel. She was at a place she had never been before. He licked and sucked her pearl with much precision as she wound her hips. Juices were flowing from her vagina as he devoured all her sweetness.

"Ahhh this is great! Please keep going!" she squealed as her back arched up. The sensation was feeling good but she was becoming breathless. She tried to gasp for air but she barely could. "Oh baby, you gotta stop, shit! Now stop," she pleaded.

"Nah, you gon' come for me, right?"

"Oh, yeah."

"Nah, I said you gon' come."

"AH Huh, I'ma cooome!" she wailed, trembling.

Her juices were all over her inner thighs and southern lips. Wanting to return the favor, she demanded that he take his dick out. Stripping out of his boxers, India's eyes widened at the full view of it. Desperately wanting him to insert his tool inside her mouth, she stared. Meek had the biggest and the most beautiful penis she'd ever seen. *I guess it's true, little man with a huge package,* she thought. Not wanting to wait any longer, India wrapped her mouth around his dick and glided up and down his manhood. Running his fingers through her hair, he groaned, feeling the semen at the tip of his dick. "Damn, ma," he moaned, pulling her head up to release his kids; he didn't want to disrespect her by busting in her mouth.

Finished with the oral sex, he wanted India to feel him and swiftly flipped her onto her back. Gliding his dick in, out, round and round India rocked her hips with the rhythm. Thrust for thrust he went deeper with more intensity, and she keep up well. Meek squeezed her breast as he pounded her pussy steadily. The pussy was just as he had imagined, if not better.

"Meek, you's a beast," she moaned softly. India exploded, but she wasn't nearly finished 'cause he was definitely taking her there. She turned over and got on all fours, signaling him to dip right back in. "Oh, you ain't gon' play, ma," he panted, reaching his peak.

Spreading her ass cheeks apart, he plunged his penis inside her and relished the way she threw the pussy back. The moans and quivering let Meek know he was putting it down. Slapping her ass caused her to shriek in sheer pleasure; he was really gutting her down and she loved every moment of it. Dazed by how wet she was, he dug deeper and deeper, stroking her from all angles possible. "This feels too damn good bay." India was reaching her climaxed and he knew it. Climaxing too, she could feel his body spasm up and pulsate inside her. "Damn ma, you gon' do something to a nigga." He groaned, clenching his jaws together. It was feeling so good he didn't even have the strength to pull out.

Lying beside him and staring at the ceiling, India wondered if she just made a terrible mistake. Was he doing this just to be able to say he fucked something that was Sump's for so long? Or were the feelings that she carried inside was mutual to his? Sensing an uncomfortable India, Meek pulled her onto his chest and nuzzled their panting bodies together tightly, letting her know that he wouldn't have taken it back for the world. He watched as she slept peacefully and before long he fell into a slumber himself.

*****

"Ayo, bay?" Meek called out, entering the house through the garage.

Several weeks had passed and India had had some of the best times of her life. Unlike Sump, Meek liked enjoying the simple things in life. He didn't think it was corny taking long walks along the riverbank or going to the drive-in and laying a blanket outside the car to watch the big screen. Meek even read inspirational novels and attended fashion shows with her. With him, India didn't always have to be a fly girl when they were out on the town. Meek thought she was still adorable in a comfortable sweat suit and tennis shoes. When India was with him she didn't feel like a trophy wife, he made her feel like a *wife*.

They weren't officially "together" but the two were more than friends. India didn't want to rush into things knowing that it wasn't right. Being with Meek was showing dishonor but while in his company India felt honored. Logic told her that this wasn't in the game, but her emotions weren't playing a game. She tried to deny the feelings that harbored inside but with Meek it felt like paradise and she slowly let the emotions emit love.

Each day that passed, Meek brought a different joy to her life. His affection was more grown - man than that of Sump's. India had always held a secret attraction to Meek but with how he stepped to her with sophistication, and a well-rounded mentality, he now held her attention in a different light. India wanted him to be her lover and moral supporter. He became her teammate and something like her lifestyle advisor. He was intelligent and India cherished his advice. She wanted him to share her world completely, but it was forbidden. Their world would be dismantled and India wasn't ready to walk into that inevitable death trap.

"On the web browsing for me a place," she replied, scrolling through the list of houses in a nice but affordable area.

"Now, what I tell you," Meek said and put his hands on her neck, causing her to slightly lean back as he massaged her tenderly. He had the softest hands and the most gentle touch.

"What you talking 'bout, bay?" India asked.

"About you needing to focus on school and getting all that done. Stack your bread ma and worry about finding a place later. Feel me?"

"But I know you getting tired of me, babe. I don't wanna be smothering you."

"I told you I enjoy your company and will be sure to let you know when you begin smothering me." Meek laughed lightly.

"Oh so you think I'ma be sweating you hard, huh?" India removed herself from his hold and stood up. "Uh-huh, not never that my dude." She puckered her lips and walked close to him. "What you gotta say, nigga?"

Triple Crown Publications presents... *Wife*

"I ain't got nothing to say, ma." He pulled her into his chest and rested his forehead atop hers. "You know I want you here, right?"

"Yeah, I know."

"So now that we got that straight for the one hundredth time ..." He grinned and stared her directly in the eyes. "We can get going."

"Where are we going now?" India blushed, loving his quality time tactics.

"Brooklyn Parade bay, you know I gotta get me a funnel cake." He leaned up and kissed her on the forehead. "You know you want some too," he softly pinched her side. "Get dressed. I'ma be waiting on you downstairs, big head."

$\mathcal{C}$hapter $\mathcal{N}$ineteen

$\mathcal{S}$ump was home and it felt good to be back. He was truly ecstatic that his money was not only long enough to talk, but long enough to have mothafuckas working their asses off to advance his damn release date. What a fucked-up government! Gibson had some folks tamper with a little evidence and once they reopened the case, they wound up ruling it as falsified evidence and an illegal search. So the courts freed him earlier.

Sump had one thing on his mind and one thing only: money. He was glad to be back to reclaim his reign in the streets. Ronnie and Mac C handled shit better than he thought and he was impressed. But to crave his appetite, he had to get back out there to grind himself.

Meanwhile, he had been living the lifestyle he envisioned. Lilly was his woman, and she was everything he needed and wanted her to be. She had become his lover and best friend. She understood the way a man was supposed to live, especially a street nigga. He didn't have to argue, be questioned on his whereabouts or hear the constant nagging. She cooked, cleaned, and sexed him when and however he wanted it. What more could a nigga want? Fuck having the best of both worlds. He had the whole world in his hands.

Lilly was loving this life. She knew love would conquer all once it was said and done. She finally was able to call him her man and be able to hold the title of wifey. She enjoyed being with him and loved his company. All his free time was spent with her. Finally, she

Triple Crown Publications presents... $\mathcal{W}$ife

didn't have to share Sump's affection with India. It was all how she dreamed it to be. She treasured them being a family and him waking up to her and their kids every day. Lilly was so grateful that God answered all her prayers and thanked him for blessing her with him.

Without warning things changed drastically. He transformed back into that same creature and visited her as he pleased. Lilly didn't know what to do because she wanted to renounce Sump and knew if it was someone else, she would've. But she was so far in love with him that he was hard to let go. Especially knowing she'd made it thus far. She knew he'd come back around and she just had to maintain her position.

Her friends told her that he wasn't right for her, but they didn't understand. They weren't the ones wearing her shoes. It just wasn't that easy to let go and she just couldn't imagine life without him. It seemed as if Sump made her life complete. Every time she saw him, her world lit up like the Fourth of July and she would fall deeper in love with him. She wanted to carry his last name. He was the only dude she could see herself actually being with.

Sump was the only man she ever loved and showed that he loved her somewhat. Around him she just felt secure. So if she had to wait a lifetime, she would definitely wait this lifetime and the next lifetime to have the only man who truly filled the void.

*****

Navigating through city traffic on the expressway, Sump banged "Something You Forgot" by Lil Wayne. Listening to rap always cleared his mind. Wayne's words resembled his current situation. He tried, but couldn't take it any longer. India was his girl no matter what she did in the past. He had already forgiven her.

At first he allowed his pride to stand in the way. Pushing that out the window, Sump knew he needed India more than the air in his lungs. There wasn't any way he could allow himself to live without her. She was his better half. The life in his soul. Needless to say, India was his queen. All the negative things he tried embedding in his mind to hate her, he just couldn't. He knew deep down inside his heart that India was a good girl; he'd just provoked her to do certain things.

Yeah, it wasn't right for her to fuck with Scrappy, but it wasn't right for him to hurt her for so many years either. And no, two wrongs don't make a right. But it wasn't her fault that she was the victim of Scrappy's revenge. He couldn't blame her for merely being vulnerable.

Although he killed her spirit countless times, India was there for the longest and he couldn't just give up this easy. He was free now, and knew she couldn't deny him in the flesh. Or could she? What woman would accept their husband having two kids on them? But India knew she held claim to his heart, so why wouldn't she forgive him?

They'd been through so much over the years. Painting the picture of his life without her in it made for a bleak black and white portrait, whereas before it was iridescent. India completed him. Though his sworn enemy at times, she also was his best friend. India was his confidante... his best half ... his rib ... his backbone ... his rock. The memories they shared ached painfully and he would do anything to turn back the hands of time.

Knowing only one person could solve his problems, he headed over to Nana's house. Inside her room, Sump watched her sleep from her bedside. She lay there hooked up to machines. He hated to see Nana in such state. Released from the hospital, she was stationed at home and received 'round-the-clock in-home medical care. She was slowly showing signs of recovery, but the doctor informed them it could take some time.

After sitting there for 20 minutes, Nana opened her eyes and smiled weakly at her grandson. She always loved when he came and sat with her. "Mother, I see you up now. How are you feeling?" He took a seat in the chair.

She replied in a struggled whisper, "I'm fine, Pookie. I'm fine." She called him by the nickname she gave him as a child.

"Dang, Momma, you would still 'member that." He forced a smile, really hurting inside.

Not even a second later, Ronnie came through the door. She was dressed in a gray hoodie, baggy jeans and a black v-neck. "Hey son, hey Ma." She leaned down and kissed her cheek, then took a seat on the edge of the bed. Ronnie looked at her son. With the dismal expression spread across his face, anybody with eyes could tell that something was bothering him.

"What up son, you got something on your mind?" she voiced in her baritone.

Sump knew that Ronnie didn't care for India, but he didn't care because he did and that was all that mattered. "Yeah, man."

Knowing her son, she already knew what was troubling him. "So you thinking about India, huh?" The mention of her name panged his heart.

He ignored and she continued. "Sump, you don't gotta tell me 'cause I already know you love that girl. When I told you I was gonna press charges on her you begged me not to. I could hear it in your voice that it would have hurt your soul son. That's why I didn't do it ... and after all I deserved it," she admitted. Ronnie was tired of hiding the facts. She'd been wanting to lift this from her chest long ago and this was the perfect time. She had to let it all out and express her true feelings.

"I'ma be honest with you, son. This has been on my mind and I've wanted to tell you for so long but I was just too stubborn." She began. "The real reason I never liked India was because I didn't want you to love and give her your affection 'cause your father never gave that to me. I was jealous of the relationship that y'all carried for so long, because it was something that I didn't have. I mean, you know Sump, I done been in plenty relationships, but none of them ever meant anything. That's why I always tried to teach you to put your money first. I didn't want to see you love someone unconditionally in front of me. I wanted you to play girls and break their hearts the way your father did mine." She paused, wiped the lone tear that slipped from her face, and continued. "When Lilly came along and you told me about her I tried everything to get you to love her so that you wouldn't love India anymore. But then when I thought about it, it prolly would have turned the same way once you gave her all of you. I like Lilly no doubt, baby, but I can't be the judge of who you should spend the rest of your life with. And although I know India and I will never become cool because I've put that girl through so much all these years, if India is who you want, go after her, Sumpter."

"Ronnie, it might be too late." He dropped his head shamefully. "I done the ultimate betrayal, but I really want her back. I mean I want to remarry her. It's like I don't wanna advance without her."

"I know son, and if you love her how you say you do, then step up and tell her. You haven't seen her since you home. I believe that it won't hurt to try, son. And maybe y'all can work something out."

Nana couldn't believe her ears. Ronnie had despised India for years, pressuring her son to leave India alone — and now she was telling him to go after her. It was great, but Nana felt they may be a day too late. She felt Sump and India were supposed to be together, but he blew his chance. One thing she knew was that she would pray for his sake that she wasn't gone forever.

"Yes, sweetie." Nana coughed and coughed, but she had to muster up the strength to voice her opinion. "It will not hurt, Sumpter, so I tell you, try. But if she won't let you back in don't blame her or yourself. Just view it as though it was never meant to be and become that girl's friend. Just carry a cordial relationship with her because y'all have kids. Those girls are smart and bright. No matter the outcome, just remember y'all share beautiful children and if y'all don't do it for nobody else, do it for the babies because they both love y'all dearly."

"I feel y'all and I'ma try. Thanks fo' real though, Momma." He rose up and kissed Nana on the cheek. "I'll be back to check on you tomorrow," he said and turned to Ronnie. "Thank you Ronnie, for keeping it real. But nobody will ever be able to ever take yo' spot. You my mother," Sump kissed her on her forehead and left with heavy thoughts on his mind.

En route to Nala's place, he thought of everything that his old birds had spoken. Sump hated that he loved India so much that he was letting his guard down. He didn't care though. He had to get his baby back and was determined to do anything it took.

As he pulled inside Gene and Nala's driveway, he couldn't believe his eyes. India's car was parked on the street. *Damn, is it fate*

Triple Crown Publications presents... *Wife*

or what? A nigga came over here at the right time, Sump thought to himself.

Emerging from the door, India could have fallen down the flight of stairs. Sump was climbing out of his car, heading in her direction. Her heart dropped and one moment later, picked up and beat erratically. She remembered his little promise. She wasn't ready for this and surely wasn't ready to face him. Entranced and disgusted at the same time, India was confused. The latter outweighed her soft emotions, but he still was fine as wine and that fresh out of the joint look still wore on him. He summoned her, but India ignored and continued walking to the car with Vanessa in tow. He couldn't believe how stunning she looked and she could feel him staring. India was happy that she wore what she had so he could see what he sacrificed for the bitches in the streets.

The fitted black blazer she wore cupped her breasts. Smoky-gray ripped leggings hugged her thighs and hips. To complete her look she rocked a pair of black Christian Louboutin stiletto boots. Draping her hand was an oversized gray Prada bag, two-carat heart-shaped screwies adorned her ears and a matching necklace dangled from her neck. She wore her hair up neatly in a loose ponytail.

"Oh, so India you on some funny acting shit, fo' real though?"

India didn't have to speak, her "assistant" spoke for her. "Boy, quit talkin' to her. Don't you see she don't want your no good ass talkin' to her? Gone wit' that bullshit."

"Yo Vanessa, don't got time for all your big talk. Now India, you ain't gon' say nothing to me?"

Reaching the car, she pressed the button on her key chain to unlock the door and finally looked up. "What is it Sumpter? What?"

"I just wanna holler at you. For a second, that's all."

"Don't do it, girl. You know he ain't for the right thang." Vanessa rolled her eyes.

"Man! India got her own mind, Vanessa. So just shut the fuck up sometimes girl. Damn, you that miserable?"

"Boy, you the fuckin' miser ..." India interrupted.

"It's cool, Nessa. Let me just see what he wants."

"Girl, fuck that!" she exclaimed. "I'm not about to sit up here

and wait. I'ma jump in my ride and you meet me somewhere when you done entertaining this lame-ass nigga."

"You wish I was a fuckin' lame." Sump chuckled, enunciating. "Not neva."

"Whatever, you gotdamn lame." She climbed inside her car and sped off.

"So, what up? What you want?" India shifted her weight and folded her arms.

"First I wanna say I'm sorry for all the troubles and tragedies in your life."

"Uh-huh. Forgiven. That's all you wanted?"

"Nah, ma. I just want you to know that I don't blame you for anything and you had all the right to leave me. But we really need to go somewhere and talk. Jump in with me, I'll bring you back in an hour."

"Naw, I can't do that. Whatever there is to say, you can say it right here, babes."

"Please, baby." He stroked the side of her face, sending chills up her spine. "Just ride with me and I'll bring you back."

India sighed and placed her hand on her hip. "Don't you have a girlfriend at home? Did you use to do this same shit to me?"

"What you mean?"

"When I was at home," she emphasized. "Were you in the streets begging the women you hurt for forgiveness?"

"Where this shit come from?"

"Boy, I see you really don't wanna talk. So I'ma holla at you." India went to open up her door but Sump gently tugged on her hand.

"C'mon now, please just roll with me."

"Where to?" she yelled, rolling her neck.

"We're going to our house."

"Our?" India cocked her head back and stared at him.

"Yes, India that's still our house. I don't know why you left anyway. Speaking of that, where you been staying at?"

"None of your business!" she spat.

"Oh, so it's like that?"

"What does it concern you?"

"Yo', fuck all that. You gon' roll or not?"

"Not!" India opened her door and got inside, shutting the door. He pulled it back open.

"So you serious?" Sump asked.

"Thought I was playing?"

"C'mon, ma. Just follow me around there then. Just give me twenty minutes."

India knew he wasn't going to stop the madness so she agreed. "A'ight, 20 minutes." She glanced at her Cartier watch. "Your time begins now. So put a pep in ya step, player."

Ten minutes later, they pulled up to their house and India parked behind his car in the circle-shaped driveway. It felt weird to be there because she hadn't been in so long.

Inside the house, Sump put on some soft music and turned on the fireplace. India knew this was going to take more than 20 minutes. She removed her boots, sat on the floor Indian-style and began thumbing through a magazine, trying her hardest to ignore Avant's convincing voice. "Don't Take Your Love Away" was playing.

Choking back tears, she tried her hardest to hold her composure. She knew he was trying to express his feelings through the lyrics. Tired of just sitting there, India broke the silence. "Your 20 minutes about to be up, B."

"India baby ... I just wanna know how long you was fucking Scrappy?"

"Oh, so we came here to discuss me?" She glanced up at him and focused back on the magazine.

"Nah, fo'real though. I just wanna know that shit."

"Well if we came to discuss that, I don't have to explain anything to you. I'm fenna go." India rose up and grabbed her boots.

"Sit down, man." He stood face-to-face with her. "Alright, we ain't gotta talk about that." He tugged on her arm and led her to the couch.

"The question is ... how long you were cheating on me with Lilly?" She rolled her eyes.

"I'ma keep it real. It's been over three years. But India, I don't love her how I love you."

"How you sound?" she shot.

"What you talkin' about?"

"How you gonna say you don't love her like you love me? But you still love her though."

"India, that shit I can let go, but you I can't let go. I mean, I done been out for a little minute and I've tried getting over you but shit, I can't ma. Since I lost you, I'm lost too. I'm very sorry for the trouble I done put you and your heart through over the years and I swear I'll do anything for a part two, baby. I'ma man so I can admit that I fucked up big time. But everybody fucks up, India. It just seems like a nigga can't advance without you though. I been so used to you, how can either of us move on without each other? We all we know, In." He hadn't called her that since they were teenagers. India knew he was serious now but that just wasn't good enough.

"So you really expect me to just forgive you like this? After you done carried on a long-term affair with some chick and had kids with her? Oh, and you know the streets talk. I know you done copped her a little business and all that shit. Which I don't care because that's your paper, fam. But for us to have been together, you loved a chick more than me evidently. I just can't forgive you for loving this girl, Sump. Cause you just didn't fuck the bitch and have a baby but you was loving this girl, Sumpter. Had two kids with her. How can I forgive that? I just can't!"

"Why can't you? I can forgive you," Sump pleaded.

"What you mean you can forgive me?"

"That shit you done was raw and uncut too," he said.

"I know it was and I know you can't forgive me for it or nothing else I do."

"I promise I can," Sump said truthfully. "Anything you've done, I've already forgave you for. You gonna always be perfect in my eyes."

"You'll never be able to get over that. So quit psyching yourself up."

"You can't tell me what I can and can't do." His forehead scrunched up.

"Boy, I know you can't and won't. Things will never be the same, even if we tried. You just need to accept it, Sumpter."

Frustrated by India's lack of interest he stood and yelled. "I don't need to accept shit 'cause you just lying to your fuckin' self India! You know this shit can work if we just tried."

No longer able to hold back the tears, India screamed, "We done tried long enough, Sump! It's just not meant to be. People have died 'cause of us! Some people could still be alive if it wasn't for our dealings!" She cried hysterically. "We done tried so long but I realized all we were doing was playing a fuckin' game. This shit was never supposed to be. You done went out on me millions of times and now I've realized that if you truly cared you wouldn't have needed anybody else. No matter if the pussy was thrown at you or not. And don't bring that punk ass excuse about it's all a part of the game. Fuck that game. If you really loved me like you saying, nothing would've provoked you to go out there and bring me back STDs. You wouldn't have spent days and days giving your affection to another bitch. But you have, so you made that choice ... not me. You done dirt first. Not India, but you Sumpter. You made your bed so lie in it. All there is to it is we share kids and that's that."

"Fuck outta here. We can try again. I done told your ass I done tried getting over you but I can't! There's no other girl I can see myself with forever, but you, and trust and believe I done tried, but I just fuckin' can't ma! All I do is think about you. I just can't get you off my mind! I love you and I know you still love me. You just gotta come back home wit your man."

"I just ..." Tired of conversing, Sump knew if trying to talk it out wasn't working, his touch just had to. He cupped her chin and appeased his desire for her with a kiss. As he passionately kissed her, he began unbuckling her pants. India didn't protest. The sensation of his soft hands caressing her body felt heavenly. Her heart was screaming no ... but her body was screaming yes. Unable to go any further, India jumped up and darted to the bathroom. *This can't happen. This will not happen. Who are we fooling?* India asked herself. She knew it would be the wrong thing to do and this needed to end. There was no way she would allow herself to be entrapped by him ever again.

Back inside the living room, Sump wondered what had happened. It was going so well. He promised things would be different and he wouldn't hurt her anymore. Deep down inside his soul, he knew he could never be what India wanted him to be. Selfishly, he was going to press the effort. He heard India's phone ringing, knocking him from his thoughts. Curiosity wore on him heavily and he just had to know who was on the other end. He quickly grabbed the phone out of her purse and answered. "Who 'dis?"

Silence.

"Yo, quit playin' on my wife phone, B." The caller hung up.

Hurriedly, he placed her cell phone back inside her bag. Seconds later, India reentered the living room and retrieved her boots from the floor.

"So you just gonna leave India?" He spoke sadly.

"I can't do this anymore, Sump. I just won't."

Ding, dong! Ding, dong! Ding, dong!

"You expecting someone?" India asked, stepping into her boots.

"Nah," he replied, confused. "I don't know who that can be." He got up and inched towards the door to find a teary-eyed Lilly.

"Who is it?" India wanted to know, walking into the foyer.

"It's Lilly."

"Well open up, 'cause I gotta go nigga."

Sump could not concede but India could. As she yanked the front door open, India stood face to face with Sump's mistress. Lilly was unable to deter the flowing tears. At that moment, she knew deep down inside no matter how submissive she was, if India wanted Sump back, she could have him.

"So, Sump ... y'all back together after all the things you promised?"

"Oh, nah baby. We ain't nearly together." India gloated arrogantly.

"So why are you here? Sump, I thought this bitch was history."

"Hold on now my nigga. Don't disrespect me while I'm standing here. That's what you're not gonna do." Any other time India would've stole on her, but she didn't need any misunderstandings about her fighting over him.

"What is she doing here, Sump?" she bellowed.

"Lilly, gone with all that bullshit fore' I beat yo mothafuckin' ass."

India was finna bounce, but this shit was better than the soaps. So she stepped to the side, leaned up against the wall and watched attentively, elated that she wasn't the one having a straight up sucka attack.

"So you gonna try to fight me because of her Sumpter? How can you still love her and she left you while you were in prison?"

India snickered. "Bay, throwing salt in my game won't get you anywhere. So please stop mentioning my name."

Lilly was heated by this time. "You know what? Fuck you. You ain't nothing but a hood-ass bitch that'll never do shit in life, but have a nigga take care of you because of a pretty face. A ghetto-ass chick that wanna fight and do shit like that. India, who still fights? We both grown with children. I really don't know what Sump see in you because you ain't nothing but a damn user."

Sump couldn't help himself. Lilly was talking a little too reckless for his liking so he snatched her up. "Didn't I tell your dumb ass to gone with the bullshit?" Choking her, he jerked her neck continuously. "Bitch, you came over here just assuming some shit."

Tears were streaming down her face and she cried hysterically. She could barely breathe. "Now you can fucking leave. Bye!" He tossed her to the floor with a thud.

"You know what? Let me leave before I beat your li'l girlfriend's ass." India directed her attention towards Lilly. "And I don't give a fuck, grown or not. If I feel like putting my mans down, then that's what it'll be. You fuckin' clown-ass girl ... and best believe you can have this no-good nigga. I surely don't want his ass. Now good luck 'cause the nigga will never fucking change. If he ain't change for me, no bitch will ever get Sumpter Jones to themselves. Believe that." India strutted off, satisfied.

Sump began jogging down the flight of steps, right behind her. "India, you ain't gotta leave. We still need to talk ma."

Sliding inside her car, she rolled down her window. "We ain't got shit to talk about. The talking session been over," she half-barked, shielding her face with her sunglasses. "Sump, please. We're done. This girl is desperately in love with you. So you can just leave me alone. I've already moved on. She loves you, so just love her back." India told him, tears blurring her vision. "Oh, and next time you speak about me to your bitches tell 'dem like it is. You didn't want me to get out here and stand on my own two, nigga. So don't just blame that shit on me. But it's all good 'cause I'm straight. Just get back up there with that girl before she kills herself." India pressed the button to start up the engine.

"I'm not gonna let you go this easy, India."

"I am already gone Sump. We're history like your girl said. I'm doing my own thang now. It just wasn't meant." She pulled away, leaving him standing in the dust.

*****

An hour later, India pulled up in the parking lot of Starland's Pub and Grill, Vanessa's favorite low-key spot. She whipped her car alongside of Vanessa's, parked and hopped out.

"Damn, bitch! About damn time you left that crab-ass nigga alone. You lucky 'cause I was about to ditch your ass but you called right on time."

"Shut up with all that. Let's get a damn drink."

Once the two cousins got inside they headed straight to the bar and slid onto the barstools. It wasn't packed at all but it was a fair crowd, exactly how India liked it.

The waitress came over. "Will you gals be ordering anything to eat and drink today?"

India was scrolling through her iPhone, texting Meek. She had been phoning him since she left Long Island and he still hadn't picked up the phone. No, that wasn't officially her man, but still he was always available to her no matter what he was doing. "Yes, can you get me a fried chicken dinner with fries and bread oh and a sliced deluxe pizza; I'll also take an apple martini and a bottled water." She never took her eyes off her phone, texting.

"And for you?"

"I'll have a chicken tender dinner with mashed potatoes and cabbage, a stick of shrimp, and a Hennessey and Coke."

"Who you texting, India?"

"Girl, Meek. I been calling him and he ain't answering."

"You know your nigga prolly handling some business so don't even trip," Vanessa said.

"Oh, nah I ain't trippin'. His ass prolly is."

"Forget all that, though. What was Sump lame ass talkin' about?" she inquired, eagerly.

India laughed and shook her head. "Girl, 'bout us getting back together. Dude almost got me. You know his manipulating ass was kissing all on me and went as far as unbuckling my pants, but I didn't let that shit go down. I'm cool as a cool breeze."

"India, you stupid."

"Nah, but why when I was leaving the bitch Lilly came over? When I say the girl was sick, I mean the broad was dying."

"Are you serious? What happened?"

"To make a long story short, Sump played her for dumb in front of me as usual. Choked the hoe up something crazy." India laughed lightly. "This was right before she 'bout got the sense knocked into her ass."

"Why was you gonna do that?" Vickie flared her nostrils up.

"The chick had big balls, fam. Start talking real reckless about I'm ghetto and a hood bitch and just chatting out the side of her neck."

"Oh yeah, you should've floored that bitch." Vanessa laughed as the waitress came over and laid napkins in front of them. She placed their food and drinks down.

"You already know I was, but I didn't want Sump thinking I was fighting over his ass. That could never be the case, fam-fam. Not never."

"I am so proud of you. To be honest, I thought if y'all was to ever get around each other you would allow him back in."

"Psyched ya mind and made ya' booty shine." India burst into a fit of laughter as she dipped her chicken into the ranch dressing and shoveled it down her throat.

"You retarded, girl." Vanessa laughed. "Now you need to stop fooling yourself, talkin' 'bout you and Meek friends cause both of y'all want more."

"Girl, you need to stop fooling yourself ... because we are friends," India defended.

"Y'all are the two closest friends I done ever seen," Vanessa said. "Friends that spends way too much time together and that fucks."

"Okay, you fucks. That don't mean you with a man."

"You're right! I fucks and keep it moving, but y'all are stuck."

India sucked her teeth. "Girl boo, we like it just how it is. Plus, Sumpter will go fuckin' nuts if he knew anything about anything."

"That's why your punk-ass scared, for real." Vanessa chuckled, seriously. "You don't want Sump to find out. But I got news for you. Sump and Meek don't kick it heavy anymore. Besides ma, you're not his wife anymore so what harm is it?"

"Still, I'm not just gonna throw the shit up in his face. Yeah, him and Sump barely talk but believe me they still got love for one another."

"Okay, but they ain't cool. How many times have they kicked it since he been home?"

"I mean none but ..."

"Exactly, that's my point."

"Still Nessa, if any of them needed anything from one another they could easily pick up the phone. Without hesitation they gon' shoot whatever's needed."

"Well, least we know neither of them gonna be calling to ask for anything. So stop it already."

"Vanessa, this for real. Sumpter would prolly kill the both of us if he knew, man."

"Why would he do that?"

"Stop playing. You already know." India gazed at her hard. "He still got love for me, that's why. Even though him and Meek ain't cool like they used to be, he still gon' act like they just the best of friends."

"Right, act! Sump doing his own thang and it ain't like he ain't ever fucked a few of your cats. Did you forget Kim was saying that her baby was his and that was like your best friend? You grew up with her so what's the difference?" Vanessa said firmly. "Girl, please."

"It's not a difference and you know that."

"Bitch, you know what?" Vanessa sighed, shouting. "Just stop fucking with Meek then, gotdamn! I don't got time to kept try'na convince you! Do what the fuck you wanna do, ma!"

"Girl, it ain't even that heavy." India took a swig from her drink.

"That's my point. So just drop the damn discussion."

"Vanessa, I ain't the one that's gon' debate wit your punk ass," she snapped. "So beat the block."

"Don't be mad at me because you a punk." Vanessa laughed.

"Yeah, whatever." India rolled her eyes. "What are you doing after you leave here?"

"Prolly go fuck somebody. Why, what's poppin'?"

"You so nasty." She turned her face up. "But I was just asking 'cause you know me and Nala going to that comedy show. You with us tonight, family?"

"Yeah, I can make that happen." Vanessa glanced over her shoulder and then took a double take. "Umm, ain't that your man over there walking towards the pool table?"

"Where?" India spun around. In full view, she saw Meek engaged in a phone conversation with a cigar dangling from his mouth. "What the fuck! This nigga ain't in a meeting and phone is working perfectly fine from the looks of things. I wonder why he ain't answer the phone or any of my texts."

"I don't know. Go 'head and see." Vanessa shrugged and took the rest of her drink to the head.

For a second India sat there in admiration. The sight of him melted her heart and lifted up her soul. As usual, he was looking causally fine in black jeans and designer sneakers. The skullcap that matched his black Gucci cardigan had never been rocked by a man with a finesse like Meek. His piercing eyes and swagger enhanced his look.

India gulped down the remains of her drink and made her way over to him. "What up bay? I've been try'na call you. You ain't answering my calls." She wrapped her arms around his waist.

"Ay, let me hit you right back." Meek hung up.

"Who was you talkin' to?"

"What up, what's good?" He slid out of his leather jacket and laid it across the chair.

Sensing the attitude, India asked, "Fuck wrong with you?"

"Ain't shit wrong with me. What up my nigga? You good?" he asked, beginning to hit the pool balls.

Furrowing her brow up, she asked again. "Meek, what's your problem?"

"Shit, you ask Sump what's his problem. Everything straight on my end, shorty."

Confused, India glared at him. "Fuck you mean, ask Sump? I'm asking you. What does he have to do with this?"

"You tell me?"

"Oh, so we actin' funny now! Where this shit just come from?"

"Baby, you know I'll never change my character ... but what up, friend? What's good, you cool?"

"Oh, I'm your friend now, huh? That's how you feel? If I'm not mistaken you the same nigga that was just saying this morning that you want me to stay. What happened just that damn fast?" India really wanted to know.

"India baby, I'ma let you do ya' thang with Sump, a'ight! I'm not the man to stand in the way. So do your thang li'l mama."

"Boy, what the fuck are you talking about?" She was bewildered.

"Yo India, quit playing these games. If you don't know anything else, you know I don't like a person who tries to play me on my intelligence. But honestly, it's cool. Real talk, do you baby girl."

"Yo dude, I can't read your fuckin' mind. So either you gonna say what's on your mothafuckin' mind or leave the shit alone."

"Yeah, a'ight." Meek moved to the opposite side of the table and retrieved his cigar from the ashtray.

"A'ight, what? What, you feeling guilty all of a sudden?" India popped. "So now you don't wanna talk to me anymore? Now you ain't gon' beg me not to find my own place? So this what it comes down to?"

"Yeah man ... you got what you want and obviously you like living like that. So I'm good." He hit the ball again.

Frustrated, India walked over to him and snatched the pool

stick from his hand. "So what the fuck is that supposed to mean? I got want I want? You sound like a fool. Guess you on the same bullshit Sumpter used to be on, huh? I should've known y'all wasn't any damn different." India felt played. There was no need for her to stand there any longer so she turned around to walk off.

"Nah, don't put me and that nigga in the same category." Meek said. "Shid ... and you must like the shit. Got the nigga answering your phone."

India took a halt and speedily shifted her body around. "What? What the fuck you mean answer my phone? You must got me mixed up with one of your bitches."

"Nah, it was you. And stop playing dumb. Wanna know when was you gonna tell me y'all were back doing y'all thang?"

"What and who the fuck you talkin about?" India's heartbeat quickened; she had no idea what Meek was saying.

"You fucking back with Sump and got dude answering your phone. But now you act clueless. Just like a silly ass broad."

"Nigga, I can never be a silly broad," India fumed. "And when did Sump answer my phone? You straight up bugging, B."

"So you wasn't just with Sump?"

Stuck on stupid, India didn't have a thing to say. She was indeed with Sump, but how'd he know that?

"Yeah that's what I thought. It's cool, we still can be cool, India. No hard feelings my way, ma."

"Okay, how you know I was around Sump?"

He looked at her like she was dumb. "You know how. Don't play me cock, yo. I know you allowed him to answer. Then you call my phone hours after you leave from with the nigga and expect me to answer." He chuckled in an attempt to conceal his anger. "Fuck outta here with that bullshit. Like I told you, you can be with the nigga. I ain't mad, ma." He was lying.

India grabbed her phone from her bag and promptly scrolled through her received calls. Sure enough, a restricted caller came through around the time she was with Sump. She knew it was him because he was the only person to block out their number. Breathless, she tried to gasp for air. She knew that wasn't a good look.

India knew that he wouldn't believe her, even if she told him that it was nothing and she no longer carried feelings for Sump.

"Meek, I swear he just wanted to talk to me. He begged me to talk, then I finally agreed to hear him out. But I swear I wasn't there longer than thirty minutes."

"I feel you. But it's cool. I told you, I'm good. You good?"

At that moment, India could've sworn Meek stabbed her in the heart. It seriously ached. She knew there was no way she could win this. She fucked up and allowed Sump to fuck it up for her. But she loved Meek so why couldn't he just hear her out? Why didn't he want to listen?

Tears welled in her eyes. "Okay, since you don't believe anything I have to say ... let's go to your place so I can get my things and leave."

"That's cool," he replied coolly. "You can just go 'head. You don't need me with you. You got a key."

"I don't care." The tears slowly escaped, obscuring her vision. "Let's just get this over with. Let me get my things so I can go. Nigga I could've been gone. But nah ... you wanna beg a bitch to stay. I knew this shit was gonna happen."

"Yeah, 'cause you can't let go of the past. But it's cool. I'll be ready in five minutes."

India felt so dumb, she couldn't even reply. How could he play her, knowing her heart was still mending? All she wanted was for him to understand that there wasn't anything left between her and Sump. But no, he didn't want to hear her out. She couldn't take it anymore. She hated the life she was living. She wanted out, and now. If Meek would allow her to walk out of his life that easily, then evidently their love wasn't meant to be.

Everything began going in slow motion. The room was spinning and she was dizzy. She had to bounce. There wasn't anything left in New York. It was more than time for a change. She couldn't live like this a second longer, and she wasn't.

India rushed over to Vanessa. "Can you go over Netta's and grab my daughters and met me at the airport with them please?" Tears raced down her face.

Vanessa jumped up in concern. "What's wrong, India? What just happened?"

"I guess Sump answered my phone back at the house when Meek called. Now he thinks we fucks back around," she said in between snivels.

"Oh In, it'll be okay. You don't gotta run away."

"No! But I do. It's just not the same. I don't like it here anymore. Too much has happened and my Mom been telling me to come out there. It's really time now. Can you please just go get my girls and pack up as much as possible? I'll just start them over once I get settled on the west coast. I gotta go. I'm about to get all my things from Meek's and I'm going to the airport. Please get my girls and meet me at the airport. Please, Vanessa."

*****

India couldn't make it to her car fast enough. Once she reached the XJ she climbed inside, and all she could do was cry hysterically. She couldn't win for losing. India knew she should've never allowed Meek to get so close to her heart. All she wanted to do was grab her things and she was out. Waiting on Meek, she called the airport to see when the next flight was leaving for California. *In four hours ... good. I can make it*, India thought and phoned her mother. Marla was so happy that her baby finally accepted her offer. Meek wasn't coming out fast enough, and India was frustrated as she dialed his number so he would hurry up. She had to go!

Two minutes later he came strolling out, calm as he usually was. India honked her horn. "Would you speed the fuck up? I gotta fuckin' go," she said as it started to drizzle outside.

"Oh, I'm coming. Be easy ma," Meek said unperturbed. That made India even more irritated; he never raised his voice, no matter what. He always stayed calm and composed.

She stuck her head out the window. "Well, hurry the fuck up. I ain't got time to fuckin' waste."

His car was parked two cars over from hers so he merely waved her off. He hopped in the 745, cranked his ignition and pulled off, India directly behind him.

Unbeknownst, Sump was in Lilly's tinted Magnum. Right after

India backed out of his driveway, he jumped in Lilly's car and followed her. He never minded Lilly because she was a woman on his terms. He needed to talk to India. He contemplated going inside the bar, but elected not to once he noticed Vanessa's car parked beside hers. He was going to wait until they departed and follow her to her next destination.

Wondering why she stormed out the bar in tears, Sump sat and waited patiently to see what was next. He noticed Meek emerging from Starland's and India screaming at him. He stayed positioned and wondered what the fuck was going on. Needing to probe further, he followed right behind them.

Oblivious of the Magnum in tow, India followed Meek closely at a fast speed, zigzagging through the highway traffic. India cried the whole way to his house. Dabbing her eyes, she checked herself in the rearview mirror. She pulled inside the driveway and parked behind his car all the while Sump parked a couple houses down, on a stakeout.

Back inside the house, India began getting her suitcases ready. Meek watched her from the bed. He'd thought about helping her, but then again he knew that would speed up the process and he didn't really want her to leave. India wasn't quite his girl but he knew that they shared some good times over the past three months. And no, it wasn't just about the sex. Matter of fact, the pair only made love three times over the course of their time together. It was just something about India's swag that he adored. Meek loved how she didn't depict that hood chick image but didn't act all stuck up either, although she was stunningly gorgeous. She was the perfect mixture of siditty and hood, which he admired. She was picture perfect and had swagger down to an art.

But he knew India still must've had something for Sump because she shouldn't have accepted his offer. If that was really the true story! After all the bullshit Sump had put her through. All the times he'd held her at night, comforting her! But she still allowed him to answer her phone. He knew something had to be going on, and Sump's words were still replaying in his brain. Meek was far from a lame ass nigga. He didn't want to let her go but if Sump was what she wanted, there wasn't anything he could do about it ... but watch her pack.

"So you're leaving now India?"

She looked at him like he was crazy. "You don't care so don't even trip." She continued stuffing her Louis Vuitton luggage. "Talkin' 'bout I want Sump!" she fussed. "You must be out your rabbit-ass mind if you think I want that sorry muthafucka. That'd be pointless to me divorcing dude."

"C'mon now, you tripping ma. It's raining like hell out there, India. You ain't gotta leave. I told you we still can be friends. We started out as friends and we still can be. Ain't shit changed, big head."

Although India knew they were just friends her heart still stung. "Nah, I'm cool. I don't need any 'friends' shit ... I 'm all I got. Fuck you and fuck what you stand for," India yelled, enraged.

"So you wanna be ignorant 'cause you got caught." He shot his head back in disbelief. "Fuck outta here wit that bullshit. You tripping. Remember, this shit ain't my fault. You did what you did. I know you love the nigga, and it's cool ma ... believe that. I ain't trippin' on you. But like I said you ain't gotta leave, I can leave until you get your own little spot."

"Oh, like hell I do. My flight leave in about three hours and I gotta go. I really do."

Confused, he asked. "Flight? Where you going?"

India sighed agitated. "If you must know, I'm moving to California with my mother and I'ma find me a place out there. I need a new start. A whole fucking new beginning 'cause shit ain't happening for me here. I'm good on everything and everyone here except my family," she said with much attitude.

"Damn, that's how you feel, ma?"

"Nah ... that's what I know."

Abruptly, they were interrupted by the doorbell ringing nonstop. India looked at him and he stared back. "Expecting hoes already?"

"Nah, baby. I told you muthafuckas don't have the privilege of knowing where I stay," he said, wondering who could be at his door at close to midnight. Without hesitating, Meek retrieved a chrome glock from his drawer.

Finished packing, India looked at him like he was silly. Since it was raining outside she kicked her boots off and replaced them with a pair of all black sneakers. "Can you at least help me take my shit outta here?"

"You gonna leave the rest of this shit?"

"What you think?" She stared at him like he was stupid. "I sure can't take it all with me on the airplane. Just have the rest of it shipped." She shrugged him off.

India grabbed her two suitcases, walked into the foyer and placed her suitcases by the door as the banging continued. Descending the staircase, Meek yelled out, "Who the fuck is it?" He placed the rest of her things by the door and looked through the side window. There he saw the face of Sump looking right at him. Nobody knew he stayed at that house. Not even his closest friends.

"Who is it?" India whispered.

"It's Sump."

India could've sworn she died and was already buried. Instantly she panicked. What in the fuck was he doing there? What would happen if he discovered that she was inside there with Meek? India didn't want anybody else to die because of her dealings. "Oh my God, I have to hide."

"Shit, why you gotta hide? You still fuck with the nigga?"

"Nah, I just know this isn't a good look," she tried reasoning.

"Open up the fucking door! I know India in there," Sump barked.

Fear spread across India's face and knots twisted in her stomach. She wished she could transform into "I Dream of Jeannie" and disappear. "Yo, what the fuck you acting all jittery for?" Meek raised his voice an octave, wondering what the fuck she was so scared for. He shrugged, "The nigga already knows you in here." India stood there scared shitless. Uh-oh, she thought. Meek sensed the fear in India so he decided to do it her way.

"What you wanna tell the nigga, we cool or the truth?"

"Just tell him we cool, please. I just need to get to my girls,"

India pleaded and Meek agreed. He wasn't nearly afraid of Sump. Meek busted choppers too. By no means was he a sucka-ass nigga. He just respected India to the fullest and if that's what she wanted to say then that's what it was. Besides, baby girl was petrified. Meek unlocked the door with his gun in his hand just in case shit got out of hand and opened it up. Sump charged through and went straight for India.

"What the fuck you doing here?" He could sniff out if India was lying a mile away; that's why asking her before assuming some shit was the best resort.

"I ... I ... I been staying here every since your mom tried to take over the house," she stuttered, nearing peeing in her pants.

"So you just been staying here doing what India? What the fuck you have to stay here for? You could've stayed with Nala, Vanessa, or Netta. Anybody! So what the fuck you staying with my boy for? You could've found you your own spot by now!" he screamed; the sounds of his voice echoed throughout the entire downstairs.

"C'mon now Sump. Don't even trip on her, she was just leaving."

"Why in the fuck you ain't been gone India?" he stated, foaming at the corner of his mouth. "This shit just don't look right to me, man." He pulled his gun from his waistband. "Y'all muthafuckas think I'm stupid! I'm far from a dumb-ass nigga. Meek you got yo gun out and shit. What, you gonna shoot me homie?"

"Check dig, playboy. Just get the fuck up out of my house," Meek snapped. He was indeed a cool and calm dude, but changed man and all ... that was still his crib and Sump was completely disrespecting it. "Don't come in my crib and get to disrespecting."

Sump cocked his head back incredulously. This wasn't his boy talking reckless to him. Not Mr. Calm Man. He then knew it was some fishy shit going on. He definitely smelled two rats. Instinctively, he pulled the gun to India's head with tears filling his eyes. "So that's why you didn't wanna get back with me? You was fucking a nigga that's like my brother. Me ... Indy, are you fo' real? How can you do me like this?"

Meek didn't hesitate. "Yo bra, put the gun down. You just gon' kill yo kids mother?" He placed the pistol on him.

Sump chuckled. "So you really pulling guns on me!? I know y'all muthafuckas fuckin' now. India, just keep it real." He shoveled the gun harder into her temple. "Tell me how long this been going on. Five, six, seven years? How many, ten? Let a nigga know?" He was beyond crushed. He couldn't believe two people he trusted and held dear were playing him all along. "That's why this nigga been distant," he realized. "This shit explains it all."

"Yo Sump, take that gun off that girl man. You buggin', B."

"Nah, y'all trippin'. That's why you was talking about you can't be with me and you got somebody. Was this the nigga you was talkin' bout, bitch?"

"Just leave, Sumpter. And even if I was, we been finished long ago. It's not your problem what I do with myself. Let's not get on you," India exploded. "You had two fucking kids on me, nigga. You done fucked basically every girl that I called my friend. Nigga you must've forgotten about Kim, Stacy and Tracy. All them was my cats and you were fucking them hoes while we were together. Me and Kim was the best of friends nigga and you fucked with her, hard," she glared into his eyes. "The bitch used to wear my muthafuckin clothes. Fuck that ... and the nasty bitch used to steal my panties." She yelled in exasperation as the sobs emerged. "Slept in my mutha-fuckin' house nigga when she didn't have a place to live. Let's not get on that shit though!" By this time India knew Sump was hurt, but she was hurt too. It was time to tell him. Hell, either he was gonna kill her or he wasn't. She had had enough. It was now he knew or never. "And yeah I have been fuckin' with Meek. And no, it was never when we were together but I can say he was always there for me when you weren't." India could barely breathe; she was crying uncontrollably. "Sump, like I told you earlier. This shit's been a wrap, even before you got locked up dude. We were holding on just because." She cried even louder. "Now if you gon' kill me, do what the fuck you gotta do. But I know you don't wanna see your daughters live without a mother and have their father in prison for killing her. Now take the gun off me," she demanded unblinkingly.

Stunned, Sump couldn't believe that India had admitted to

messing around with his boy. India was right about them not being together but that wasn't the point. This was about respect and Meek had disrespected the G-code. He yanked India up by the throat and threw her against the wall violently. Her head hit the wall with a thud and he directed his attention towards Meek.

Standing face-to-face with guns pointing at each other, Sump spewed, "I can't believe out of all the fucking hoes in the fuckin' world you picks my baby's mother. We was supposed to be niggas from way back. You knew she was off-limits but you still ain't give a fuck. How you betray me and we been friends since the playground, B? How you show disloyalty to somebody you love? Somebody that love you?"

"Look man, I knew India was your girl and I been wanting her from back in the day fam. But she was yours," he began. "So I tried to repress all the feelings inside. But when it was over between y'all, fam, what was I supposed to do ... wait for the next man to get her?"

"You damn right, nigga. At least I wouldn't have to kill a nigga I had made love for, yo. But now I gotta kill you."

"You think I'm gonna just let you kill me and I'm strapped too nigga?" Meek eyed him and cocked his gun back. "Shit nigga, you fucked up. That was you nigga, least she didn't leave you for me. You basically left her and allowed me to get her my man."

Sump didn't give a fuck if he had fucked India's momma. That still didn't justify her sleeping with his mans. And he was certainly getting tired of conversing back and forth. With his finger on the trigger, bullets were about to began flying ... but the doorbell rang.

Three minds wondered who in the hell was at the door. India popped up and darted to peek out the window. Fate must have been on India's side once again. She had never in her entire life been so happy to see the men dressed in blue uniforms. She turned to Sump and Meek and whispered, "It's the cops."

"What the fuck!" Meek hissed.

Sump knew it was fate, too. He knew he wasn't going to be able to get away with this murder. He would be the first suspect.

"Put the guns inside that closet," India told them both. It wasn't anything like hood niggas and the police. That shit just didn't mix, no matter how hard niggas thought they were. Meek and Sump grabbed the bags as if they were taking them to the car while India opened up the door. "Hello, officers. May I help you with anything?" she asked, trying her hardest not to look as if something was about to go down. Truth be told, the cops saved the day.

"Yes, do you have any clue who drives the Dodge Magnum that's out front?" The officer eyed Sump.

"No sir I do not, but what's the problem?" India replied.

"The car was called in stolen and a cruiser spotted it here." The officer never took his eyes off Sump. "Do you know anything about that, sir?" Sump knew the routine. Lilly must've described him down to his drawers because both cops eyed him as if to say, *We know it's you and don't make this ugly.* Sump knew he had to surrender.

"Yes officer, I do. That's my girl's car and we got into a disagreement. I guess she called y'all saying I stole her car."

"Oh, okay. Well you're going to have to come down to the precinct with us so this can get straightened out."

"No problem, officer." Just like that, they were gone and so was Sump.

After putting all her belongings inside the car, India and Meek stood staring at each other. "India, all I have to say is I'm sorry I didn't believe you."

"Oh, well you should be. I told you I didn't have any reason to lie so I don't know why you were even tripping. I been over Sumpter and for you to play me like a liar really hurt my feelings," India lowered her head in sadness. "But I can't blame you for it. All I can say is it was good while it lasted. But it's over now and I thank you for everything, Meek."

"Nah, India it don't gotta be over." He tugged on her belt loops.

"Yes, it does have to be over. I can see you might not ever be able to trust me. So like I said, whatever there was that we shared is over," she slightly backpedaled as their gazes met. With each step backwards India felt her heart break into another piece. His stare penetrated her soul and she knew if she stayed a second longer she would break down.

"I have to go before I miss my flight." India walked out of his life.

Meek couldn't say anything because India was right. He hated to let her go but maybe this was the best thing for the both of them. Speechless, he watched as she slid inside her car, tears streaming down her face. India drove all the way to the airport replaying the day's events in her head.

Chapter Twenty

Once India arrived at JFK International Airport, a queasy feeling overcame her. She felt sick. India knew she was dead-ass wrong for indulging in a sexual affair with Sump's boy and even more wrong for being in love with him. But the girl couldn't help it. Meek was everything she'd wanted a man to be and more. Wondering for a fleeting moment if she should stay, India quickly replaced those thoughts with new beginnings. She had to forget the past and press towards her mark. India turned on Lefferts Boulevard and parked her car in the long-term parking area.

After making her way through security, she made her way to her departure gate. She spotted Vanessa seated in the waiting area with Italy sleeping in her arms and Summer positioned beside her,

"Hey, Vanessa. Come to the restroom with me," India said with a tear-stained face, sitting her bag down.

Vanessa rose up, placed Italy's sleeping body back inside the chair and they made their way to the restroom. India could no longer take it; she had backed up vomit rising from her throat. Just on time, she burst into the restroom stall and throw up expelled from her mouth into the toilet.

"Baby you a'ight? What the fuck happened?" Vanessa asked, rubbing her back.

India recounted the entire episode from Sump and Meek nearly about to kill each other to the police coming to save the day. All the while she cried.

"That shit was drastic, India. It's over with though baby, so why are you throwing up like this? You don't throw up, no matter what ... unless you're pregnant."

"I'm not pregnant, Vanessa. I'm on the shot ... there's no way," she hissed, hurling over the toilet.

"Girl, beat it. You was on the shot when you got pregnant with Italy. You know ain't none of those methods 100 percent."

"You don't understand, Vanessa I can't be pregnant. I'm already a single mom of two. No, this can't be!" she tried convincing herself.

"I hate to bring it to you baby girl, but I was thinking you was. Your face been looking a little fat. That's why I stopped by the drug store and grabbed you this pregnancy test." Vanessa retrieved the test from her bag. "Here, now just let's see."

"Girl, you trippin'. I'm not pregnant but to prove you wrong, I'll take it." Vanessa closed the door and India took the test. Finished, India opened up the stall and headed over to the sink to wash her hands. Neither Vanessa nor India said anything. Two minutes later, she picked the stick up and the positive sign caused her to burst out into more tears. Vanessa hugged her cousin soothingly tight.

"It's okay, India. Everything will be okay. You're a strong black woman. I promise everything happens for a reason ... and please keep this baby," Vanessa pleaded.

"I can't, Nessa. It's too complicated. I don't know," she sobbed.

"Attention, all passengers: Flight 1241 for Los Angeles, California is now boarding at Gate 15A. Flight 1241 for Los Angeles, California is now boarding at Gate 15A."

"This is you baby girl so you gotta go. Everything will be fine." Vanessa assured her and handed her some tissue. Once all the items were gathered, Vanessa walked India and the girls over to board their flight. "I'll ship your car and the rest of the girl's things Monday morning." She hugged and kissed her family and walked off.

Once aboard the plane, India couldn't believe that she was in another bad situation. She knew she was supposed to be happy about welcoming another life. And if the day would've turned out different, India would have been overjoyed. She thought about the long talks she and Meek had on how he wanted to have a baby, but didn't want to have one by some random chick. He wanted his first born to be with someone he loved. India wished things could be, but they just couldn't. Meek didn't want her for real; if he did he wouldn't have allowed her to walk out of his life.

She glanced out of the window at the darkness that surrounded the sky and couldn't help but feel darkness hovering over her life once again. But she was damned to go through it anymore. She was determined to leave New York behind once and for all.

Once her flight landed at LAX, India felt a new beginning already. She and her girls stepped off the plane and walked straight to baggage claim. As her luggage came rolling down the conveyor belt, a familiar voice came from behind.

"Hey, baby. I'm sure happy that you and the girls finally came. It feels so good for y'all to be here with me."

India embraced her mother and Marla embraced her tighter, for all the years that she lost her daughter to the streets. "Look at my grandkids. They're so adorable like you, India." Marla embraced them tightly. "Now, c'mon. I have a home for y'all and I already know India ... I know you don't wanna stay with me and we can go looking for you a place next week. But for now, let's enjoy each other's company. There's a lot I've missed out on."

India and her girls followed her mother out to the car and smiled all the way to her mother's condominium. India knew leaving was the best decision she'd ever made.

"Oohh, Mommy this place is beautiful," a happy Italy squealed.

"I know Momma! Aww this is exquisite," Summer added, also ecstatic.

"I'm so happy y'all like it." India beamed. She was delighted because she assumed her daughters would've despised it, being that she separated them from the only place they knew. It felt really good to have the most important people of her life enchanted.

Marla pulled her car into the parking garage. "This is it, girlies." She popped the trunk so they could retrieve their bags. They climbed out of the car and followed Marla through the building and into her luxurious home.

"India, go 'head to that back room and get you and the girl's things situated. I'ma give them a tour around and I'll be back."

"Okay, Ma," India said. She walked inside the kitchen and poured a glass of punch, gulped it down and carried some bags to the back room. Surprised, stunned, and confused, India stood at the doorway frozen. She felt paralyzed.

"You thought I was really going to allow you to slip away from me that easy?" Meek asked, peering out the window at the beautiful skyline view and then gazing at her.

"How did you get here?" India gushed.

"It's amazing how private jets fly, huh? They'll get you to your destination in no time."

"How did you get in?"

"I called Vanessa once you left. I couldn't allow you to walk out of my life. She put me on game and I called your mother with Vanessa on the three-way and she explained everything. Your mother and I planned for me to be here once you got here."

"Oh my God, are you serious?"

"C'mon now, India. All that time we got to know one another wasn't a waste. I told you I love you. I promised myself to never allow you to walk out of my life until the death. I want you to understand I love you, and was willing to do anything to have you ma. I have never loved a chick before except you and I want to love you forever and a day."

Her eyes flooded with tears of joy. India couldn't believe that he came after her. She thought she had lost her lover and best friend forever. But now he was there and flew all the way to the west coast to convey his true emotions. "Now tell me one thing, India."

She wiped her face. "Now what is that?"

"Do you love me?"

"Boy, boo. More than life itself. Do you love me?"

"I love you, your girls and our new seed," he smiled, pleased. "We're gon' be the family that you always wanted to have, bay. I promise to love and be with you and our family until my last breath."

India had an enormous smile spread across her face. She

couldn't believe this was happening. Seeing them all as a family was the only way she could picture life. Many would say it was grimy, but fuck what anyone thought. Only a person who wore her shoes could judge her and then again, not even then.

"Now, c'mere big head," he demanded.

Raining tears, India tottered over to him and fell into his arms, feeling like she had conquered the world. Meek knew this was what he had been waiting on his entire life and knew no matter what, no other woman could replace her. He grabbed her by the waist and pulled her close to his chest. Gazing down into her beautiful brown eyes, he kissed them softly. India looked up at him and was glad to be in his comfort. She was finally all his and he was more than gladly to be the one to show her the way. Now and forever, both of their lives were complete.

Triple Crown Publications presents... *Wife*

Epilogue

Life on the other side was glorious just as India (now) Hamilton had imagined. India felt L.A. was the place she was supposed to be years ago. Weeks after her arrival, Meek wound up selling his properties in New York and decided to make his move to the west coast too. The pair quickly found a nice crib out in Beverly Hills, California. Meek already had two thriving businesses nearby, one back in New York and he was also a silent partner in a corporate enterprise.

Everything was certainly good financially, but India vowed that she would never fall off her feet again and have to depend on a man. She was determined to become independent. She promptly enrolled back into fashion design school, pregnant, using her determination to succeed. Meek also began attending college for a degree in Business.

Six months after settling into the city, they welcomed a beautiful baby girl into the world. Meek instantly fell in love with his daughter. Not even thinking about it, they named her Da'Kyla Ton'na Hamilton. She was sure to be a daddy's girl, inheriting all her father's features. India thanked God for the struggle. She knew that without the struggle, she wouldn't be who she had become. After several months of schooling back in New York and the nine months she attended CSULA, India decided it was time to move forward in her life. With Meek's connections, she immediately went into business and it didn't take long for her clothing line to get off the ground. Her first fashion show at Smashbox Studios was a success, with many top designers and buyers in attendance. And India was working hard to have her line internationally recognized in all the high-end department stores and exclusive boutiques.

Vanessa wound up moving out West. Before long, she found herself an NBA baller for the Los Angeles Lakers. Within six months, they got married and he opened her up a lush salon on Sunset Boulevard. Vanessa was grateful to have found her soulmate.

Nala wasn't too far behind and purchased herself a pleasant loft in downtown Los Angeles. She divorced Gene and had to begin focusing on her persona. She, too, had finally gotten fed up with all his bullshit in the dope game. It didn't take her long to put her degree in communications to use. Plus, being on the scene with India got her noticed. She had become a stylist and fashionista. Word was spreading. She was being considered as a potential cast member of a new reality show on VH1.

After the incident at the house, Sump finally accepted the fact that he couldn't have India anymore. And after a little persuading, Lilly forgave Sump and they got married at city hall. Shortly after the wedding, Sump and Gene ended up going back to prison for drug trafficking. They were both sentenced to serve fifteen years in the federal penitentiary. Mac C was still in the streets, unstoppable.

Italy and Summer were doing wonderful. India was so proud and thanked God for giving her daughters a better direction in life. But this day in particular was sure to be a heartbreaking one for her girls.

Their Nana was being laid to rest. Nala, Vanessa, and Meek accompanied India and the girls for support. Arriving in Queens brought back so many memories. For India, it was mostly memories of the strife, but it was what made her strive to be the woman she turned out to be.

Nana was a well-known elderly lady around the town. Her funeral brought in church folk to children that she fed over the years. Even local drug dealers that she knew came to pay their respects. India and the girls sat in the front row with the family, while the rest sat on the friends' side.

India hated for her daughters to see their father in attendance dressed in an orange jumpsuit, covered in shackles and guarded by four armed officers. India also loathed that she had to be seated at the end of the bench. That gave Sump an opportunity to communicate with her. His chair was directly next to her and the guards were posted up against the wall, inches away from his chair. And just as she assumed, he whispered in her ear. "I'm so proud of you India. You really did your thang ma. I see you taking care of our daughters very well."

She nodded. "They're the reason why I grind so hard. The reason I breathe." She didn't give him any face. She was trying to focus in on the sermon.

"Just make sure you keep taking good care of my girls, a'ight? And tell Meek I said thanks for stepping up on my behalf and I forgive the nigga," he admitted. "I love you and my daughters too much not to. If I don't know shit else, I know he's a good-ass nigga and he'll take good care of y'all fo' sho. Know I wish you and yours nothing but happiness!" He paused briefly and continued on. "And I'm sorry I will never be able to change India. It's rooted in my blood. I guess it's true what they say ... like father, like son. You know I'm the splitting image of Mark so I gotta get on some reckless shit. It's a must!" He whispered so low he was almost inaudible. "So make sure when this over with, leave straight out. The block might get kinda ugly."

Heart racing in fear, India turned and looked at him. "What you got planned, Sump?"

"Just listen to what I said ma. They won't bring me out until the church is cleared all the way out and most cars are headed to the gravesite. Just make sure y'all all are gone. Ronnie already told the fam. I'm just letting you know, baby. Be safe and take care of my daughters!"

At that moment, India wanted to get up, grab her peoples, and leave; she was damned to be caught in a massacre. He added, as if he read her thoughts, "You don't gotta go now. Mac C ain't that crazy. But I'm just saying don't stick around longer than needed ma."

Before they closed the coffin, everyone walked up and took one last look at Nana. It seemed as if everyone was prompt and in unison, following right behind the pallbearers.

Back outside, Brianna came strolling up to them and hugged everyone as they were climbing inside the truck. She took India by a total surprise. The entire service she was so focused in on Sump, she failed to pay her or T'ionna any attention.

"Hey India, what's up wit it fam?" Brianna beamed and pulled her designer frames from her eyes. India couldn't believe this was little Brianna. She looked absolutely beautiful. If she didn't put her in the mind of her when she was her age, India didn't know who could. She looked better than chicks in magazines and the videos. She wore a banana-hued blouse, black skinny jeans and yellow pumps. Draping her shoulder was the exact same ostrich Hermès bag India bought when she had recently done a fashion viewing in Europe. India couldn't believe how time had transformed this little girl into a little lady.

"Oh, what up Brianna? How's life treating you? I see you don't call me much anymore," she said sarcastically. "What have you been getting into, li'l ma?"

"Don't even trip India. You know I'm just living the life," she spoke proudly. "I just moved into my own spot across the Hudson River. When you gon' let my little cousins come visit me?"

Never is what India really wanted to say, but she didn't wanna seem like she was too good for "the life." But she sure as hell wasn't going to allow her girls to get caught up in the same life that caused so much heartache and pain. So instead of telling her never, she simply replied, "Y'all can just come out there because the girls are involved in too much stuff for school, even in the summer time. You know I got the girls in a little bit of everything. But y'all are more than welcome to come chill with us."

"Yeah, when my man takes me on a shopping spree on Rodeo, you know I'ma swag through and holler at the fam." She danced around, seemingly excited.

The sounds of a honking horn came from the truck that pulled up alongside of them and as the door opened up, out stepped someone equivalent to Brianna's whole appearance and walked over to them. "What it do India, baby?" T'ionna asked.

"Oh, nothing much. How's everything going, family?"

"Good baby, definitely good." She nodded, agreeing with herself. "Yeah, life is certainly treating a sister right." She then looked at Brianna. "Now c'mon Bre. The limo that's carrying Nana about to pull out and you know what Ma said."

"Oh shit girl, I totally forgot! India I'ma call you later. You know we gotta get the fuck from around here 'cause of your crazy-ass baby father." India had completely forgotten what Sump had informed her on; she was utterly flabbergasted by the girls. India stared at the lasses as they scurried off and climbed inside an all black Range Rover sitting up on chrome rims with personalized license plates that read: *Wifey 1* .

India couldn't believe that the dope game was still appealing to young girls. She desperately wanted to school them, but knew they wouldn't listen even if she tried. Shit, she hadn't listened either when people warned her that everything that glitters wasn't gold; especially living in the dope life. To India, it was time repeating itself, but she'd be damned. She was ending that family curse with her girls, like yesterday. If that's the life T'ionna and Brianna wanted to live, she knew there was nothing she could say that would change their minds.

Snapped out of her trance, India quickly slid inside the truck. Meek drove off as she thought about the girls. She knew that she'd have to reach out to them eventually, before it was too late. The least she could do was enlighten them and become their confidant; she knew they had a long journey ahead.

Cruising down the street, India realized she no longer even liked the smell of the city's air. She told Meek, "I'm just ready to get back home. Nana knows we love her dearly but I don't wanna go to the burial site."

Everyone in the truck agreed and Meek headed back towards the airstrip where the private jet was located. As Da'Kyla cried from her wet diaper, they heard the piercing sounds of an AK-47 spraying incessantly. India wondered if Sump was hurt or if his plan of escaping at his Nana's funeral actually worked. She prayed he was fine for the sake of her two daughters, but knew they would never be able to see him even if he was to survive. He was a fresh corpse or a fugitive; either way, she couldn't fret about it. She was living life on the other end for once, and wouldn't trade it in for the world.

Whisking to their destination, India glanced back over and said to her everything, "You know without you, I would prolly feel like nothing ... with all my success."

"And without you ma, I would be nothing."

India grabbed his hand and kissed it softly. "But together bay, we're everything. Everything we've ever needed and wanted to be. Plus more. You love me?"

"I'ma love you to you be like that's enough!" He smiled and gently caressed the side of her face. "You got my back, right ma?"

"Got your back, front and anything in between. You already know that's for certain! It's the long way down!"

 Triple Crown Publications presents... *Wife*

CPSIA information can be obtained at www.ICGtesting.com
Printed in the USA
LVOW131804301112

309542LV00002B/264/P